Time Well Bent

TIME WELL BENT

Queer Alternative Histories

Edited by
Connie Wilkins

LETHE PRESS
MAPLE SHADE NJ

www.lethepressbooks.com   lethepress@aol.com

Book Design by Toby Johnson
Cover Image by Ben Baldwin   benbaldwin.co.uk

Published by Lethe Press, 118 Heritage Avenue, Maple Shade, NJ 08052.

First U.S. edition, 2009

ISBN 1-59021-134-0 / 978-1-59021-134-2

Library of Congress Cataloging-in-Publication Data

Time well bent : queer alternative histories / edited by Connie Wilkins. -- 1st U.S. ed.
     p. cm.
  ISBN 1-59021-134-0 (pbk. : alk. paper)
  1. Homosexuality--Fiction. 2. Gay men--Fiction. 3. Lesbians--Fiction. 4. Bisexuals--Fiction. 5. Gays' writings, American. 6. Alternative histories (Fiction), American. I. Wilkins, Connie.
  PS648.H57T56 2009
  813'.0108352664--dc22
                                    2009038493

Acknowledgement

To the writers who shared their visions and then waited so patiently after upheavals in the publishing world made a new home necessary; to Steve Berman at Lethe Press who provided that home; and to all our spiritual forbears whose voices, whether heard or silenced, call out to us through all the years: Thank you.

Table of Contents

INTRODUCTION

W E HAVE ALWAYS BEEN HERE. FOR as long as there has been such a thing as sex, even before we late-coming humans began etching a record of our existence into stone or clay, alternate sexual identities have been a fact of life. When our forebears first stood erect, when they used the first tools, hurled the first spears, began to paint visions of their world onto cave walls, we were right there, some of us quite possibly shamans who drew power from the blurring or bending of gender lines. We were there when civilization dawned on the plains of Abyssinia, flourished in ancient Greece and Rome, spread through the Dark Ages and Medieval era, flared into the Renaissance.

We have always been here, in every era and every area of society.

So why have we been so nearly invisible in recorded history? Plato gave us a nod, while the scribes who put their spin on the Old Testament railed against us, but on the whole, viewed through the prism of so-called Western Civilization, our historical presence has been either ignored, glossed over, or vilified.

This has been true in popular fiction as well as in academic works, with a few outstanding exceptions such as the work of Mary Renault. A decade ago, when Nicola Griffith and Stephen Pagel published their *Bending the Landscape* series, it seemed to me that the obvious next step—after fantasy, science fiction, and horror—would be GLBTQ alternate history. We'd been portrayed in future worlds, fantasy realms, and nightmares; wasn't it time to claim our place in a speculative past? What could be a more natural theme for altered history than this aspect of human experience that has made millions hot under the collar one way or another for thousands of years, and has brought on oppression and repression of truly biblical proportions?

But no such anthology came along, and finally, after my alter ego Sacchi Green had edited or co-edited four anthologies of lesbian fiction and published more than fifty stories, many with historical settings, I decided to take on the job myself. Now Lethe Press has made it possible for me to edit the book I've wanted to read for so long.

In *Time Well Bent*, the perspectives are those of gay, lesbian, bisexual and transgender characters, some entirely fictional, many based on figures from history. Since these are short stories, not novels, the chief emphasis is on the differences, the points of divergence from "known" history, leaving the reader to ponder the long-term consequences. Some will be obvious—what if Isabella of Spain had never backed Columbus?—while others are as subtle as the publication of E. M. Forster's *Maurice* early enough to inspire many young soldiers in The Great War. In a few cases the plots cross into the related genre of "secret history", where history remains more or less as we learned it, but the events behind the scenes are far different. A certain degree of fantasy is also included, in settings where it would be considered natural in the cultures of those times and places. On a slightly different note, one story departs entirely from "known" history with the assumption that Coleridge's *Xanadu* was more than just a pipe dream.

The fourteen contributors to this book have done extensive research, and their stories generally adhere to accepted history right up to the point where they take a sharp and dexterous turn. They offer more, though, than clever twists. In these works, as in our lives, you will find humor, heroism, tenderness, brutality, violence, joy, loss, love, poetry, philosophy, pain, and an occasional spark of eroticism. The alterations to history are not uniformly idealistic, but have implications that may be positive, negative, or unknowable. The characters share the wide range of human experience common to all of us.

We have always been here. Recent cultural trends make it more possible for us to be visible in society, and academic trends in historical research have followed along, but fiction has its own power to intensify our perceptions and beliefs. Stories that center on GLBTQ people living lives that alter history can rescue our past from invisibility, and affirm our place and importance throughout all of history, past, present, and future.

I hope *Time Well Bent* will accomplish some small part of this mission.

Connie Wilkins
Amherst, MA

Time Well Bent

A WIND SHARP AS OBSIDIAN

Rita Oakes

A wind sharp as obsidian blew with the conquest.
Ernesto Cardenal

MALINALLI FROZE AS THE JAGUAR BOUNDED across the stream, scattering water droplets like silver flower petals. She let the clay water jug topple onto the bank, cushioned by moss and fern, so it did not break. Her heart beat as fast as the hummingbird's wing, and her belly clenched.

The jaguar rumbled deep in the chest and rubbed a broad head against Malinalli's thighs. She staggered from the force of the great cat, fell upon her backside to the grass. She pushed the jaguar aside, fretting over the green stains she would need to beat out of the white cotton of her huipil.

Xochi was persistent, and Malinalli found laughter bubbling up within her. She reached anew for the jaguar's great head, wished she possessed the tautly coiled strength, the celestial beauty of the star-mapped pelt, and the burning, yellow eyes. But Xochi was a goddess and Malinalli a slave and outcast.

At her touch, the skin split along the jaguar's spine and Xochi stepped out to play.

The jaguar pelt lay to one side like a discarded melon rind. Xochi's hand cupped Malinalli's chin.

Xochi was tall, with skin the color of rich earth. Broad and muscular, yet smelling of sweet flowers, Xochi always made Malinalli's legs tremble like wind-blown grass. Eyes yellow as sunlight, earlobes filled with jade spools green as a newly unfurled leaf, Xochi's power and beauty always made Malinalli feel drab.

She did not know how she, a sparrow, first captured Xochi's notice. She was grateful for it, grateful for Xochi's warmth and passion, grateful for the few moments when the dead feeling inside her went away and she could feel a treasured part of earth and sky for a brief time.

"I smell the stranger upon you," Xochi said. "What is he like?"

Malinalli shrugged. "He is a man." But not like any other. Unwashed, hairy, pale as the maguey worm.

"Is he Quetzalcoatl come again as fools say?"

"I do not believe so."

Xochi laughed. "My little diplomat. You do not say yes or no, but only what you believe or do not believe, knowing full well you are only a woman, and may be mistaken."

"I am wary of offending gods." And men.

Xochi lay beside her on the long grass, slid her hand beneath Malinalli's cotton dress. "Tell me about the stranger."

Her hand was warm, callused like the paw of the cat, but unfailingly sweet. Xochi's hand paused between Malinalli's thighs, like a butterfly settling upon a flower, then smoothed its way upward, thumb stroking over her navel.

Malinalli curled her fingers about Xochi's strong wrist. "He will plant a child in me, like maize. I do not want such a child."

Xochi kissed her, rubbed her face against Malinalli's dress, jade earspools cool through thin cotton. Malinalli's heart whirred within and she thought she would need no obsidian blade to cut it free—it would burst through bone and skin with flashing, iridescent wings. She sat up, pulled the huipil over her head. Xochi kissed her again, and swallowed the dark moons tipping her breasts. Malinalli forgot about pale strangers from across the waters.

They lay drowsy in the moist breath of day. The quetzal sang from green concealment in the trees. A cloud passed overhead. Bumps broke over her bare skin. Xochi spread the jaguar pelt over Malinalli, but the warmth could not touch the ill-omened worry that squeezed her belly.

Xochi gazed at her with golden eyes, dark hair loose and wanton about her shoulders. "What do you love?"

"Life."

"What else?"

"You."

Xochi smiled. "What else?"

"The Land."

Xochi kissed her again, but the playfulness had left her. Her eyes sharpened with the far-seeing intensity of a cat stalking prey. "The Fifth Sun will sink. The Land will fail."

Tears burned Malinalli's eyes. "I have Dreamed it so."

The golden gaze settled once again upon her. "A sleeping Dream or a waking Dream?"

"A sleeping Dream." Malinalli wrapped her arms about her middle, hugged herself tight in misery. "The first night when the stranger took me. He pushed into me and pushed and pushed, then grunted and fell asleep. I lay awake upon the mat a long time afterward, too timid to move and risk waking him. And then I slept and had the Dream of Endings. It frightens me more than their jabbering tongue, or their white mountains that float on the sea, or the strange deer without antlers that carry them on their backs."

"A waking Dream is stronger. You must Dream again."

Xochi made magic, and in her palm appeared a few black seeds, a tongue-piercer of glittering obsidian, and a length of twisted hemp.

Malinalli took the seeds, chewed them, waited patiently.

Xochi asked, "What is the Blood?"

"The Red Flower."

"What does the Red Flower bring forth?"

"Maize."

"What else?"

"Rain."

"What else?"

"Life."

"What else?"

Malinalli hesitated. Her mouth burned. She stared into the spots of the jaguar pelt, felt herself sinking into the skin, into the stars. She did not wish to disappoint Xochi. "Wisdom," she said.

Xochi smiled, revealed pointed, jaguar teeth.

Malinalli took up the bit of obsidian, put the point of it against her tongue, turned the polished shard between her palms. The blade sank deep into the meat of her tongue. Blood began to flow, spattering petals of red over her chin, her breasts, upon the ground. When her tongue was pierced through, she placed the obsidian back in Xochi's callused palm. Malinalli took up the hemp, threaded it through the hole she had made, worked it back and forth while the red flowers streamed from her mouth.

Xochi cupped her palms beneath Malinalli's open mouth, caught the blossoms offered, delicately lapped at the red petals. "Enough," she said.

Malinalli removed the rope from her tongue, tasted salt. Pain remained distant as the Dream took her, Xochi's gift in return for the gift of blood.

She stumbled through a great city, a city she had never seen, but Malinalli knew it for Tenochtitlan. It should have been beautiful, but the fine canals were choked with dead warriors. Sick city dwellers lay too weak to help themselves, skeletal and covered with running sores. Statues of the gods crumbled. Stones shattered like broken teeth.

The strangers rode their great deer over the fallen, or hacked about with gleaming swords, or fired weapons that belched like small volcanoes. Women screamed as the victors took them with violence, planted worm-pale seeds in their bellies.

Part of Malinalli rejoiced. Her mother had cast her aside—sold her as a child into slavery to merchants from Xicalango, who sold her in turn to the Maya. And *they* carelessly gave her to still other men—strangers who babbled unintelligible words and possessed skins white as the sap cut from the sapodilla tree.

Betrayal upon betrayal upon betrayal. If a child could not depend upon a mother's love, why should Malinalli weep for people she did not know?

Let destruction rain fire upon those who despised Malinalli. Let the Fifth Sun go black. Let everyone and everything slide into nothingness. Only rage would remain, Malinalli's rage—a whirling storm in darkness.

She shuddered, cried out in pain. These were not sacrifices to nourish the gods, filled with dignity, music, the solemnity of holy men and women in sacred dance, the glitter of obsidian blades. No, this was brute butchery and pestilence, which would leave the gods with none to honor them. And how vile a creature must *she* be to allow herself to overflow with so much madness, like a clay pot in a downpour?

Xochi held her as she sobbed, arms strong and warm and loving. Malinalli's mother had never held her with such tenderness. Nor had any man, though many had lain with her throughout her years as a slave.

Xochi's jaguar rumble soothed her with low music. Malinalli felt treasured as a perfect piece of jade warmed by an artisan's hands, as revered as a beating heart exposed to the gods by the most holy of priests. Malinalli clung to Xochi as she had once clung to her mother. But unlike her mother, the flower goddess did not tug free of her embrace, give her over to the greed of merchants. Xochi stroked her hair until Malinalli grew drowsy.

Xochi asked, "Must the world end because your mother could not care for you?"

Malinalli scrubbed tears away with her palms. "She thought I was ill-omened."

"Perhaps you are."

Stung, Malinalli pushed Xochi away. She donned her huipil with trembling hands. She gave no voice to her hurt. Gods were faithless creatures. Faithless as mothers who sold their children into slavery. Faithless as men who...

Xochi rose with an agile grace Malinalli had always envied. Malinalli retreated a step, knowing her fury could not face down the wrath of a goddess. Xochi's broad hand reached out, but only to sweep a tendril of tear-dampened hair back from Malinalli's cheek.

"Do not be angry with me because you dislike your Dream. Dream a new one."

From Xochi's palm a snake vine sprouted, twined about Malinalli's wrist. Flowers opened like mouths and sang. Malinalli's anger faded. Xochi had taken her blood and returned beauty.

The flowers sang, their breath fragrant. They sang of language and healing. They sang of unity. They sang of the endurance of the Fifth Sun and a confederation of many against few. Let the strangers return to the Sunless Lands, or let their red flowers nourish the earth. Let the new Dream spin like time on the sun stone. Let the Dream of Endings transform to a Dream of Beginnings, as Xochi transformed from the jaguar.

And let Malinalli, ill-omened slave, transform into something more.

Yes, she liked this Dream. But was she strong enough for it?

"You are strong enough," Xochi said.

"What will happen next?"

"What do you desire?"

Malinalli considered. She had wanted vengeance, but that was a child's tantrum. She was a child no longer. "The pale strangers have powerful weapons and will trample all the people of the land beneath the hooves of their stags. And then who will remain to remember our gods, to feed them the blood that keeps them strong? I want to drive the strangers away. Or bring them captive to the greatest of temples in sacrifice."

Xochi nodded. "You are ambitious for a woman. And a slave."

Malinalli's face grew warm with more than the sun. "You mock me."

"No. I am proud of you. Here, then, is *my* Dream: You will return to the strangers and make yourself useful to them. Already you speak Nahuatl and Mayan. You will learn the strangers' babble and translate for them. Their leader will call you his Tongue, and keep you by him constantly. His followers will call you Marina, but the people will honor you with the name Malintzin. You will learn this man's secrets—and then use them against him. In time you will unite the people in Tlacopan, Tezcoco, Tenochtitlan, Cholula, Huexotzinco, Tzintzuntzan, and all the lands between the waters against him."

Malinalli's confidence wavered, like lake water in wind. "I am only one woman. How can I do this thing?"

"You are the Dreamer. And you are my Beloved."

Warmth bloomed in Malinalli's chest. Despised and alone no longer. Beloved. Beloved of Xochiquetzal.

What might she not accomplish with a goddess for ally? She might even attempt to forgive her mother.

Pride and love swelled inside her, as maize, nurtured with water and sunlight, swells within the husk before harvest. But worry wriggled inside her, too, like a worm. She pressed her hands to her belly.

"And the child? I do not want a child made like chalk." She could not meet Xochi's eyes for shame. Had her own mother not felt the same? Could this be the real reason she had sold her to the men from Xicalango? Heat flushed Malinalli's face as she worried that she might have moved the goddess to anger. "If only I could bear *your* child instead? The strangers need not know."

Xochi drew her close and Malinalli, tense at first, molded herself against flesh firm as stone, welcoming as water.

A bird swept past, a blur of green and red. A long plume drifted toward them, a prized feather from the quetzal. Malinalli plucked it from the air in wonder.

Xochi laughed, took the feather from her, traced it down Malinalli's lips and chin, partly in play, partly in blessing.

"A child," Xochi whispered. "Our child."

"I would treasure such a child."

Xochi motioned for her to sit. Malinalli sank once again into the grass, watched with unabashed curiosity as Xochi's palms filled with kernels of white and yellow maize, and tiny grains of amaranth, and specks like the black seeds Malinalli had eaten before the bloodletting.

Xochi poured these onto a metate that appeared suddenly before her, began to grind them together.

She worked in silence. Wind tugged at her hair, plucked at the hem of Malinalli's dress, eager to blow breath into the mix of seed and maize. Xochi smiled, pointed teeth both lovely and fierce.

"Give me your hand," she said.

Malinalli surrendered her hand and Xochi sliced her palm with obsidian. Blood pooled from the shallow cut, and Xochi let it fall from Malinalli onto the metate. She cut her own hand next, and let divine blood mix with Malinalli's own.

Xochi worked all into a thick, coarse dough, and then sprinkled it with bits of quetzal feather. She fashioned it into a cake the shape of a child. Xochi blew upon it. The wind shook the glossy leaves all about them and joined its breath to the breath of the goddess. They baked the child-cake with their breath, as the sun bakes mud into brick.

"Hold out your hands," Xochi said.

Malinalli spread open her palms. The seed cake was warm in her hands, firm, and heavy.

"Now eat."

Malinalli nibbled at the cake. The corn was sweet, but held an edge of bitterness. The amaranth crunched between her teeth like nuts. She had not eaten more than a few bites before feeling full.

"All of it," Xochi said.

Malinalli obeyed. The cake sat in her belly like one of the balls from the strangers' belching weapons, but she had only eaten half of it.

Her skin flushed and sweat trickled down her face like tears. Malinalli could no longer be certain the green grass remained below her—no longer sure the blue sky stretched above. Was she flying? Or was she falling? It did not matter, so long as Xochi's arms remained about her.

Her stomach stretched tight like a drum. She would burst if she ate any more. Bitterness now outweighed the hint of sweetness against her tongue. She fought down the urge to bring it all up again.

Xochi kissed her, and pressed a palm against Malinalli's middle so firmly it hurt. She covered Xochi's hand with her own, thinking at first to push it away, but clasped it tightly instead. *Beloved.*

Xochi's tone was gentle, but unyielding. "Finish the cake."

Tears of pain pricked at Malinalli's eyes. "I cannot."

"Yes, you can. Let not even a single crumb fall, if you would have our child be whole and strong."

Malinalli choked down the last of the cake in spite of the pain in her belly, the increased burning in her mouth, the dry clawing at her throat. A child was borne in pain—perhaps magic required a child be made in pain, as well.

When she had swallowed the last of the cake, the heaviness in her belly vanished so quickly she gasped. Had she somehow spoiled the magic?

"It is gone," she said, bracing herself for Xochi's anger. Stupid, useless slave to undo the magic of a goddess. Truly her mother had been wise to sell her so many years ago.

But Xochi laughed, hugged her so close Malinalli's ribs creaked. "Do not be so sad. The child merely waits to be born. He will have a great destiny."

"So our child will be a son?"

"A son strong and fine. What his mother does not accomplish, he will finish. Where there is war, he will bring unity. Where there is pestilence, he will restore health. Your strangers will claim him, but his heart will always belong to his own people, his own gods, his own land. That is *my* Dream."

Xochi released her, drew on the jaguar pelt, but did not change immediately back to the great cat. Her yellow eyes shone with pride and love. She kissed Malinalli sweetly upon the mouth.

"The strangers will wonder why you take so long to fetch water," she said. "Return to them, my beloved. You must keep their trust for our plan to work."

Xochi sank to all fours, became a jaguar once again. She rubbed her face against Malinalli's thighs, rumbled with pleasure as Malinalli scratched her ears. Then Xochi lifted her broad head, catching the scent of prey—tapir, or peccary, perhaps. She bounded away, tail lashing.

Malinalli usually hated partings. But Xochi would find her. Xochi would watch over her. She would want to see the birth.

Malinalli bent and filled the water jug, imagining she could already feel the child taking root within her. She would bear the touch of Hernán Cortés with patience now—the pale, ill-smelling flesh, the coarse scrape of the hair upon his chin, the grunts as he pleasured himself upon her. He would mistake her son for his own. He would make many other mistakes. With her guidance. And Xochi's.

Author's Note:

Malinalli, variously known as La Malinche, Malintzin, or Doña Marina, is a controversial yet intriguing figure, often reviled as a traitor. How is it she never received the acclaim of a Pocahontas or a Sacajawea? Her early life is a mystery, but she was a slave, given as a gift to Hernan Cortés. She bore him a son, often said to be the first mestizo. *She served as an interpreter of Nahuatl and Chontal Mayan languages, which allowed Cortés to communicate with the indigenous peoples of Mexico and convince them to ally with him against the Aztecs. Certainly the conquistadors could never have defeated Moctezuma so quickly without the aid of these allies.*

Unfortunately, history has not recorded Malinalli's thoughts about her foreign companions. I found myself wondering what might have happened if she had actively worked against the Europeans. What if the Spanish Conquest had failed? Suppose the multiple groups of Mexican Indians united against their common enemies: the invaders from across the seas and the predatory Aztecs? This story lays the groundwork for that possibility.

For more information, I heartily recommend the books, Malinche's Conquest *by Anna Lanyon and* Matlintzin's Choices *by Camilla Townsend.*

THE FINAL VOYAGE OF THE HESPERUS

Steven Adamson

MODHUN BLINKED, BUT THAT DID NOT disrupt the blackness, so thick it pressed against him with an insistent, liquid touch. The air reeked of damp and salt and human waste.

Around him, the others spoke in whispers, their throats too dry for anything else. If Modhun listened hard, he could hear the scraping of the *chokidars'* boots on the deck above.

Someone grabbed his arm. "Do you have any food?" asked a woman.

"If I did," he said, "why would I give you any?"

"Not me. My daughter." The woman took his hand and placed it on the girl's smooth, skinny shoulder. "She needs to eat."

Modhun recoiled. Scrambling over random knees and shoulders, he found a corner to explore the folds of his *kurta*, fingering the hidden seams that held money.

Five minutes later he was on the *Hesperus'* deck for the first time since leaving Calcutta. Moonlight streaming through the rigging painted pale wedges and swathes in the shadows. Four other men who had paid for the privilege of clean air lingered near the rails, ignoring him. Their eyes said, *Keep away.* Modhun sympathized.

He made his way forward. Above, the sails, propped up by the wind like dead things, made flat sounds. Below, the ocean, so black that the moonlight only made it seem darker. Dizzy, Modhun turned away from the water.

A figure near the bow drew his gaze. The man's brown skin and white *dhoti* marked him as a fellow coolie, but he stood with his feet wide, and looked to the horizon as if lord and captain. Curious, Modhun approached him.

"You're not allowed here," said the man. "Coolies are to stay near the hatch." His voice carried a sense of control which defied a place in the ship's indentured cargo.

"You're here," said Modhun.

"This costs extra."

"You think I can't pay? You think I'm just another destitute hill coolie?"

"Not everything is paid for with money."

The man's hair was regal, long and free. He was a full head taller than Modhun, with big shoulders and a strong neck. His wide forehead gave a sense of intelligence, and his eyes ordered the world. Small gold hoops in his ears were the only soft note in his appearance.

"So how come you get to be here?" Modhun asked.

"One of the *sahibs* in charge of the ship—the one always polishing his sword. He lets me come here if I give him some of what I have in my pants."

"What?"

"He likes to suck my cock," the man said simply.

The idea stunned Modhun. For a *sahib* to engage in such acts seemed to contravene the laws of the universe. The shock must have shown on his face, for the man asked, "Is my language too blunt, young one?"

"I'm no child."

The man took Modhun's face in a firm hand and looked close at him. "Hnh, a few hairs on their chins and they think they're men." After he let Modhun go, he asked, "Does the idea of two men together surprise you?"

"Hardly. I've sucked more than my fair share of cock. No one's ever making me do that again, let me tell you."

"Is that why you're throwing your life away and crossing the *Kala Pani*? To secure fortune and power?"

"I'm looking for something better," said Modhun. "Isn't that why you're here? Or are you one they kidnapped?"

"No. I'm here because Garrison Commander Plunkett decided that he didn't want to make a martyr of me. By sending me to Demerara he can erase me from existence without upsetting my followers."

"Followers?" asked Modhun, on guard. "Are you a holy man?"

"My name is Akash Lall. I'm a bandit. Or at least they call me a bandit."

"Oh." Modhun relaxed. "You're political."

"Yes. The people in my village suffer terr—"

"Please," said Modhun, holding up a hand. "I'm sure you and your *followers* had wonderful reasons for breaking into homes, and stealing money and ravishing daughters. That doesn't matter to me."

"Human misery is not—"

"The only misery I care about is my own."

The ship's bell rang out. Modhun went below rather than bribe the next watch.

Once in the hold again, his mind kept picturing Akash Lall standing on the bow with a *sahib* kneeling before him. A warmth flushed Modhun's thighs. He fought his thoughts down. Better by far for him to sleep and leave this cursed vessel behind. He would seek new images in his dreams, visions of his new life to come. Visions which had guided him out of the Golden Temple with promises of deliverance.

The land is flat and green—wild with life and loud with heat. Dark water pours through its veins. Modhun is glad for the heat in Demerara. It comforts him, his bones still shivering from the ship's icy passage through the far south.

He is pleased that Akash Lall is sent with him to the same estate. The young girl, Kavita, and her mother are with them too. The woman has married on the ship, taking a higher-caste husband to replace the one whose death sent her seeking into this land. No one remarks on the difference in the couple's status; they have crossed the Kala Pani, *the Black Water, and such distinctions no longer have meaning. There are only four other women in their estate's group of seventy and those are soon 'married' as well. Not surprisingly, Akash Lall secures a wife.*

The women are to cook and clean for all the men of the estate. The school for the children will be built soon, the overseer tells them. The coolies live in the former slave quarters of the now-emancipated blacks—a dozen shacks made of ragged board, into which they crowd. It is almost like being back on the ship again.

The work starts immediately, though everyone is weak from the voyage. During slavery, new arrivals were given three years of light work to become acclimatized. Since the coolies' contracts will last only five years, however, the planters give no such concessions to them. Sunrise to sundown they are in amongst the sugar cane, slashing at waist-high weeds. Modhun is ill almost immediately, the adjustment too severe. There is no respite for him. The overseer lets him know that unless he collapses he has to work. Three other coolies who insist that they are not well enough to work are placed in stocks. One is whipped. All are fined a full week's pay.

Within a month, Modhun recovers and settles in. This is not the kind of labor that a person can love, or even become accustomed to, but he knows now that it will not break him and that knowledge strengthens his broadening

*back and straightens his spine after every day spent folded over, hacking and
tearing.*

By the end of the first fortnight on the ship, everyone had a cough—all
except Akash Lall, who would smile as he moved about the hold among the
coolies, greeting many of them by name. Modhun was thankful the journey
was near its end, for the strain of the crowded hold was becoming too much.

Akash Lall seemed a tiger given human shape. His muscles and movements
told of restrained strength. Whenever he felt these thoughts bubbling, Modhun
would look away. That part of his life was over. He would let no one hold
him back or hold him down. Never again, he'd sworn. But his resolve never
held and soon he would be back to nourishing his eyes with the golden-brown
image of Akash Lall. Something about the man sparked the cravings at the
back of Modhun's brain.

The second time Modhun went on deck, he found Akash Lall smoking a
cigarette at the bow again.

"And what did you have to offer the sword-polishing *sahib* to get tobacco?"
he asked.

Akash Lall said nothing. Modhun joined him in watching the horizon.

"I know your secret," Akash Lall whispered in his ear.

Had he been so obvious with his gazes? "H-how can—"

"I know thieves," said Akash Lall. "I've seen it in your eyes." He smirked.
"I've seen it in your *dhoti.*" With that, he grabbed Modhun's crotch, producing
a metallic jingling as he pressed the hardness there.

One fear gave way to another for Modhun. Had Akash Lall simply guessed
that any valuables Modhun had hidden would be there, or did he actually know
of the necklace of silver skulls that Modhun had stolen in Benares? "So you
want a share of it? Or are you planning to take it all from me?"

"There is no honor in stealing from such as you."

"You think you're better than me? You think that kind of thing matters
where we're going?" He pointed at the sea ahead. "This is the *Kala Pani.*
It erases everything. The past won't matter anymore. Laws, crimes, caste,
loyalty, *honor.* None of it is worth an ounce of goat dung! When we reach this
new place, we'll start equal."

Akash Lall puffed at his cigarette. "You're right," he said. "This water
will wash away Bengal, but remember this: Where we're going I will have no
reason to fight, so no one will name me criminal, whereas you will always be
a thief."

"I took nothing that I was not entitled to. Nothing that I had not already
paid the price for."

"So it was simply fair trade, I suppose?"

"Were your crimes any different?"

"Of course they were different. I was fighting for freedom, for our rights."

"Freedom from what? The British? They're the best thing to ever happen to us."

"The East India Company does nothing but take and bully."

An hour later, their argument remained unfinished when Modhun went below deck.

Within a year, eight of them are dead. Sores, fevers, dysentery: Disease finds the coolies easy prey. A dozen are in the sick house. There is a doctor, but he offers little treatment except a place on the floor of a shed built for seven. To miss work, even for sickness, is to lose pay and feel the whip. Modhun has twice escaped the lash by bribing Jacobs, the overseer.

Beatings are given out for the least offense. Zaman and Paltu get five strokes each for laughing while they worked. The two run away with the next full moon. They will walk all the way back to Bengal, if they have to, they tell the others. The decomposed bodies of two unknown men are found not long after, in a canal fifty miles to the east.

Naturally, it is Akash Lall who organizes the coolies' first protest. They steal two boats and cross to the estate on the other side of the river. When the police come, Akash offers their terms: They will not go back until Jacobs is removed. So resolutely does he argue, and so skillfully keep the coolies from breaking ranks, that their demand is met.

Things change only slightly, however. No one bothers even asking about the long-promised school anymore. The sick house remains a horror. Modhun sees the inside only once and it is enough. The smell of putrid flesh and the moans of men too delirious to recognize their coming death make him vomit on the bare floor where they lie.

He reacts much the same when Kavita is found unconscious in the horse paddock, naked and bleeding from between her legs. The girl never manages to speak and dies from her injuries soon after.

A month on the ship. They should have arrived in Demerara twice over already. The *chokidars* told them only that they were almost there.

Modhan made his third trip topside. He and Akash Lall would never speak in the hold, but when they met at the bow they greeted each other.

"Has your *sahib* told you how much longer we are to endure this misery?" Modhun asked.

"He has better uses for his mouth than speaking to me. Maybe if you…"

"My mouth is for talking. There's something I want your opinion on."

Akash Lall grunted.

"I... I'm having dreams," said Modhun. "More like visions. I see this place we're going. I see what is going to happen to us."

"Do we make it back home?"

"I can't tell. The closer we get, the more I see, but it's still not clear."

"What do you see, then?" asked Akash Lall.

"I see the work. It's hard. Very hard. I see us suffering and living like prisoners. I see you and me..."

"Yes?"

"We change," said Modhun, handpicking each word to hide the true depth of the suffering ahead. "We grow."

"How do you know these are true visions, anyway?"

"Because I've always had them. That's how I ended up at the temple in Benares. When I was a boy, I could find lost animals and money and tell when the rain would fall. I was declared a holy child. All the attention and the wonder got to be too much, though. I started making false predictions and they gave up on me soon after, made me into just another servant, but I never lost the talent."

"So why do you need my help?"

"Because... About a year ago I started having dreams about a statue of Kali at the temple. It's made of black marble and uglier than your mother. The fifty-one skulls in its necklace are made of silver, with rubies for eyes. These dreams showed me where to find tools so I could prise the necklace off without making a sound. They showed me how to smuggle it past the guards. They showed me the road to Calcutta—who would help me and where danger waited.

"And the whole time I could hear whispering in my head, telling me that the necklace was mine by right, telling me of all the riches and power I would find if I would just have the courage to take what was so easily taken. That voice was like a snake's tongue tickling my ear. It was the voice of Kali herself. I'm sure of it."

"Kali is no goddess to play games with," said Akash Lall. "She holds dominion over time and reality. She has no sense of boundaries and she delights in playing tricks."

"It was no trick. She showed me this ship while I was still a hundred miles from Calcutta."

"*This* ship?"

"Yes. Right down to the patches on the sails and the writing on the bow. She was right about everything, only now..."

"Now what?"

"Now I see things in store for me that make me think it is a trick after all."

"I have no experience with such things," said Akash Lall. "Maybe the priests at—"

"Priests." Modhun scraped the word off his tongue. "Saddhus and Yogis and Gurus and Swamis—scoundrels all! I lived in The Golden Temple for thirteen years. I know priests. They do nothing but chant words at the people and pretend to be enlightened. Always touching what doesn't belong to them. Frauds. Liars."

Akash Lall smiled. "Sounds like a good place for a thief. You should have stayed."

"No. I'll not be like them."

"What makes you think you aren't already?"

"You have such disdain for me," Modhun said. "I keep wondering why you let me stay here. Your pet *sahib* could throw me below, but you don't order him so."

"Boredom, I suppose," said Akash Lall. "The rest of them, they're nothing but hill coolies. They know crops and they know herds and nothing else. You at least have something to say." Modhun turned away, biting aside the small smile stirred by the compliment.

The whip bites like a hundred dancing scorpions on his back. Modhun starts weeping immediately. He would collapse, except that his arms are tied to the post that holds him up.

When the six strokes have been administered, Modhun struggles to imagine what insane reasoning led him to submit to this beating. As the roar of pain recedes, he remembers—it was Akash Lall. The last time Modhun had bribed his way out of a whipping, the big man had looked at him like he was a worm. What is it about Akash Lall that makes him abandon sensible thinking? Modhun wonders.

The next day, he is back in the field. It is harvest time and Modhun is on a gang fetching fifty-pound bundles of cane to the punts that will transport them down the canal to the factory. Some of the others help Modhun with his share out of sympathy. Akash Lall, however, makes no acknowledgement of Modhun's pain, or his attempt to be honorable.

Cholera struck the *Hesperus*'s cargo full-bore in the fifth week. The five casualties were dumped off the side without fuss. Once, when they were on the disposal crew, Modhun saw Akash Lall flinch as the victim's body met the dark water with no more splash than a pebble would make.

By the end of the second month they were in the far south and the weather was too cold to walk the decks. Pressed together in the hold, Modhun heard the whispered conversations of the others. The confinement was tearing down barriers between castes already. Ramesh, a *brahmin*, and Haimant, a *sudra*, discovered their mutual love of flute music and became friends arguing over how the best flutes were made. Kavita's mother told everyone that there would be schools for the laborers' children in Demerara and she thought that Kavita would do well there. Kavita seemed to take the crowding better than any of the two-hundred-odd coolies. To her, Demerara would be a place of ease and opportunity and she talked constantly about owning her own cow. Modhun tried to avoid her and her doomed ambitions, but she seemed to sense his sympathy and sought him out. He became her favored confidante.

Even with the unfaceable cold outside, the body heat of all those people and the stillness of the air made Modhun sweat precious water constantly. One of the older coolies suffocated in his sleep.

By the third month they sailed warmer waters, but despair was more prevalent. They had been lied to about the length of the voyage. Some of the coolies attacked the *chokidars*, demanding that the ship turn back for Calcutta. One man broke another's arm over a disputed bowl of *dhal* and rice.

On the evening that Haimant jumped overboard, Modhun was topside and saw it all. There was a look of deadness in the man's eyes. He was with Ramesh, who was talking in earnest with much hand movement. Haimant turned to the ocean and smiled as if he saw comfort there. He simply climbed the rail and stepped off. It seemed as if Ramesh was jumping in to rescue him before Haimant had even reached the surface. In the little time the Captain allotted for the search, the two men were not found. They belonged to the *Kala Pani* now.

Modhun paid to visit the deck twice. On the first Akash Lall was not there. The second found him avoiding the ocean.

"Thinking about Ramesh and Haimant?" asked Modhun.

"For Ramesh to jump in like that, for a mere *sudra*, knowing what it meant. I can't comprehend it."

"I thought it was brave of him."

"Crazy," Akash said. "I can't believe you admire him."

"You're scared? Not of drowning, but this water. What it means for your soul."

"I'm terrified," said Akash Lall. "I've seen death, Modhun. Terrible death. Bullets smashing men's faces into pulp. Bodies ripe and rotting after weeks in the rain. This journey we're on, though, it's far worse than death. This is the end of everything."

There is no identifiable moment when Akash Lall begins to die, but it starts in his mind. For Modhun, the first troubling sign is when the big man hacks off his waist-length hair, muttering only something about the heat when Modhun asks about it. Then, Akash Lall stops taking the headman position that he is so good at in work gangs. Whenever the coolies take a rest break in the field, he sits in a corner and stares at the ground instead of joining in the gossip and the jokes.

When Akash Lall misses two days of work, Modhun goes to investigate and finds a group of coolies taking him to the sick house. Modhun tries to stop them, but they knock him to the ground.

It takes him a week working during his free time, but Modhun builds a small shack away from the other coolies. At the sick house, he hardly recognizes Akash Lall because he has lost so much weight. With hardly any effort, Modhun carries him back and places him on a mat in his new hut.

Though she has already found herself a new man, Akash's wife agrees to supply Modhun with vegetable broth and mashed plantains for the sick man to eat.

"He was good to me," she tells Modhun. "He treated me like I was his own sister. He's a kind man. Very sweet."

That is not the Akash Lall that Modhun knows. But surely there is something to the man? After all, why is Modhun so determined not to abandon him to the sick house?

Akash rarely speaks. Mostly, he demands covers, for the fever makes him constantly tremble. The rest of the time he stares out into a distance that only he can see, fear on his face.

Modhun dresses the sores that climb Akash's legs. He bathes Akash's emaciated body with a warm washcloth. He combs his ragged hair. But the care is futile. Akash's skin goes ashen and scaly and his hair thins and hangs limp, with gray corrupting the black.

The effort of tending to Akash strains his endurance, as he must still work in the field during the day. He feels himself getting weaker. More and more, he takes the necklace of Kali from its hiding place and stares into the haunted ruby eyes of her fifty-one victims, questioning them. Were they also led to their demise with promises of riches and glory?

Sometimes, when he remembers their arguments on the ship and the way that Akash seemed to bend the world to his will, Modhun wonders if the ragged scarecrow on his floor is the same man he knew on the Hesperus.

In the middle of the August heat, Akash dies, the fear and hopelessness still there in his wide-open eyes. Modhun has had the fever for two days himself by that time. He convinces the others to clear some space in the middle of a field and they cremate Akash on a pyre of canes.

That night, Modhun is awakened by screams and angry shouts. His vision swirls and his feet refuse to hold him up. He crawls to the doorway to find all the fields ablaze. He thinks that this cannot be, that they doused Akash's pyre thoroughly, but every bit of the horizon is burning and the heat makes Modhun sweat. The smoke streams upward like a waterfall in reverse. All through the air, bits of charred cane leaf float like dark butterflies.

As Modhun loses consciousness, the smoke parts to reveal Kali, standing as tall as the sky, her dark face lit up from below by the conflagration. The giant goddess is dancing, her tongue stretched out to taste the panic and dread of the coolies. With each step she tramples the thin, bloody corpse of Akash Lall into the mud.

Then, there is blackness.

The sickness does not kill Modhun. He is one of the few to ever walk out of the sick house. However, the nightmare vision of Kali from the fever-induced delirium of that night rides along in his memory for the rest of his time in Demerara.

A few of the coolies choose to stay on when their contracts end, but Modhun takes the next ship back to Calcutta. He sells the necklace of Kali the first chance he has and the money he gets for it multiplies in his hands with every investment. Clothes of silk, jewelry, servants, and a mansion are all his within a year.

Supervising the embarkation of a load of tea one day, Modhun is accosted by a beggar woman. He raises his hand to push her aside then recognizes that she is Kavita's mother.

She tells him that she returned to India with her new husband and two children. At the train station, her husband told his family to wait while he bought tickets and then he disappeared. It seems he was too ashamed to return to his village with a low-caste wife.

Modhun gives her a room in his house, but acts like he is hiring just another servant. He wants to ask her if she ever thinks of Kavita. 'What a stupid question,' he thinks and stays silent. That night, he leaves the strong arms of his latest lover and gazes over the ocean from his balcony. The wind is cold and he knows why: It is the breath of the Kala Pani, whispering to him and bringing him dreams of the past.

Modhun was careful to pick a time when Akash was below deck to visit the bow of the *Hesperus*. Once there he removed the necklace of Kali from his *dhoti* and stared at the poisonous thing in his hands, as though he were holding not the necklace of Kali, but the serpent of Shiva.

His visions were truth, Modhun knew. If he were to keep this stolen prize, all the ambitions that had burned in him as a temple servant would be realized. But were those his ambitions still? Modhun coiled the necklace in one hand and contemplated the deepness of the black sea.

No matter what he did, there was no reason to think that his shipmates would escape their fates. The memory of Akash's despairing eyes and the pain of those last days still to come was too insistent to defy, however. "Kali Mai," Modhun prayed, "I give this back to you. Save us. Save him." The necklace of Kali blazed white in the moonlight as it streaked from Modhun's hand and struck the ocean like a burning meteor.

Behind him, slow handclaps. Akash leaned back on the rail, approval on his face. He said, "That Kali is bitch, isn't she? The thing most people forget, though, is that she's a force for good."

"You know, Akash, I don't believe you're a bandit at all."

"No?" Mischief lit up his smile as he approached Modhun. "Then I confess—I am really a Rajput prince, heir to a wealthy throne, who is running away from the demands of courtly life."

"A prince of demons, you mean," said Modhun. "Sent to torment and confound me with—"

Akash took Modhun's hand, brought it to his lips, and kissed the top of it. "My sweet thief." Akash pulled him inward.

As he let himself be held, his forehead against Akash's chest, Modhun felt the tightness in his muscles evaporate. For the first time in his adult life, he was at peace. This was love without payment; pleasure without shame. He was finally in charge of his life. It was not long before—among many other delightful things—he discovered for himself what it felt like to kneel before Akash.

In the quiet, misted dawn of the next morning, they awoke on the deck. When Modhun lifted Akash's heavy arm from his waist and sat up, he sighted land for the first time in four months. Modhun knew the landscape of mudflats and heron-dotted trees immediately. This was Demerara, the land of his visions. But where were the lighthouse and the red-roofed clock tower? Where were the donkey carts and the fields? Where were the *sahibs*?

"There's no one here," he said. "There's supposed to be a whole town."

"There's no one on the ship either," Akash said.

Instead of shouting and hustling, the topside of the *Hesperus* echoed only with silence. Where were the officers yelling orders and the sailors readying their lines for port? Where were the sneering *chokidars*?

Modhun smashed open the lock on the cargo hatch with a crowbar he found. By the time the other coolies had all climbed up to the deck, the ship had drifted up what was unmistakably the Demerara river and run aground far from either bank. A search of the ship found no crew, but the stores were intact and a lavish lunch was soon underway.

It was afternoon before the first boats showed up. They were small, pointed things with round bottoms that looked impossibly unstable. The men inside were brown-skinned, with dark, straight hair, and wore little clothing. In the confused communications that followed, with hand waving and raised voices and strange-sounding words, one thing became clear: These Demerarians had never seen people like the coolies or a ship like the *Hesperus*. Somehow, through the shifting tides of the *Kala Pani*, the coolies had come to a Demerara where the British had never set foot.

The coolies soon convinced the men in the boats to take them ashore. When Modhun stepped, barefoot, onto soft soil he felt like he was coming home.

This is a gift from Kali, he thought.

Thirty years later, not far from that same spot, Modhun watched Kavita's grandchildren play on the shore, chasing Akash, whose hair still streamed regally about him. This new world had been kind—everything Modhun had asked for that night on the *Hesperus*. But the tears still ran down his cheeks when he remembered the coolies of the other Demerara, stranded on the far shore of the *Kala Pani*.

Author's Note:

In real life, what I've called the final voyage of the Hesperus *was the first in a century of immigration from India to the West Indies, starting in 1838. The conditions on the sugar estates shown in Modhun's visions are based on historical documentation of the way the early immigrants were treated. The British government actually suspended the immigration program from time to time until better guarantees about safety, health and justice were put in place.*

Today the descendants of Indian immigrants have created a unique home and culture for themselves, better by far than what their forefathers left behind. It is the pain of those forefathers that made this new world possible, however. It may seem strange to honor them by erasing their struggle from history in the story, but I felt that they deserved a world where they could escape the indignity of the estate, even if it was only in fiction.

ROANOKE

Sandra Barret

Eᴌɪsᴀʙᴇᴛʜ Wʜɪᴛᴇ ᴄᴀᴍᴇ ᴛᴏ ᴛʜᴇ ᴅᴏᴏʀ, bringing her latest gift from Sampson. "It is more food than we need."

Her eyes glanced over me, showing the unquenchable spirit I so admired in her. I took the offered rabbit. "Were it not for your beau, we would have nothing to eat in this household." The spinster cottage had no men and thus no hunters to bring in meat regularly. We survived on the kindness of those like Elisabeth.

She held my arm. "Not my beau, Miss Payne, though he may think otherwise."

Her adamant statement heartened me. Of the three men who ran Roanoke, Sampson had the least respect for unwed women and would have left us all behind in England, were he governor. As it was, he ignored our needs as much as he might, insisting we should wed if we could not care for ourselves.

I held the rabbit to the waning sunlight. It would not fill the bellies of the four women in this cottage, though it would be a welcome addition. Elisabeth bid me good-bye, but I begged her wait as I left the rabbit to those women more able at cooking than I. Staring at their gaunt faces, I could sit by no more. "I would return with you to speak with your guardian."

I grabbed my thick woolen shawl, and Elisabeth led the way across the frozen ground to the building she shared with her sister, Eleanore, and Ananias, her sister's husband, one of the men left in charge of the colony when our governor returned to England for supplies. Their cottage held the same sparse contents as most here, bare floors and a solitary hearth used for both warmth

33

and meal preparations. So much we had left behind for the chance of a new life in this new world. Yet, as I considered the plight of those of us without husband or brother to provide for us, I wondered anew if this land would give us life or slow death.

Eleanore sat by the hearth, spinning the last of the season's wool into the yarn she would use for her first born. I could see the barest swell of her belly, showing that she had many months before her child would arrive in the coming summer.

The cottage had bedrolls brought from England, unlike the straw bed covered in cloth that I slept on. Ananias sat in conversation with Manteo, our guide and a prince of the Croatan tribe. I thought my courage would leave me as I looked into Ananias' cool gray eyes, but Manteo's presence emboldened me. On our long voyage from England, he had taught me his language and much of his tribe. Mayhap he would support my cause.

Ananias stood from his stool and welcomed me. "What brings you to us, Rose Payne?"

"The women, sir. I fear we may not survive without more food."

"The winter has been hard on all."

As the only midwife, I had some training with sickness, but it proved little help against scurvy and the sweating sickness that had already claimed half of our colony, including the families we spinsters had been indentured to. "I know our men hunt and trap as much as they can, but they feed their families first. No one looks to the needs of the spinsters now that the Lord has claimed our masters."

"What would you have us do?"

I had but one idea. "Teach me to trap and fish."

"That would not be proper work for a woman. No one would teach you."

Manteo, squatting next to Ananias, stared at me, his dark brown eyes searching for I know not what before he spoke in his own language. "I know one who could guide you, if you wish."

Ananias, like most in Roanoke, had not learned Manteo's language, so I translated his proposal. In the end, I was not encouraged, but neither was I prohibited. On the morrow, I would meet Manteo's tutor and soon, God willing, I could provide for us near-forgotten souls.

I was not prepared for Manteo's tutor. Maigan was older and smaller than I, but broad of shoulder with an intensity of spirit that amazed me. She spoke not a word of English, but greeted me in Croatan. I had seen the women of Manteo's tribe and none looked as she did. She tied her long black hair in one braid, as did the men, and wore men's leggings under a woman's long tunic. Intricate necklaces bespoke her privileged rank within the tribe, and I was not surprised to learn that she was Manteo's aunt and thus sister to his tribal king.

There was more to Maigan's rank than that, but Manteo used words unknown to me to describe her.

When he left us, it seemed he took my courage with him. Left alone with this enigma, I knew not what to say, but followed her silently beyond the wooden palisade that surrounded our village. We moved along a frozen path through the surrounding woods. Once beyond the sight and sound of the village, I could smell the sea that surrounded our island.

Maigan stooped by a felled tree and motioned me to join her. She pointed to a cluster of ragged brush, bare of leaf and weighed down with snow. "To trap an animal, you must know how it lives." We watched for long hours, moving from area to area. Maigan taught me where to fish and how to gather the best material to build my own traps. It was a hard lesson, but she had a patience about her that welcomed me and emboldened me to ask questions.

Days passed before I snared my first rabbit, using one of Maigan's traps. She gifted me the trap, advising me how to use it to build my own set. It was trying work to find the right branches and other material in such cold weather, but the thought of providing for the other spinsters fortified my spirit.

At the end of that first fortnight, as I set my first, weak trap, I asked the question most on my mind. "Why are you the only woman in your tribe allowed to hunt?"

Maigan's dark eyes studied me. "You and I are not women. We are *okitcitakwe*."

"She is a woman. She should stay within the palisade in winter." Sampson's scratchy voice bespoke the illness he had yet to recover from, the fever so many of our colony had died of this winter. Still, God forgive me, I had not prayed for his recovery as I had the others, so many men, women, and children who deserved more from this harsh land of Virginia than did he.

Ananias gave me not a glance, but rubbed his weary eyes. "The Croatans have taught her to trap fish and snare rabbits. Have we so much spare food that we can deny her skills? How many in this village have not tasted meat today?"

I stood a stone sentinel as they discussed my fate. Had I been born a boy, I would not be here. I would be hunting for meat in the woods of this island, skills Maigan had taught me. She spoke to me on other subjects as well, secrets I dared not speak of.

Sampson gave up his argument, yet I saw the stamp of disgust in his eyes as he left, as did Ananias. "You have not made a friend of him with this new trade, Rose, but we need what food we can get."

I left Ananias's cottage, saddened the more for not meeting Elisabeth. She alone encouraged my new skills. The spinsters accepted the food I brought, but I felt their hard glares. I was something they did not comprehend and thus did not trust. Yet the men seemed to welcome my skills, all save Sampson. Maigan's words echoed in my thoughts, and I felt an inkling of understanding. I was changing, becoming something different, and some feared what they did not know.

I walked across the hard-packed snow to the back of the cottage where I kept the traps Maigan taught me to build. With Ananias tempering Sampson's objections, I made haste to set my traps and catch what food I might. Little meat there was to spare and the spinsters saw less and less of it each week, save those who had caught the eye of a suitor. I, with my plain skirts and odd ways would not attract such a man, nor did I seek to. God have mercy, but my desire sought none but one I could not have.

Maigan came three days later, gifting me a knife of good quality and a bow for which I must attend her for lessons. I followed her out through the wooden palisade gate to the cedar forest south of Roanoke. Silently she walked, her thoughts ever on the secrets of her trade. She was tribal healer, spiritual guide, and advisor. She had taken me to her village more than once, and I found that the reverence with which the Croatans treated her seemed to encompass me while I was in her presence. There is so much to the Croatan ways that cannot be expressed with English words. I knew not what to make of it.

I walked behind Maigan, envious of the freedom her men's garments gave her as I pulled my skirts from another trailing bramble bush.

"Your tribe accepts you as hunter?" she asked, breaking the long silence.

"Most, yes. The women are glad of the extra fish." The spinsters accepted me once they recognized that I was no threat to their search for a husband. "Hunger forgives many differences."

A turkey pecked at the muddied ground in front of us, the first sign of warmer weather. Maigan showed me how to nock an arrow and draw my new bow. "And you are shaman." She spoke a mix of English and her Croatan language, but I knew her meaning. She'd seen me give last prayers to the dead. "But still you dress as a woman."

I retrieved my spent arrow, having missed the wild turkey. "I am a woman."

Maigan held my bow, covering my hand with hers. "I am hunter. I interpret the Gods for my people. I have two wives. Am I woman?"

"You are *okitcitakwe*, but we have no such kind in England."

"This is not England."

The argument was old. Maigan showed me the path, but I could not walk it. The colony would not accept me as *okitcitakwe*, as a person who walked in the worlds of both men and women as Maigan did.

Elisabeth came to my cottage after prayers, bearing a tightly wrapped package. The rest of the women had stayed in the meeting house, but I had traps to repair. She closed the door against the pelting rain and stood in the dim light of the hearth fire, breathless and, God forgive me, beautiful. She held out her package. "These are for you."

I saw the mischievous glint in her eye as I accepted the gift. I untied her careful wrappings to find a pair of workman's breeches, shirt, boots, and jacket. My hands drifted over the material, unsure how to react.

"I saw the state of your skirts when you come back from your hunting, so I spoke to Henry Berry. He gave me these. They belong to his brother, who is tall, like you."

I was dumbstruck. Ananias and the other men accepted my skills because they needed me, but I knew not Henry's mind on the matter. That he would encourage me seemed unthinkable. "But I cannot wear men's garments, Elisabeth."

"Not within the palisade, no. But Henry suggests you hide them without and exchange your skirts for these while you hunt."

I fingered the clothes, wanting to try them on, but afraid of what it meant. "Sampson already despises what I do and calls me deviant."

Elisabeth's hand was on my arm in an instant, its warmth penetrating to my core.

"The Lord knows and loves each of us for who we are. We live in a new land, with new possibilities." Her delicate hand touched my cheek. "Would that I could see you in them, my Rose."

Speech would not come as I was lost in her touch and the closeness of her. The approach of voices made her drop her hand, and I hastily wrapped her gift back in its package and hid it under my straw mat. Elisabeth slipped out of the cottage as the other women entered. Thoughts of the gift and the bearer kept me awake well into the night, debating the possibilities of what it all meant.

Elisabeth was right, the men's clothes made my tasks easier, and Maigan taught me to hunt larger prey within the forest. Bringing the meat back to the palisade proved the most difficult. Ever wary of being found in men's garments, I had to change clothes before approaching the village. The pride in Elisabeth's eyes pleased me greatly when I brought home my first deer. That we were constant companions was known by all, but secretly, my heart prayed that we could be more, a wish I felt Elisabeth shared as well.

That Sampson hated me, I did not doubt, both for my skills as a hunter and for my friendship with Elisabeth. I know not whether he followed me from the village that day or happened upon me in the hunt. Before I checked my first trap, he was there.

"You are an abomination." His hands seized my shoulders. "Deviant woman. You may wear our clothes but you will never be a man."

"Nor do I wish to be if you are the icon of your kind."

He slapped my face, then marched me back to the village. I walked through the palisade gate, my face awash in shame as he pushed me forward to Ananias's cottage. Ananias was in bed with the fever. Elisabeth wiped his brow with a damp cloth, her hand stopping in mid wipe when she saw us enter. Color flooded her cheeks as her gaze swept over me. Sampson pushed me to the side and Elisabeth stepped back from him, her color fading.

Ananias's bleary gaze took in all this. "What brings you here, Sampson?"

"Can you not see for yourself that Rose Payne has gone too far?"

Ananias lifted himself from his bed to gaze at me. "Rose?" He coughed and collapsed back on his bed.

Elisabeth came forward to cover him. "He is too sick for this. Take your complaints to Mr. Berry."

Sampson grabbed my arm and led me away, but not before I saw the anguish in Elisabeth's face. Henry Berry had not the courage to stand up to Sampson, letting him dictate my punishment—five lashes. I would no longer be allowed to hunt or trap. I was to be kept within the palisade, allowed beyond only to tend the crops when needed.

Henry insisted on administering the lashes himself, for which I was grateful. Had Sampson carried out my punishment, I would have had more than the stinging welts upon my back. Afterward, I returned to my cottage and changed back to women's clothes. No one came for the men's clothing. No one came at all, leaving me in my shame.

Maigan came the next day. I know not how she discovered my plight, but she met me in the field where I was sowing the beans. "The English do not understand," she said.

I stood up, pressing a hand to my sore back. "No, they do not." Yet that was not a fair statement. Some had come to me in the morning, expressing their distress at my treatment, but none dared oppose Sampson, not for my sake.

Maigan stood at the edge of my field. "Come with me. My tribe honors our kind."

I looked back at the wooden palisade surrounding our small village, seeing a glimpse of Elisabeth through the open gates. "I cannot leave whilst my heart stays here."

Ananias succumbed to the fever a week later and Eleanore, in her distress, went into labor. Only then did Elisabeth come for me, for my skills as midwife. She stood in the doorway, her paleness expressing how difficult her days had been of late. She stopped me before I could leave the cottage. "Forgive me," she said. "I dared not come sooner. Sampson has been watching over Ananias night and day. I fear he watches over me as well."

Dread enveloped me in its dark embrace. "He will marry you now that your guardian is dead."

I could see the fear in Elisabeth's eyes. She stepped closer to me, cupping my face in her warm hands. I held my breath as soft lips touched mine, lips I had longed for. Bittersweet was the kiss as we parted, breathless. "I have prayed so long that it would be otherwise, yet there is no escape for me."

She stepped away from me, overcome by sadness. I closed the space between us and kissed her again, wrapping her in my arms. When our kiss ended, she rested her head upon my shoulder. I kissed her cheek. "Do not give up on us, Elisabeth. I will find a way."

Eleanore's labor was mercifully quick, and Virginia Dare was born at midnight with a healthy cry and rosy complexion. Elisabeth took the babe whilst Eleanore slept. It was then that I presented my idea to Elisabeth. It was not the first time I had thought of it, but I knew Sampson would wait no more, nor would Henry step in on Elisabeth's behalf, bachelor though he was.

"Come with me," I repeated. "Maigan's tribe would give us a home."

Elisabeth cooed at the baby, and I thought she had not heard me until she spoke, a mere whisper in the dimly lit room. "Am I to leave Eleanore and my niece? No, there is no hope for us, my Rose."

My thoughts whirled. "There must be a way, please. Give me time."

There was little else I could say, and so I left. The walk back to my cottage solidified my plan. With the moon near full, I could make it to the Croatan village by dawn. I gathered my shirt, trousers, and boots and made my way into the woods. The warm night was thick with the sounds of crickets and the rush of some night creature my passage disturbed. I had been often enough to the Croatan village to know the paths to it by night.

The hum of insects announced the dawn as clearly as the graying sky. I could smell the cooking fires of the Croatan village. I was greeted by a pair of young men who took me into the small village. Their houses were more round than square, topped in thatch, much like our own in Roanoke. A long mat stretched across the central walkway and the women were already placing out the morning meal. Unlike Maigan, the women wore their hair braided on both sides, their late spring skirts covering them mid waist to knee.

Maigan emerged from her home. Without a word, she left the village and I followed her. We walked to the shore before she spoke. "You are English no more."

It was not a question and yet I answered. "I cannot come alone. Elisabeth will not leave without Eleanore and the new babe."

Maigan eyed me critically. "You come with two wives?"

I faltered, knowing what she meant but not how to explain myself. "I would provide for Eleanore, but I cannot marry both."

Maigan laughed, her hands resting on my shoulders as she looked up at me. "You are English no more."

It was the last I would hear from her. A shot splintered the quiet morning and I watched the life drain from her dark face. I grasped her as she fell, sinking to my knees. When I heard the heavy footfalls behind me, I turned, expecting to see one of Manteo's tribe. Instead, the sweating face of Sampson emerged from the overgrown trail. My heartbeat galloped within my chest. Like a coward, he had shot her in the back. My hand grasped the handle of the knife Maigan had given me.

Sampson raised his rifle, a cold smile crossing his face. "You make my task too easy, Rose Payne."

He could not have reloaded so soon. In a flash, I knew his plan, but it was too late. His rifle came down upon my head before I could react. I collapsed across Maigan's still form, seeing Sampson drop the rifle beside me before he fled into the woods. My eyes drifted shut, but I fought the darkness that threatened to envelope me. He would not win.

I shifted, forcing myself off the ground. Maigan lay before me, lifeless. I lifted her, then stood, ignoring the pounding in my head. Step by step, I carried her. I was met again before the village, but this time, there was no happy greeting. She was taken from me and carried to her simple house. No one spoke to me and I knew not what to do, so I followed.

An older woman entered, chanting in words I could not comprehend. She cut a lock of Maigan's hair and a snip of her nails, placing them in a small pouch that she left resting on Maigan's still chest. Then I was left alone with Maigan. Some came later to clean her, but still, no one spoke to me. As the silence and the isolation surrounded me, I cried silent tears for a mentor who'd given me more than anyone else. *Okitcitakwe* and friend.

As night fell, the village came alive with the haunting sound of a slow lament. Manteo, whom I had not seen in months, came, along with an older man who knelt by Maigan and wept. Two young women came in and wrapped Maigan in an ornately beaded blanket. A leather string was attached to the pouch the old woman had prepared. I was told to follow as Manteo and his father lifted Maigan's sleep pallet and carried her and the pouch beyond the village to the burial ground.

I watched as the old woman came again to chant and cast oils upon Maigan. As Maigan was lowered into the ground, the old woman clutched the pouch and brought it to me. Manteo stood by me, translating her lament into words I could follow.

"You came to be adopted into our family," he said. "Accept now, the soul of the one who brought you."

The woman draped the pouch over my head. Manteo waited until the ceremony ended before he explained the ritual. "When one as important as

Maigan dies, our custom is to encourage her spirit to live on in another. You were more than kindred to Maigan. The elders selected you to bear her spirit and take her place."

The pouch hung below my chest and I felt the weight of its meaning settle on me. I would be not just a member, but *okitcitakwe* to the tribe, honored as Maigan had been.

Two days later, the elders met in council and I was asked to join them. Maigan's death would be avenged. I saw the sadness in Manteo's eyes, a match to my own. The hunters of the village, old and young, set off to Roanoke the next morning, with Manteo and I at the front. I felt heavy of heart and spirit. There were many I cared for within the palisade walls beyond just Elisabeth. And yet I clutched Maigan's bow in my hand, for I would not let Sampson take both Maigan and Elisabeth from me.

The palisade gates were barred and the village quiet as we approached. Manteo bid us stop outside of gun range. A stillness settled without, but not within my heart and mind. When the palisade gate creaked open, I felt the stir of anticipation sweep through our party. But instead of a rush of armed Englishmen, only one man emerged, Henry Berry. The gates closed behind him.

I stood apart from the group, and with Manteo at my side, I met Henry as he approached.

"Rose." He took a step closer. "He told us you were dead." His bloodshot eyes glanced between us both, then he addressed himself to Manteo. "We cannot make up for Sampson's crimes, but know that he has been justly punished. We ask now only for peace between us."

"Punished?" I said.

"When he bragged of killing Maigan and you, Elisabeth shot him with Ananias's pistol."

The palisade gate opened again, letting loose one more soul, my Elisabeth. Heedless of all around her, she ran to my side. Her hands cupped my face as if to prove I was real and not a ghost. I spoke not a word, but she saw my pain, the loss of Maigan, and understood. I would have left with her then, but my place in Manteo's tribe required I act as mediator between the two villages, English and Croatan. Man and Woman, *okitcitakwe*.

Within a year, the villages were one. There were difficulties between English and Croatan, but time and patience taught us understanding. Over time, the English accepted me as advisor, much as the Croatans did by tradition. We thrived, with no threat to our unity. Not for another year, not until we saw the sails of an English ship.

It was late summer, and had we left but a day earlier for the annual meeting of the tribes, we would not have seen the ship. Mayhap the Lord, or the spirits of the Croatans, were guiding us, for I know not what would have happened had most of our village been away when Governor White returned.

Manteo and Henry walked to the seaward shore to verify the ship. I would have gone with them, but Elisabeth bid me stay. Her face was a mask of worry, for White was not just our Governor returning after three years, but her own and Eleanore's father. I lived now in the cottage with Elisabeth and her sister. Little Virginia toddled around the dirt patch in front of the door under Eleanore's watchful eye. Elisabeth waited within, sitting in the dark by the cold hearth. Would that I could assuage her fears, but none amongst us knew what to expect from the English ship.

When White entered the village, few came out to greet him, so great was our uncertainty. He could tell with a glance that we were preparing to leave, the packs of food and bedding piled outside each cottage. His face was unreadable until he recognized Eleanore and quickened his pace with a broad smile.

He wrapped his arms around his eldest daughter. "I should have taken you both back with me." He glanced at me but did not recognize me in my Croatan clothes. I wore my hair short, as the English men did, but my garments were Maigan's, and I still filled her role within our combined village.

I stepped out of the shadow of the cottage. "Your daughters have fared well, Governor." He stared at me, but still did not recognize me. "Rose. Rose Payne," I said.

He had no words for me, but addressed Henry when he approached with Manteo. "I thank you Manteo, for your help in keeping our village safe. Know that you and your people will always be dear to us, but this island is claimed by England, and this village must return to English ways." His gaze slid over me again, but his manner bespoke no tolerance, no acceptance of what we had become in his absence, what I had become.

"The land may be English," I said. "But the people are no longer."

His frustration rose at my defiance, but that was nothing to his ire when Elisabeth stepped into the light and stood by my side. "You are not our Governor anymore," she said. "Our life, our loves, are set by the this new world, not by English rule." She slipped her hand in mine.

His eyes narrowed as he blustered. "If you will not submit to me, you will to English guns and English sailors."

I gave the only peace offering I knew. "Any in this village who would return to English life are free to join you. Take the willing with you and start the town of Raleigh as we were chartered to do three years ago."

His eyes never left my face, so vivid was his anger. He would not take my offering, not just because it was a compromise he could not face, but because he still saw me as a woman, with no voice or authority. He could never understand, nor would any of the English. It was the first time I acknowledged how much I had gained through Maigan's guidance, and how little I'd lost by accepting who I was.

He raised a hand to strike me, but my knife was in my hand and at his throat before he could react. His eyes spoke hatred, as did his voice. "You are a demon! None here will follow you."

White left us, refusing any further discussion. The tribe, English and Croatan, came together to decide our future. I voiced my choice to leave, welcoming any who would join me. The decision was unanimous. White would return with his sailors and his guns, but he would find naught but an empty shell. None would wait for him, none would join him.

With our preparations already made for a long journey, we slipped out of the palisade gates for the last time shortly before sunset. I knew not what he would tell his sailors, but in his heart, he'd know the cold stab of rejection our departure signaled. Neither English nor Croatan, we had become something more.

Neither man, nor woman, I had become something more.

Author's Note:

I've always had a fascination for the Roanoke colony. I remember learning about it in grammar school and wondering—what happened to all those people? While historians can tell us more about those events than my grammar school class did, I still feel drawn to those colonists. What sort of person would leave family and all that's familiar behind to come to a strange land? And how would they react to tenets of Native American culture that had no counterparts in Western culture?

In "Roanoke", I explore the fundamental changes in one such colonist when these two cultures meet. The colonist embraces the two-spirit tradition to lead the colony to a new place, both geographically and culturally. "Roanoke" posits an alternate resolution to the mystery of America's early colony, a twist in time driven by Native American gender roles.

A MARRIAGE OF CHOICE

Dale Chase

Aʟʟ ᴡᴀs ʙʟɪss ᴜɴᴛɪʟ Mʀ. Jᴇꜰꜰᴇʀsᴏɴ, my Thomas, announced plans to return to America. Months have passed in his company—and his bed—while my happiness has risen to a level heretofore unknown. I have seen the best of Paris in his company. I have been entertained, doted upon, caressed, and repeatedly and most pleasurably ravished, and as a result have fallen into that incomparable state wherein lovers reside.

I knew all along that my holiday would at some point come to an end, but Thomas swept away all such care. In his embrace time passed unacknowledged; forever seemed well at hand. Then came his announcement of the return, which sliced into me with the sharp blade of practicality, catching me unawares and far from prepared.

I wait for him to address our personal situation but thus far he offers no indication of a future together. In his favor, I allow that he has larger concerns than that of a young lover. He is lately consumed by plans for a Bill of Rights for our Constitution, exchanging frequent letters with James Madison, and he is as a result often agitated at the prospect of setting down guaranteed freedoms for all citizens.

Further complicating things is a rebellion of sorts by his slave, Samuel Hemmings, who has said if he remains in Paris he is, by French law, a free man. This greatly upsets Thomas as he is much attached to the handsome young man, both carnally and otherwise. He thus has on his mind not one but two considerations, and I find myself an unacknowledged third, which causes me terrible strain, for I cannot envision life without him.

I think at times to approach him about our future, but he is caught up with Samuel's uncharacteristic demand, and when that quiets, a letter from Madison invariably arrives. Thomas is lost to me as he becomes once again the statesman. The only time I have him to myself is in bed, where the last thing I wish to approach is a difficult situation. That I entered the scene at all has complicated his life, but I never meant to intrude. Our meeting was, after all, mere happenstance.

Introduced at a grand soiree, the attraction was immediate and surprising, for I had no knowledge that the American statesman preferred men to women; yet, as the evening progressed, it became most obvious. When Mr. Jefferson invited me to his villa after the party, I went most willingly.

As some sense of decorum must be observed in the telling of such things, I shall relate only that Mr. Jefferson was most ardent, most competent, and most rewarding during the ensuing night. And again in the morning. When his Samuel then entered the room he brought an air of scorn and I saw only then that it was he who usually satisfied the master.

Mr. Jefferson asked me to stay on a few days, which I did, as I was on extended holiday. After an initial week of intense bedding, we took trips to the south of France and to Italy, always accompanied by Samuel. Perhaps this was prophetic, my usurping his place, for it is upon our return to Paris that the slave announces his intention to remain in France.

"I must have him with me," Thomas declares, pacing the room after Samuel has been dismissed.

"Surely there are other slaves able to assume his duties," I counter.

"Of course there are. That is not the issue. Samuel has been with me all his life. I took him as my personal servant when he was just fourteen; he is now twenty and knows my ways as no other."

"Can you not, as his owner, force him to accompany you home?"

Thomas shakes his head. I watch his impressive figure, and see the concern which brings on my own longing, for how am I to continue without him? I can return to America, but I no longer wish to do so on my own; yet I cannot bring up my personal wishes when he has so much on his mind. And Madison's latest letter only complicates things.

Thomas fell into silence upon reading of James Madison's effort toward a Bill of Rights, and I know a lengthy reply is forming, put off temporarily by Samuel's rebellion. Thus I fall to third place—until bedtime, however, when I am again courted by the dashing and romantic Thomas, the devil who tells me dirty stories and gets himself so worked up that we sometimes do the deed in the library, clothes all but torn from my body. I am later cosseted in his bed, fondled, kissed, and on occasion taken again.

A day passes in which Thomas speaks at length with Samuel and for a time the two disappear upstairs. I remain in the salon, knowing what takes place above, forcing myself to accept that Mr. Jefferson, the master, will always have his Samuel. The slave is far more a given than I.

Renewed attentions and assurances ultimately cause Samuel to relent and he at last declares loyalty to his master. He will not remain in France. Only then does Thomas turn to me, but even then he is distracted.

"Madison has sent the twelve proposed amendments," he tells me, "asking my opinion, so I am in contemplation of individual freedoms, which serves to remind me of our great distance from home. Madison needs my help before he faces Congress. It will be a battle with the Federalists to even allow a Bill of Rights."

I say nothing. Since I usually engage in spirited discussion, my silence causes him to look hard upon me. He becomes concerned because he is, after all, a caring man. "Caleb, what is it?"

I draw a long breath before speaking, as this conversation will direct the path on which my life is to be set. "You have had much to deal with and I seem to be omitted, which I do understand, only now you make plans for your return to America and I am not considered."

We are at table on a bright May morning that is marred only by this difficult topic.

"My dear boy," Thomas begins, "oh, my dear boy, you are very much considered and I am sorry not to have spoken as such. You know my present preoccupations, but you, Caleb, you are my everything. Have you not gained such assurance from my attentions?

"In your bed, yes, but otherwise I seem overlooked."

"You are right, of course, it does appear so, but please know you are in my heart every second of the day. Perhaps it is your being so present in my life these months that has allowed me to look toward other things. I never meant for you to be less, for surely you are not. So now, tell me, will you join me on my return home?"

"Monsieur Le Beque has offered me a position in his law office. I have no such guarantee at home."

Thomas shuts his eyes for a moment, as though he has suffered a wound, and for that moment I do feel that I've inflicted one, justifiably so. "You have every guarantee, Caleb. Reside with me at Monticello. There is much to do and I cannot envision any of it without you at my side. You can be my secretary, assist me with my work, my farm."

He is leaning forward in his chair now, flushed with concern, and for the first time in days I feel returned to him. "I would like to remain with you," I tell him, and he offers a long sigh and the smile I so adore.

"Then it is settled," he declares.

"Will you go to the Congress in New York?" I ask.

He shakes his head. "Madison wants it but I prefer he come to Monticello. We can make our plans there."

We fall to silence as we finish our breakfast, after which we stroll out onto the terrace. At the railing Thomas puts his hand over mine. "You do know I love you," he says.

"Yes, and I you."

He then takes me upstairs to seal the declaration.

Aboard ship en route to America, Thomas begins to exhibit a restlessness I have not seen before, one which sexual activity does not relieve. He appears satisfied in those immediate moments after I have been wonderfully ravaged, but he then retreats into a kind of uneasy contemplation that renders him silent. When I inquire if something troubles him, I am dismissed with assurances that all is well and yet I can see it is not.

We have become friends with a giddy young couple recently married, who return from a Paris honeymoon. George and Felicia Randall are handsome and bright and though quite young, possessed of the finest manners. At supper we four sit at table, I beside my Thomas, and I note how engaged is my lover, how enthusiastic for this couple embarking on life's great adventure. Thomas speaks highly of marriage, which stirs my interest, seeing as how it is doubtful he shall ever enter into such a union, but I take this simply as part of his curious way and also his unfailing good grace.

Later, when he asks me to his cabin, he is not as urgent as usual. He is pensive, even as he undresses me.

"What is it, Thomas?" I ask.

"Hmmm?" He is as distracted by the question as by his own thoughts.

"Something is on your mind, has been for days. Can you not tell me?"

He settles me onto his bed, my chest bare, and slips an arm around me. Nuzzling my neck, he observes that the young married couple might at that same moment be doing the same thing. I am taken aback by such a statement.

"They are in love, and that particular state brings on an eagerness, does it not?" he asks. "One wishes to commune with one's wife in the most intimate manner."

"I suppose so."

"He removes her clothing much as I remove yours." Here he pushes me back and removes my trousers, my underdrawers. When I am naked he looks upon me at length.

"He might have her naked now, his manhood erect." Now he opens his own trousers, reaches in, pulls out his cock. "He then might fuck her."

This inflames me beyond all reason and I reach for his organ, begin to pull at it, which puts conversation asunder. As I work him he quickly strips away his clothes and I am mounted most ardently. The young couple is, for the moment, forgotten.

The following day we are on deck taking the air when Thomas notes that a man is free to place an arm around his wife in public but should he, Thomas, express himself likewise with me, there would be frowns and talk. I cannot deny what he says.

"A ship is a small world," I offer, "unlike your Monticello where you may enjoy your freedom."

The Randalls pass by at this point and Thomas nods, bids them good-day, and the greeting is returned, but I feel him tense. "Is it fair that we are denied such expression?" he asks.

"We need not make a show of such things," I counter. "We are confident with one another and that must suffice."

"But is our love not equal to theirs? Am I not as committed to you as George Randall is to his Felicia?"

"Of course," I assure him as the Randalls recede.

"Then don't you see?" he asks. "Were I to place an arm around you, as I surely long to do, there would be questions of propriety when, in fact, we are no different than George and Felicia Randall."

"Where our love is concerned, we are not," I reply, "but you must look beyond feelings. They are man and woman; they are married."

"Exactly!"

I am now at a loss. He compares apples to oranges and asks me to declare them similar.

"Equality, Caleb. Are we not committed to equality in our new Constitution, and will I not be assisting Madison with the formulation of his Bill of Rights to ensure that equality? How then can we stand here and accept inequality?"

He turns to me then. "I declare my love for you and ask that you be by my side always. I ask for your hand in marriage."

I am shocked at such a statement. "Surely you jest."

"I most certainly do not," he insists.

"It isn't done."

"Perhaps it should be."

The sky soon turns gray but Thomas refuses to go to his cabin. His unrest on the subject of marriage seems no less than that of the churning sea.

"Some things are not meant to be changed," I offer some time later. Huddled beside him under my great coat, I shiver as I try to make a point. "Marriage is a sacred trust between man and woman."

"Would you not marry were we able?"

My heart flops about, leaping one second, falling the next. I am at a loss because he strays beyond reality. "Of course I would marry you, Thomas, I love you, but even saying such words feels awkward, intrusive. Two men do not belong in that particular institution."

"Two men," he says, "have no rights whatsoever. We may not hold hands in public nor embrace nor kiss. We must, in the interest of society's delicate balance—which is in reality no balance at all—remain forever unacknowledged."

"You would condemn propriety?"

"In this case, yes, I would."

That night he has Samuel to his cabin instead of me. I do not complain as I must tread lightly where Samuel is concerned. He and I have managed to craft an odd coexistence in sharing the master's bed and I sometimes wonder at the slave's feelings for the man I love.

The following day as Thomas and I take the air he tells me he will conduct an experiment, and as we stand at the railing he slides an arm around my waist, which causes me to flinch.

"Relax," he says. "A show of affection is in order for one's true love. We shall see how it plays to our audience."

"I fear you do yourself damage," I tell him but he only smiles and pulls me close. "After this we'll retreat to my cabin."

"Which will surely set them talking."

"So be it. We are men free to do as we please and I rather fancy a good fuck."

I blush at such talk here in the open, especially when an elderly couple pause nearby to gaze seaward. Mr. Jefferson does not remove his arm from my waist and I see from the corner of my eye the turning of heads.

Later, as Thomas undresses me in his cabin, I tell him talk of our salacious activity will be all over the ship.

"Talk of what? Affection? How ghastly that one man could love another."

He has me naked now and kneels to get at my morsel. Nothing more is said.

"Madison has agreed!" Thomas announces, rushing into the sitting room at Monticello, letter in hand. "He has read my proposal for the amendment's wording and says we have much to discuss. He arrives Thursday."

"Is he in agreement about the proposal or merely the visit?"

"The visit, but that is of little consequence. He is a thinker, a listener, a man of reason who cares as much as I for the rights of man. I know I can convince him to make the change I propose."

"I wouldn't be so certain."

He smiles. "Skepticism?"

"Practicality," I counter. "He may not see your point."

"He will be here three days. In that time I shall make my point his."

James Madison, I find, is as close to my thirty-two years as he is to Jefferson's forty-three. At thirty-eight he is frisky, kind, but above all articulate. I see why he was elected to Congress. While I adore my beloved Thomas, his soft voice and shy manner make him a reluctant public speaker. Madison, on the other hand, is a veritable whirlwind. The two are soon settled in the library, hashing over the proposed wording.

Madison began his Bill of Rights with George Mason's Virginia Declaration of Rights, and both he and Jefferson champion that great statesman for what he has given Virginia. Before him, there was no such document, and it has proven the ideal starting point for something similar at the federal level.

Thomas has read Madison's amendments over and again, aloud to me and quietly to himself, and now debates with his close friend and ally in the effort toward guaranteeing all citizens certain specific freedoms. They agree entirely on the need for the Bill of Rights, declaring that the Constitution as presently written does not guard against abuses of power, but the phrase Thomas is now determined to add has set them apart. Madison fails to see things as does his friend. I need not sit in the library to hear them argue as their voices rise with their passion.

"The freedoms of speech, press, and religion are the choicest privileges of the people," Madison declares, and Thomas heartily agrees, yet says they are not enough. "The freedom I speak of must also be included."

"You go too far."

"I think not. It is a rightful liberty and we must insure it is never violated."

Madison goes silent. I picture a furrowed brow. "Government must not intrude on such a private matter," he finally says.

"Aha!" Jefferson seizes upon this to make his point. "Would not denying this most basic freedom become that very intrusion?"

"But government would do no such thing. The right to marry whomever one pleases is well established. It need not be addressed."

Thomas does not immediately respond. I believe him to be pacing the room, as is his habit. At length he frames a reply.

"My friend, I am afraid we approach the matter from opposite ends and I fear you are unable to see across to my side."

"I'm sorry, I'm lost as to your meaning."

I hear Thomas utter a long sigh and when he begins to speak his tone becomes intimate. I rise from my chair to stand just outside the doorway so I may continue to hear.

"A marriage of choice," he says, and in the ensuing pause I assume Madison is nodding, not having grasped what as yet remains unsaid. And how on earth is Thomas to say it?

"James, you have a good marriage to a woman you love and I fear this good fortune blinds you to the plight of those less fortunate...such as myself."

"You have not met the right woman," Madison declares.

"But I have met the right person, my friend. I am deeply in love and wish to marry."

"Wonderful! I am truly happy for you. What is her name?"

"Caleb Carr, the young man I have taken as my secretary."

To his credit there is no outcry from Madison, only a long pause. To my lover's credit, he does not intrude as his friend works to grasp the situation. At length, Madison manages only an "I see."

"Do you?" Thomas asks, seizing upon the meager reply. "Do you truly? Because it is the basis for what we must make into law, that a person must be guaranteed the right to contract a marriage of choice."

Madison chuckles. "And I thought..."

"Understandably," Thomas adds. "Your frame of reference is marriage to a woman and I do not dispute that glorious union. I only wish to make a similar union available to each and every citizen without discrimination as to sex."

"Two men to marry."

"Yes, or two women if they so desire."

"Dear God."

Footsteps then and I hurry to my chair, my book, lest Thomas catch me eavesdropping. He strides into the room, flushed, and asks me to join them. I follow him into the library where he seats me beside him. Madison faces us, looking quite grave.

"We are but an example," Thomas begins. "Consider us representing countless others who by some quirk of creation fall in love with a person of the same sex. Are we to be blamed for our nature and therefore denied the right to marry?"

Madison looks to me and I see concern in his eyes. I possess enough intuition to know he sees me as having caused a breach in Thomas. Heat rises within me; I wish to leap up and defend my Thomas who by way of me now stands diminished in his friend's eyes. I also wish to point out to the brilliant Mr. Madison that he has failed to note that Thomas has not only not married, he has not courted, has not pursued any of the ladies he has encountered. He has told me in private of his lack of interest in them but apparently he has never shared this with his good friend, and as a result his good friend dismisses this great statesman as a confirmed bachelor. How ignorant of Madison not to read the true meaning of such a label. All these thoughts pass in but a flash, and then Thomas is at my rescue.

"Do not blame Caleb for any of this," he declares, leaning forward, soft voice become quite insistent. "It is not as if he has absconded with my sanity as well as my heart. James, I have no attraction toward females. This is so from birth. My entire experience is with men and now, at long last, I have fallen in love and wish to marry. What I ask is that my government not deny me the right you enjoy."

Madison is slowly shaking his head during this outpouring. He looks down at his hands, gripped fast together in his lap. "I know that the Greeks..." he manages, but cannot go on. "It is too much, Thomas. Let me go and rest. And think." He hurries away. Thomas is then at my side, oddly elated. "A fine start," he declares.

I cannot help but scoff.

"He is merely stunned," my lover insists. "It is much to absorb, the personal revelation behind the phrasing for the amendment. Do not worry, he will come 'round."

"I am not so certain. Marriage is sanctified and holy."

"And that is the problem! It is a legal union, not a religious one, and it is this Madison must be made to see."

I blow out a sigh. "Such a task."

"One I relish."

Supper this night is awkward to say the least. Madison and Jefferson engage in conversation that purposely avoids the issue at hand, and when Thomas inquires after Madison's devoted wife, Dolly, the response is brief. I watch a master at work as Madison deflects even this polite inquiry into marriage and turns the talk to farming, something Thomas cannot resist.

It is a relief to see the tension broken for the moment in favor of plant propagation but soon Thomas catches himself. He is stubborn when in the grip of a wrong he sees must be righted. At this point I attempt a rescue and fail miserably, my question regarding the upcoming Congress only compounding things. Where I had thought to discuss the body as a whole, Thomas soon has it narrowed to Hamilton and the Federalists, who see no need for a Bill of Rights, and we are back from whence we came.

When the meal ends Madison excuses himself, pleading an early night to write letters. He will see us in the morning. I follow Thomas to the library, where he does not sit. When I suggest cards or chess, he waves me off and I see he is lost in thought, so I take up a book and leave him to it.

He is at his desk for hours, jotting notes or simply staring ahead. I am amazed at his prowess in this regard, possibly the only thing superior to that he exhibits in bed. As I watch him wage the internal battle—for he is surely imagining Madison's every argument and crafting a response—I know what he truly needs is a sexual interlude and I consider approaching, but at that very moment, as if that incredible mind can see into my meager one, he looks up and suggests I go on to bed. "I may be at this for some time," he says.

"Should you not rest and be fresh for tomorrow?" I ask.

"I am better served with preparation. He will undoubtedly offer the religious basis for marriage and we shall be at loggerheads if I cannot dissuade him."

"And he must then dissuade Congress," I offer.

"If Madison can see the logic, I have no doubt he can convince the others. He remains the key. Now off to bed with you."

Madison's second day with us is a remarkable effort by two old friends to maintain that friendship while engaging in an argument so serious that at one point Jefferson excuses himself, pleading a need to take the air. It is clear to Madison that his friend does not want company.

In the interim, Madison comes to me. Unfailingly thoughtful and the ultimate diplomat, he nevertheless skirts the issue as much as he addresses it, and I see in this the genuine discomfort of one not so inclined as we.

Seated opposite, he studies me as if my proclivity might show on my person. I watch him calculate, for is it not, in the end, an adding up? The sum of one man against another? "I am no different," I finally offer.

"No, of course not," Madison replies, "and yet..."

I wait for him to complete the thought, but he does not, and therein lies the root of his dilemma. He cannot even bring himself to speak of the union of two men, though it sits before him. I smile, thinking perhaps it would be easier for him to accept were it some detailed legal abstract instead of two men inhabiting the same household and revealing that they share a bed.

"It is no fault of our own that we love each other," I say, and Madison again agrees, but still with difficulty. I try another tack.

"What would you have done had you been prevented from marrying your dear wife?" I ask.

He smiles and shakes his head and I see I will be indulged, but he does answer. "I would have been crushed."

"Exactly. So Thomas is crushed by our being denied marriage, and he sees in this the future, others so denied through no fault of their own. We did not choose to love men. It is simply a fact of our birth."

Madison gets up, goes to the window to look out across the lawn. Our conversation is at an end. I take my leave to find Thomas striding about the grounds and I share with him my effort. "He does not see the two situations alike," I say, "and I doubt he ever will."

Thomas stops, turns, takes me at the shoulders. "But he will. He will. He must!"

With this declaration we return to the house and after a hearty mid-day meal, Thomas suggests we three sit on the porch as it is a fine summer day.

The argument resumes when Thomas asks Madison what, specifically, is his objection to the phrase "the right to contract a marriage of choice," pointing out that it denies nothing, only insures a basic right.

"As I said before, it is unnecessary," Madison answers. "Marriage is a custom of society that was long in place before this country was born and it will continue as such long after we are in the ground."

"A custom of society," Thomas repeats. "Is that not an intentional misnomer so you may avoid your true meaning: a custom of the church?"

"There is no wrong in the church sanctioning marriage," Madison argues.

"Of course not, so long as it does not trample legal marriage. We have a Constitution purposely separating church and state and it is on this principle that marriage should be addressed, as a legal contract."

"But society sees it as a religious union," Madison insists, "man and woman together as stated in the Bible. You cannot negate such a thing."

"The Bible! You retreat to your Bible when it has no weight in law. Do not bring it into this discussion, my friend, as it has no bearing here."

Madison frowns, and I fear Thomas has gone too far. It is one thing to separate church and state, another to tell a man to discard his Bible.

"I support your separation of powers," Madison concedes, "you know that, but I will not have my Bible tossed aside like a mere pamphlet."

Thomas is out of his chair. He looks skyward as if some higher power might intervene, but this is surely my thought projected onto his. His sole resource is his own mind. He appears to be trying to hold back a storm. At last he speaks.

"Do you think me a heathen because I separate church and state? Do you think I blaspheme in declaring myself equal to you in matters of the heart?"

"Thomas, please," Madison says, "you must not make this a personal issue. We are talking of a Bill of Rights, a Constitutional amendment. I know your belief is rooted in your own situation, but you must look to the larger world. Society is fixed in its views of marriage, and I doubt any lawmaker will look to change that."

"But they must!"

"Then perhaps you should accompany me north and speak before Congress."

"No, I'm no orator. You are the speaker, the persuader. You must get them to look up from their Bibles and see the common good."

A pause ensues, one of many during which the two friends try to contain themselves as they remain at opposite ends of the issue. Then Thomas resumes. He has taken his seat again.

"We have no idea what lies ahead," he says, "but mankind has a long and terrible history of oppressing that which it does not understand. It is our task to educate those who can prevent such a thing."

As Madison considers this noble position, it occurs to me that Thomas is blind to his own dichotomy, for does he not hold slaves and as such inhabit the role of oppressor? It is something I dare not speak. I sit quietly as the war of words continues.

"What would be lost with the phrase?" Thomas asks late in the day when we are all tired. "What damage would it do?"

"None," Madison concedes. "What it will do, Thomas, is draw attention to you, for I must cite you as the source when I seek support and all will then be revealed."

"Then let it be so. If that is your sole concern, we need not argue further. I am proud of my love for Caleb, as every man should be proud when he loves another human, be it male or female."

Madison looks everywhere but to Jefferson and he says nothing. Clearly he is uncomfortable with the path the conversation is taking. Thomas sees this. "Please, my friend, I do not wish to give you discomfort, but perhaps it is precisely that discomfort which is most telling. You look away from the idea of two men who, let us say it, share a bed, so how can you guarantee our government will not at some future point do the same and possibly worse? If not guaranteed, it might even deny such a right."

"All would look away," Madison manages and Thomas seizes upon this.

"So now we're to the heart of it," he says. "Fucking. Is that what you must hear? Yes, the right to marry whomever one chooses means the right to fuck whomever one chooses. The two are inseparable and you are afraid the Congress will see only this and be repelled. Well you must stand up for all creatures of all natures, for we are equals, all of us. And the right to marry the person of our choice deserves to be set down by law."

Madison visibly wilts at this point. It isn't so much acquiescence as just a wearing down. He takes a long look at his friend and Thomas smiles as if the battle is won. "Take it to the Congress," Thomas says. "Speak of it as the most basic of rights and they will see. Do it for all citizens."

Madison sighs, nods. "I shall, Thomas, but I do it for you."

We do not know the outcome until months later. Letters come from Madison about his progress or lack thereof. Already the first two proposed amendments have been discarded, so that the third, the one Thomas asks altered, is now the first. There are ten in total and agreement is finally reached. When the letter confirming this arrives Thomas finds me in the garden.

"It is done!" he declares, pulling me to my feet, embracing me. "Madison has done it!" He then reads from the letter.

"It is as you wish, Thomas. The first amendment in the Bill of Rights, which I shall heretofore think of as yours, reads thusly: 'Congress shall make no law respecting an establishment of religion, or prohibiting the free exercise thereof; or abridging the freedom of speech, or of the press, or the right of people to peaceably assemble, to contract a marriage of choice, and to petition the government for a redress of grievances.' While the states must still ratify the document, I do believe it will be done at last, but I must in all good conscience, my friend, tell you I am still not convinced the phrase is needed."

I cannot help but seize upon this last. "There are undoubtedly others who feel as he does."

Thomas nods. "Indeed, but with the amendment as written, we need never suffer to find out."

Author's Note:

Changing the sexual orientation of an historical figure and having that change affect history was an enticing prospect. Thomas Jefferson, my favorite founding father, immediately came to mind, and since he had a hand in drafting the Bill of Rights, a story evolved over a right that could have been guaranteed from day one—same-sex marriage. Jefferson's widower status lent itself to his being gay, and Sally Hemmings easily transformed to Samuel. Bringing James Madison onstage to argue the merits of "a marriage of choice" was fun, as was putting words into the mouths of these great men. Adding a fictional character and sexual content brought still more delight, as did tinkering with a Constitutional amendment. Had the events of the story actually taken place, countless gay and lesbian couples would now be celebrating long marriages instead of fighting a battle for this basic right.

THE HIGH COST FOR TAMARIND

Steve Berman

Ivan wondered why Sandro took him down to the docks; the only open cinema remaining in Tampico was not near the waterfront. On a late Saturday morning, the docks were quiet except for a few tired gulls, which squawked at the boys in annoyance for not bringing any offerings. Sandro walked slowly down one rickety wooden platform to the edge. Ivan winced at how his best friend—no, Sandro was more than that, they needed a new word for all he meant to him—favored one leg. The one without the sick bone.

Wary of loose boards and rusty nails, Ivan sat down next to Sandro. The air held a terrible smell, worse than spoiled eggs or meat or milk, that made both their eyes tear.

Ivan leaned forward. The water beneath them was murky and dark with spilt oil and whatever else the old factories had poured out. Somewhere along the docks, they had passed a sign that warned against swimming. Ivan couldn't imagine anyone crazy enough to let that water touch bare skin. It would seep into the flesh and cause sickness. Maybe turn the bones against the body, as Sandro's did.

"Think they have tamarind candy at the Regio?"

Sandro shrugged and began searching the inside pocket of his worn jacket.

Ivan thought he might be looking for a pack of cigarettes. He hated when Sandro smoked. It made the boy's mouth taste awful. "Or maybe they'll have hot chocolate?" Rich and semi-sweet. That would cover any hint of ash on Sandro's tongue.

But Sandro took out, not a cellophane wrapped package, but tiny red box. The one Ivan had given him at the last *El Día de los Reyes*.

"Your ring." Ivan felt his stomach fall out of his torso and land in the stinking water. Did Sandro mean to give the ring back? Ivan had saved up for months of sweeping the crosswalks in town to afford a band of gold that didn't look brittle.

A plaintextual edition of the Zapata Telegram (1917), as found at the Imperial Prussian Archives in Berlin in 1968:

"The President and I have conferred about your proposal. We are interested in supporting the efforts of Germany in return for diplomatic, financial, and military assistance. We shall begin sending troops and munitions north along the border. Should the United States of America enter the war we will reclaim our lost territories. General Villa expressed interest in Zeppelins. von Kardoff recommends submarine presence at Tampico." Signed, ZAPATA.

"Chalina saw some news program on the television."

Sandro turned the jewelry box over and over with his brown fingers. "Showed an American hospital. It was so white and clean."

Ivan had visited Sandro at the Hospital Vera Cruz and remembered how cramped and dingy each room felt.

"Your sister watches so much television she thinks she could speak New York."

"It's empty."

Ivan laughed. "Not as crowded as Mexico City, but empty?"

"No, this box." Sandro placed it on the dock between them. "Maybe. I whispered a prayer into it and tightly shut the lid. Maybe it's still inside."

Ivan reached for both of Sandro's hands. All the fingers were bare. How had he not noticed? Sandro always wore his gift when they went to the morning show. The Regio was never crowded then and they could sit in the seats and lean against one another and hold hands in the cool darkness.

"What happened? Did your father find it?"

Sandro shook his head. "There's a small shop in town with grimy windows. He buys jewelry without asking questions."

Ivan wiped at his eyes. He blamed the chemicals rising off the water. "Why?"

"I can hitch north to the occupied territories. If I get to Austin they have vans there that will cross into América."

"We could go to New Orleans maybe?" Ivan had always wanted to go there ever since he heard of Mardi Gras. Soon after Tropsch Petrochemicals GmbH transferred his father from Berlin to Tampico, Ivan's family attended

Mass at Saint Boniface. He had first seen Sandro sitting quietly, with his head down. The only reason he went without complaint each week to church was the hope of seeing the Mexican boy again. After they finally became friends, Ivan had avoided Saint Boniface. New Orleans had grand churches but he wanted to really worship the streets where they laughed and danced. Tampico lacked both.

"No."

"Then New York?"

Sandro gripped Ivan's fingers tightly. "Just me. If you went, they might arrest you. I would not know where you are."

The entry for the Battle of Tampico in the 1963 *Zedler Universallexikon*:

The Battle of Tampico was an engagement of the Great War (April, 1914) fought in and around the prosperous port town of Tampico. This event served to bring Mexico into the war. In the winter months of 1914, a diplomatic relationship, the Concordar, *developed between the German Empire and Mexico through the efforts of the Foreign Secretary, Arthur Zimmermann, and Emiliano Zapata Salazar, military advisor to President Adolfo de la Huerta.*

Imperial undersea boats arrived in early April of 1914 at Tampico and surprised the American fleet, commanded by Admiral Henry T. Mayo, which had settled in the area to protect American petroleum interests. The Dolphin, flagship of the American Atlantic Fleet, was among the vessels sunk (though some current historians debate whether sabotage may have been involved). The attack successful, the undersea boats continued to safeguard the Gulf of Mexico. Financed by the Empire, Mexico invaded the bordering American states of Arizona and Texas. By securing the Tamaulipas region, the Empire ensured the success of the Concordar *and the explosive growth of the Mexican petroleum industry.*

Bibliography: See M. Stürmer, *The Concordar's Role in America's Defeat.* Bertelsmann, 2000.

"So you'd leave me so easily?"

"I want to see the insides of their hospitals. They must work miracles. Clean and white miracles."

Ivan nodded. "Fix your bones."

"Then I can come back here."

Ivan wondered why anyone would ever leave such a wondrous place. Did such hospitals find people hiding in the corners, wanting to stay forever? Would a Sandro that could dance on good legs without cancer ever return to the dirt of Tampico?

His first and only love picked up the box and reached back with his arm to throw it into the Gulf.

"Wait." Ivan gently but firmly stopped his arm.

"I want to throw out my prayer. Maybe if it floats out to clean water—"

Ivan pried open Sandro's fingers. The box felt warm, almost sweaty. "I'll keep your prayer." He brought the box, which felt heavy, as if the ring remained still hidden inside, to his lips and kissed the lid once.

Protesters Burn Waters and Damage Docks
Marcela Valente

TAMAULIPAS, 5 Apr (MPS) - Residents from the region converged on the small port of Tampico to stage a waterfront rally, protesting the role Petroleos Mexicanos (PEMEX) has played in allegedly polluting the Gulf. Wearing carnival masks resembling buzzards and demons, the protest escalated into violence when police arrived. Oil poured into the water was set ablaze, generating thick black clouds that could be seen for miles. Official reports estimate that property damages nearing two million pesos will hamper the recovery of the impoverished district for years.

Ivan spent a week fashioning the ogre mask, coloring it angry. The time felt nearly as long as the past year without Sandro. Behind the wall of paper mache, he could barely see the woman light the gas-soaked rag stuck in the bottle he held. One eyehole was too low. But he could feel the heat.

He rushed down the dock. The sirens chased him, but not yet the police. He felt like a hero from the movies.

Even with the burning bottle spreading acrid smoke, he could still smell the stench of the waters. He knew they had made Sandro's bones turn against him. Like bullets left too long in the body, poisoning a man's blood, the ships war had sent to the bottom had left the Gulf weak, too sick to resist PEXMEX's dumping. Ivan's father could tell the long, complicated names of every chemical swirling in the tide. Ivan only cared that they would burn, cauterizing the water. He tossed the makeshift grenade as far as he could, hoping the fire would never end.

Strong arms grabbed him. In that last moment of freedom, his other hand opened. The tiny gift-wrapped box fell to the dock. He had whispered to it his own prayer while taping gold paper salvaged from his Weihnachten presents around it. After a haunting year, Sandros had not returned to him.

Ivan managed to kick the box with his foot, so that it would fall into the blaze that erupted. As the officers beat him down, he caught, for only a moment, a smell like perfume—no, more like tamarind candy—rising off the water.

Author's Note:

I remember attending a convention and sitting in the audience for a panel discussing alternate history. I wanted to read stories that presented an alternative England where Oscar Wilde wasn't jailed or an America dealing with James Buchanan's admission that he loved William Rufus King. The panelists seemed content to argue over battles and terminology, while I wondered how many of us retold our own history.

Would it be better to retell our own histories more to our liking?

Just shy of eighteen, I sold my first story, something silly, to a Midwestern digest. At the time, writing seemed so easy. Words fell upon the page and I needed only care a bit how they were arranged. Nothing prepared me for the forthcoming drought; I didn't sell another piece for a couple years. But knowing that any day that magazine with that first story would show up at my door helped hold back so many disappointments in my life.

I was a sophomore at Tulane when I found the fat package from Kansas City stuffed into our mail slot. I shared the apartment with three other guys, but only Mike mattered to me. The other pair has all but faded from memory.

I remember eagerly tearing open the package. A dozen of Lighthouse Magazine *fell into my lap. I'd more than spent my first meager check on additional copies.* Lighthouse *looked homespun and the Script typeface could have come from my mother's Selectric typewriter (which used these cool metal domes covered in raised characters), but I found my by-line and, for several minutes, I had a taste of bliss. Until I read the story and discovered the editor had stolen its magic. Literally. Without my permission or even a warning, he'd substituted a filthy king for the villainous wizard.*

In my room, I worked through my disappointment by carefully autographing issues with a felt-tipped pen. I struggled to make each cursive letter perfect, as if my penmanship would distract any reader from the story's flaws.

When I handed one to Mike, he didn't even turn a page to read the inscription. That hurt me. But then, Mike would often hurt me.

Later, he wanted to wrestle and pounced on me. I was a scrawny boy of twigs caught in his grasp; he outweighed me by sixty, maybe seventy pounds. When I grew frustrated and started to smack at him to let me go, he became furious and ground my face into the rough carpeting. The skin of my cheek and forehead burned. That eye went dark.

I wondered aloud if I should go to the hospital. He didn't offer to drive me but gave me several aspirin. I was more frightened than resentful. I remember thinking, if I hadn't resisted wrestling, he would never have grown so violent.

My vision cleared in a couple days. Mike acted more bothered by the raw patches on my face that took longer to heal. One night he sat besides me on the second-hand sofa and told me his darkest secret: once at a family gathering, one of his uncles had drunk too much and then made a pass at him. That Mike had taken me into such confidence was empowering, yet terrifying. His disgust for the man was clear and vocal. I grew scared that Mike had known my feelings for him, that he'd injured me as a warning.

He went into the kitchen. I heard him puttering around there. Mike rarely did any of the apartment chores. I did them for him. I stayed seated, thinking about the story he'd told me. If it were a fairy tale, even one so simple as what I'd written at seventeen, would the uncle still be the villain? How could anyone resist anyone as strong and handsome as Mike?

Understanding the uncle's weakness, I sat there and rewrote the story in my head and allowed a torrid moment between them. That would have created a precedent, one that offered me hope.

Mike returned with a thermos and two mugs. He poured hot chocolate laced with peppermint schnapps. As he stretched out on the sofa beside me, our legs touched. He did not seem to mind.

I thought to myself, now I'd like to read to Mike my story. Not the one from the magazine, but the story he'd given me. But, I kept quiet as we sipped from our mugs. I never let the happy-ever-after ending loose.

A SPEAR AGAINST THE SKY

M P Ericson

CARTIMANDUA LEANED ON THE PARAPET THAT topped the stone wall. From this high up she could see for miles, over the fields and pastures that surrounded the massive hilltop fort, past the scattered homesteads and enclosures of her subjects, even as far as the line of forest to the south that marked the boundary separating her domain from that of Venutius.

He was out there, she knew. Somewhere past that dark wall he waited, hoping she'd offer some chance for him to march on her territory and claim it as his own.

Vain hope. She would never give a finger's-width of it away. Not to him, nor to any crazed fool who thought war and destruction brought anything but grief.

Soon she would have to tell his messengers so. The riders approached from the south. She could see them from here, a small clump sliding toward her across the rolling expanse of fields.

"Too few to be a threat," Vellocatus said. He was standing beside her, sniffing the breeze. "Too fast to be friendly. My guess is there is war in the south, and our help is wanted. Again."

"Why not send a lone rider, if they only want to ask for our help?"

"Maybe the others are going further. Northward, perhaps." He squinted. "There's a cart in there."

Cartimandua stared at the clump.

"Impossible. A loaded cart would not travel that fast, and why would they bring an empty one?"

"It could be lightly loaded. A woman, a child, an injured man. Who can say?"

65

"You can say. Go out and greet them."

He slung his cloak back over his shoulders and strode off. From his swagger, she guessed him to be well pleased with himself.

Silly man. He could take the power from her with a word, but he was content to run as her hunting-dog, savaging whatever prey she set him to. The hunt was his joy, not possession of the carcass. She loved him for that, if nothing else.

She watched as he sped across the fields, a single rider bringing challenge to the minions of Venutius.

The parties slowed, met, stopped. There was a quick exchange, lasting no more than a dozen breaths. Then Vellocatus wheeled around, and flew like a spear back toward the hill fort.

Ill news, most likely. Cartimandua cast a final glare at the forest, then walked down the wooden steps into the enclosure of her fort.

"Boudica, Queen of the Iceni, and her daughters." Vellocatus raised his spear, which had blocked the doorway, and stood aside.

Cartimandua rose. She had taken the time to comb and pin her hair and adjust her dress, to give the illusion that she had been calmly seated throughout the visitors' approach. Now she advanced to greet them, unhurried, dignified. Inwardly, her heart pounded so fast she thought it would burst.

"You are welcome." She held out both hands.

"I am honored." Boudica stood tall as ever, and her grip was as firm as it had been sixteen years ago. But her tawny hair fell to her waist in a tangled mass, and her eyes blazed with a fierce light.

"You are a widow?" Cartimandua studied the unkempt hair. "I'm sorry. Your husband was a great man."

"He was a fool. And you can spare me the pretty words. I have no time nor wish for ceremony. You and I must talk."

"Can I at least offer you a meal and a drink?"

"Not now. Perhaps later, when I know your answer." Boudica gestured past Cartimandua's shoulder to the alcove closed off by thick curtains. "We'll talk in there. My daughters are coming with me."

Seated on the bed, with her daughters huddled close to her, she spoke sharp, harsh words about the Romans. The girls, perhaps ten and twelve years old, listened in silence.

"You must have known Prasutagus died. Do not tell me how sorry you are. That would be a lie. Well, it means Iceni territory is Roman now. Do you know what that means?"

"The Roman army will take over administration of the province."

"It means we are slaves. Less than slaves. Within a week of Prasutagus's death, I had Roman soldiers in my house demanding money. 'Taxed like any other subject,' they said. I hadn't burned the corpse yet."

"What did you do?"

"Told them to go back to their commander and tell him to send decent men next time. So what do you think he sent me?"

"More soldiers," Cartimandua said wearily. Boudica positively reveled in inciting fights. There was not a tactful sinew in her body. "Of course he did. What other option did you leave him?"

Boudica shrugged off her daughters and shot from the bed. She threw her fur cloak aside, whipped out the brooches that fastened her dress at the shoulders, and swung around. With one hand she tore aside her mass of hair, baring her back.

"This is what they did to me," she snapped. "This!"

White lashes ran across her skin, thick and taut as ropes. The flesh had been cut deep, its edges flaking back like sneering lips.

"And my daughters." She swung around to face Cartimandua. With sharp movements she thrust the brooches back in place. "Do you know what they did to my daughters?"

The girls turned dark eyes on Cartimandua. The younger shivered, but the elder blazed with the fury of her mother.

"I think so," Cartimandua said, wincing.

"Raped them. A gang of ten soldiers each. It took weeks before my little girls could walk again. They said we were animals—less than animals—and we belonged to Rome now. They could do what they liked. Well, they will not. Not again. I have the Iceni, I have the Trinovantes, and I want the Brigantes as well. Together we will destroy the Romans and all who support them, and set this island free."

"You intend a rebellion?"

"I intend a fight. Will you help me? I have your husband's word already."

"Vellocatus will make no decision without consulting me."

"I meant your other husband. Him across the way." Boudica tossed her head, probably meaning to indicate Venutius, but the true direction was more toward the north. "He has never bent to a Roman yoke. Never will. Him I can rely on. What about you?"

They stared at each other, hot eyes meeting cold. In Cartimandua's chest an old rage sparked and burned.

"You left me," Cartimandua said. "You made a choice. Now you are reaping the harvest, and it is not to your taste. So you want me to sweeten it for you with the blood of my sons."

"If they are of age to carry weapons, yes."

"It does not matter if they are or not. We cannot defeat the Romans—there are too many of them, and they are too strong. Caratacus was a fool. You will fare no better. And I won't have you drag down my people along with yours."

"You are a coward, then." Boudica flicked her hair back over her shoulders.

"A realist. What was done to you—all three of you—is an outrage. You are welcome to stay here for as long as you wish. I would be happy if you made this your home. But I will not rise up in rebellion with you."

"Then we will leave." Boudica held out her hands to the girls, who climbed off the bed to join her.

"Do not go yet," Cartimandua said. "Stay and take something to eat. Spend the night. You have all traveled far—you need a rest."

Boudica shook her head. But the youngest girl turned pale and faltered, clinging to her mother, and for a moment seemed about to cry.

"Has she eaten?" Cartimandua demanded.

"Of course." Boudica gave her daughter a stern look. "We had a meal at sunrise."

"That was hours ago," Cartimandua protested. "Stay. Let the girls sleep comfortably for one night."

Boudica looked at her daughters. Her features softened.

"Only the one night." She glanced at Cartimandua, with something of the old light in her eyes. "We will sleep here."

They lay with their arms around each other, whispering. The girls, tucked in close behind their mother, slept with deep, regular breaths.

"You left me," Cartimandua said.

"It was necessary. You know that. We both had to marry, sooner or later, and Prasutagus was a good catch. Besides, I wanted children."

"I did not."

"You still had them, though."

Cartimandua shrugged, her movement stifled against the wadded wool of the mattress.

"There was not much I could do. Venutius was my husband."

"Where are the boys?"

"With their father. And they are hardly boys any more."

"Do you miss them?"

Cartimandua tried to say no, but a fierce pain burst inside her, drowning the word.

"Of course I miss them. They are my sons."

"I miss mine, too."

Cartimandua knew of the one that had died. She was not sure whether there were others.

"Where is Vellocatus?" Boudica asked. "I hope he does not want his bed."

"He is with the men," Cartimandua said. "He has his own interests. One of the many reasons I like him better than Venutius."

Boudica made a sound that was suspiciously close to a giggle.

"I had heard as much," she said.

"Did you find it difficult?" Cartimandua asked. "With your husband? I did."

"Awful. I just kept thinking about the children I would have. That got me through it. You?"

"No. I never really wanted children."

"I don't understand that," Boudica said.

"Oh, I loved them once they came along. Eventually. But I did not want them in the first place. I detested Venutius, and..." Cartimandua broke off. Her voice had risen, making the girls shift and snuffle as if about to wake. "I hated it all," she concluded, more gently. "I do not want to talk about it."

Boudica's hand stroked her shoulder.

"I'm sorry. I shouldn't have asked."

The touch awoke memories of laughing together, holding hands in the sunshine, secret caresses in the night. It had been a glorious summer, full of promise and joy.

"Why did you leave?" Cartimandua asked. It came out close to a wail. "You could have stayed here. You could have married here."

"I could," Boudica admitted. "But I did not like my options here."

"You could have married my brother. He wanted you."

"I did not want him," Boudica said. "Prasutagus was...gentle. Usually."

"But if you had married my brother, you could have stayed here. With me."

This time the silence was longer, and more uncomfortable.

"You expected too much," Boudica said. "All of me. As though you wanted to control me."

"No!"

"It felt like it. And you would have been jealous when the children came. I know you would."

Cartimandua didn't answer.

"It was what I wanted," Boudica said. "I had to leave. I'm sorry."

"What you wanted," Cartimandua said coldly, "was to be first. You knew you could not be that here, not with me in the way. So you went somewhere else, where no woman was more important than you. And you did not care that it meant leaving me behind. You never cared until now, when you need military support for your own schemes. You never wanted me—I wasn't important."

"There was that, too," Boudica said. Her hand squeezed Cartimandua's arm. "But I did care. Always."

Beyond the alcove, on the other side of the heavy drapes, the night was thick with the hushed breathing of sleepers. Someone stirred, someone snored. A child snuffled.

Cartimandua turned on her side, away from the woman next to her.

"I am going to sleep," she announced. "Talk to yourself, if you must."

"I did care," Boudica whispered, her breath warm against the back of Cartimandua's neck. "I still do." Her hands caressed Cartimandua's breasts. "Remember?"

Cartimandua swallowed. Her breath grew light and fast, urgent.

"I had not forgotten."

Boudica kissed the skin at the nape of Cartimandua's neck. The touch sent shivers through Cartimandua's body, down her arms and out through her fingertips, down the inside of her thighs and legs and out through her toes. She had forgotten, after all. The intensity of her response sent her mind reeling. She turned around, and caught Boudica in her arms.

They made love quietly, breathlessly, while all around them the household slept.

The din rose to the sky. Thousands upon thousands of men stood naked in the field, clashing their spears against their shields, yelling at the top of their lungs. They would rape the Romans, they boasted, cut them open and splay them over their own swords.

It was doubtful that the Romans heard that, though. They stood ranged at the opposite end, cowering behind a wall of rectangular shields, not daring to show their faces.

"Pitiful," Boudica sneered. "Look at them. Too scared to look our men in the eye."

"Safe from thrown spears," Cartimandua said.

"You are absurd." Boudica raised her spear and shook it against the sky. Her hair blazed around her like fire. A new roar went up from the men, powerful enough to shake the earth.

Boudica gestured to her driver, who turned the pair of horses neatly and sped them out into the field. The chariot rattled past the horde of men, past the thousands of other chariots ranged along the front. Fearless she stood, holding on to the side with one hand only, while the other kept her weapon raised in glorious defiance.

"We should join them," Vellocatus said. "We will be the only men left without heads or honor by the end of today."

"There will be heads enough," Cartimandua said. "Trust me."

Boudica shouted an order. At once the ranged chariots crashed forward, closing on the enemy ranks. A storm of spears flew toward the Romans, smashing into their shields with a din like a thousand blacksmiths striking anvils. Another, and another. Then the chariots turned and sped away. The swordsmen leapt to the ground and ran toward the Romans, screaming. The men already on foot, not waiting for the chariots to pass, tore out among them, wild with the lust to kill. Many fell and were trampled. Some, careless or blind with rage, were caught by the chariot teams and mown down. Wounded Britons littered the field, and still the Romans had not spoken.

Then their answer came. A black cloud of spears sprang from within their ranks and struck down into the attacking Britons. What had been a mass of charging men became a scatter, while the main part of the body writhed on the ground. Another cloud, and a third, and few were left to crash into the Roman lines. Those that did fell quickly, gored by sharp blades.

Then the Romans advanced. Across the field they crept, still hidden behind the metal of their shields. A second wave of Britons poured against them and were beaten down, and then a third. The Roman line pressed on, relentless.

British courage failed. Men turned and ran, fleeing in a craze of sudden fear. They reached the carts and pushed through them, some grabbing their children as they ran, others heedless of anything but their own impending fate.

Cartimandua turned to Vellocatus.

"Now," she said.

He turned and raised his arms, then crossed them above his head. Men barged forward through the gaps between the carts. They met their compatriots and shouted at them, bullied them to turn and face the enemy. Many did, shamed. Thousands of men poured out among the falterers, roaring defiance. Blades glittered against bare flesh.

The Romans paused. The British forces hurtled towards them, drawing new courage. The wave crashed against the line of shields, crashed over it, destroyed it. Roman soldiers fought like snakes, writhing on the ground, stabbing with short fangs. The Britons hacked down at them, cleaving helmets, severing limbs.

It took an age. So much slaughter, so much death. The Romans did not yield. They fought to the last man, and took more than their own number with them. When the eagle standards fell at last, a shriek went up from a hundred thousand women and children who still watched, burning-eyed, as their men bled and died.

It was over. In far-off Rome such slaughter might now make the conquest of Britain seem more trouble than it could be worth, or it might not, but for now, they could claim victory. Cartimandua gripped the edge of her chariot. She stared across the forest of corpses at the flame that still burned, far away on the other side of what had once been the British line.

"I told you we would win." Boudica raised her drinking-bowl to Cartimandua. She still carried the spear, but now she thrust it into the earth, point first, to rest there while she drank.

They had to shout to make themselves heard above the din. All around them, men and women sang of victory. Huge bonfires had been lit in thanks to the goddess of war. Out on the battlefield, the Morrigan's ravens took her share of the fallen. Great flocks of them crawled over the bodies, pecking at stumps and wounds. Severed heads hung from the belt of every survivor, staring in futile fear.

"You did." Cartimandua drank in return, honouring the dead. Her mind whirled from the stench of blood and smoke. She was exhausted, and wanted nothing more than to sleep, but the woman before her seemed to burn with an unquenchable flame, never to tire, never to grow dim.

"What will you do now?" Cartimandua asked. She had a fleeting, crazy sense that Boudica would reply: 'March on Rome, of course.'

Boudica only shrugged.

"Go home, I suppose." She glanced at her daughters, nestling together beside an upturned cart. "Not that we will ever be happy there again."

"You could come back with me," Cartimandua said.

Boudica turned sharp eyes on her, brutal as spear points.

"I am still a queen."

"You are a king's widow. That is not quite the same thing. You will feel the difference, I think, when you return. If you want your hand on the reins, you will have to marry again."

Boudica grimaced.

"Whereas with me," Cartimandua said, "you could live as you pleased. You won't be first. But you will be listened to, and honored, after this day's work. You will never have to marry. Your daughters would be safe and cared for. And I would love you." The words rushed up from within her, fierce and untamed. "I do love you. Always have done. Always will."

Behind her, a roar went up from the men as the drinking-horns were carried around again. There would be a mess of drunkards in the morning for grim-faced women to clean up. But tonight, for one magical night, there was only celebration.

"Will you stay with me?" Cartimandua asked. "You have no need to go back. An Icenian man can take your husband's place. You and your daughters would be welcome in my house."

Boudica gazed at her steadily.

"Would Vellocatus mind?"

"I think he would be relieved, to tell you the truth. He is happier among the men. It would be a good excuse for him not to share my bed."

Boudica smiled.

"I shall think about it." She strode past and joined the feasting men.

Cartimandua tugged the abandoned spear out of the ground. It came away easily, its firm rooting a mere show. She tested the point. It was not as sharp as it looked.

She turned, and watched the tall flame-haired woman stride among the men. No warrior, this. A dream of one, a vision of a spear-queen, but in truth a girl still, vibrant and alive, under the trappings of age.

Cartimandua tossed the spear aside, and went to claim her.

Author's Note:

Cartimandua, queen of the Brigantes at the time of the Roman invasion of Britain, commanded a territory that extended throughout the north of England. She was clearly very powerful, and could have resisted the Romans, but instead she allied herself with them.

Boudica, queen of the Iceni, staged a revolt against the Romans in AD 60-61. It was spectacularly successful at first, but ended with bloody defeat at what we now call the Battle of Watling Street. She died shortly afterwards, possibly from suicide.

In this story, I speculate that if Cartimandua had supported Boudica's rebellion, the British would have won the battle and ended the Roman occupation.

We have no evidence that the two women ever met.

SOD 'EM

Barry Lowe

BROTHER FRANCIS BLEW ON HIS FINGERS as he stretched them in an effort to prevent their freezing. He was cold. Bitterly cold. Not only from the icy fingers of the draft that lapped at him, but cold from the admonitions of the abbot. He didn't know why he should stay perched on a high stool at the workbench when his fellow monks had been allowed to sit round a penurious fire to warm their blood.

This penance was too much. He looked at the parchment in front of him. Not the bloody Book of Genesis again! It wasn't that he minded transcribing the Bible over and over. It was his job. And for that, in return, he got to rise far too early each morning to spend much too long on his knees in the chapel praying to a god who obviously didn't feel the cold or else was still snug in bed under a mound of blankets. He giggled to himself. It was that kind of thinking that had got him into trouble in the first place. Well, not so much the thinking as the espousing. That, and his too-intimate friendship with Brother Finan.

It was all perfectly innocent. The whole affair was a misunderstanding. They had simply been trying to keep warm. He was sure God didn't mean for his priests to freeze their balls off in His name.

There he went again. His mouth was always going to get him into trouble, just as it had when he reached over to kiss the cold trembling lips of Brother Finan, trembling not from the wind but from anticipation. No one had explicitly mentioned the kiss. They just alluded to it with the words "unhealthy" and "against nature."

"Well," he'd retorted, "If nature is going to be the arbiter of all things natural, it must be just as much against nature for a man and woman to kiss, as I've never seen horses, nor fish, nor bears, nor swallows kissing. Nor bats, nor cows, nor sheep, nor…"

"Enough!" roared the abbot. "You dare to question the word of God!"

"I suppose I do," thought Brother Francis. "Or at least the Word as interpreted by the abbot." He just couldn't see God as some miserable old fart sitting around telling people what NOT to do.

Brother Finan had been banished to the kitchen. At least there he was warm. Brother Francis was sent to the Scriptorium, scattered with parchment pages of illuminated manuscripts. He supposed he'd got the colder of the two punishments because he was the older of the two and had, therefore, been seen as the instigator. Too, he did have a beautiful hand. He smiled at his own healthy lack of humility. His copied manuscripts were the talk of Ireland. They changed hands frequently and were in great demand; it was only that which prevented the abbot from throwing him out on his unnatural ear.

He didn't mind laboriously copying out the Latin texts, but he did prefer some books over others. He knew why he'd been assigned Genesis. It was salient to his situation.

What *was* his situation? He was perched in a monastery on a rock in the North Sea off the coast of Ireland. Tick. He was a lowly scribe. Tick. With a self-confessed beautiful hand. Tick. His manuscript copies were traded for gold. Tick. He was in love with Brother Finan…

Tick. There, he'd admitted it. He had been in love with Brother Finan since that first day he came to the monastery. He had attempted by every meager means at his disposal to inveigle his way into a friendship. "An unhealthy friendship," the abbot called it.

Every three hours when he was called to prayers he would seek out the company of Brother Finan. Just to be close to him was enough. And eventually Brother Finan had reciprocated. During that period when they had been comparatively free to pursue their friendship, Brother Francis was acknowledged to have produced some of his most beautiful work. The script was the best he had ever managed. He himself marveled at how his quill flowed across the parchment, his decoration becoming more colorful, more luminous, more spiritual. Even the prior was moved to remark on the improvement to already superb craftsmanship.

But the abbot, whose demeanor was as brittle and desiccated as some of the old papyrus in the library, papyrus that was falling into decay and had to be copied swiftly, had turned against him. The pilgrims who made the arduous journey to the abbey to gaze upon the finger bone of blessed St. Catherine were much impressed by the manuscript from which the abbot read the service, but the abbot was an austere man, and regarded it with a contemptuous sneer.

He abhorred beauty for its own sake. Beauty was the work of God and was functional, just as Brother Francis's work on the manuscripts should be functional. He believed Francis took too long embellishing, distracting with decorative delicacy from the real beauty: the words.

Beauty was what Brother Francis lived for. Beauty made his heart glad. It took his cold morning breath away. As did Brother Finan. He didn't understand it but he realized beauty was a gift from God to be enjoyed. As he enjoyed Brother Finan; his company, his beauty, his friendship and, finally, his love.

They had never, ever consummated the love in the manner the abbot seemed to think. Oh, they had both wanted to, but their love had been expressed in chaste kisses and quick fumbling under lice-ridden sackcloth. When they lay down at night in the miserable god-forsaken cells, for Francis genuinely believed God had forsaken this hellhole, he dreamed of Brother Finan. And Brother Finan dreamed of him.

His fingers would sometimes cramp until he could no longer hold the quill. On those days he toiled in the rocky, stunted abbey vegetable garden. Occasionally, he faked his own indisposition in order to feel the warmth of the sun's rays on the rare occasions when it shone. He wanted to fling off his robes and feel the strength of the sun all over his body, but that was forbidden. As so many things were forbidden. Either by God, or by the abbot.

The candle gave off a stench of seabird fat which made him bilious. He was allowed two candles so that his eyesight would not suffer. After sharpening the end of his quill, Brother Francis dipped the writing end into the horn of ink at his side. He was always careful to keep it away from his elbow as he was occasionally clumsy and had spilt it over a nearly completed manuscript once. Now he knew better than to have it perched on his writing table. He was also responsible for the manufacture of the ink that the copiers used: carbon ink, a mixture of charcoal and gum. He had experimented with its manufacture until he achieved an ink as black as the lonely nights, as black as the abbot's heart.

He glanced around and retrieved some parchment leaves hidden among the general disarray in the room. Spoiled pages were scattered about to be used in experimenting with inks and handwriting, but this parchment was special. It had none of the imperfections of that made from animals with ticks or diseases.

These were Brother Francis's poems. He wrote them in praise of his friend's beauty. They were among his finest work, and he would make a gift of them to his friend when they were completed. They were the most beautiful things he had ever accomplished. His masterpiece. He gazed at them and knew they were good. They were his gift to the world, but the world would never read them, not his world, at least. Only Brother Finan would read them.

Before Brother Francis embarked on the poems, he had whiled away his boredom in writing amusing anecdotes about the abbey, or else improving on the bible stories. They were so lacking in poetry, he thought. You could boil down much of the Bible to a series of strictures and do away with the rest. It would save a great deal of time and effort. Particularly the begats. The long list of names was so tedious that, on a few occasions, he had left out whole verses and renumbered the others to cover his sin, but no one had noticed or, if they had, they didn't care.

Sometimes he would add a word that made the narrative more exciting. Once the abbot had read from one of these books and had raised an eyebrow when he came across a word which was not in the official handbook of God. Nobody else noticed. This emboldened Brother Francis to try his hand at further improvements, as he saw them. He was pleased with his daring, although his work began to come under more intense scrutiny. But no one complained, and the Pope himself had requested one of Brother Francis's illuminated manuscripts for his library in Rome. It was through such patronage that he had managed to survive to his thirty-fifth year.

He ran his fingers lightly over the flesh side of the vellurri bearing his poetry, hoping to feel the love with which he had imbued the words. If only he could feel the same love when he wrote out the words of God, as he once had. Now he felt a more carnal love, and with that he had begun to see how dried up the word of God was without the chance to live it.

Confined to the abbey on Rathlin Island, six miles from the Irish mainland to the southwest; to the 3500 acres of sheep meadows, cow pastures, bird cliffs and the meager farmland they eked out from the salty spray; this was his world. A world of prayer and meditation. And of continual frustration.

He put away the poems because the abbot would look in shortly, not to check on his progress, but to ensure he was still at his writing table and not in the company of Brother Finan. He dipped the quill in the inkhorn and shifted his elbow so that he could read the manuscript he was copying.

19.1. The two angels came to Sodom in the evening; and Lot was sitting in the gate of Sodom. When Lot saw them, he rose to meet them, and bowed himself with his face to the earth.

2. And said, "My lords, turn aside, I pray you, to your servant's house and spend the night, and wash your feet; then you may rise up early and go on your way." They said, "No; we will spend the night in the street."

Brother Francis put down his quill. He had heard of the beauty of angels, but there was no description. He had assumed they had wings. But did they? He had assumed they were the most beautiful creatures ever created by God. He imagined they must look like Brother Finan. And that was why the angels in the decorations to his manuscripts bore a striking resemblance to the young monk.

Francis found Lot and his wife tendentious. At least Lot's wife got her comeuppance when she was turned into a pillar of salt. He had once illustrated the moment she was struck dumb and lifeless for her inquisitiveness, but the abbot had found it so repulsively realistic he had destroyed it. Francis had to admit he, too, would have been tempted to turn back to watch the destruction of the Cities of the Plain: Sodom, Gomorrah, Admah and Zeboim. As he wrote the names he felt a frisson of excitement, not at their destruction but at the life that had bubbled in the cities.

4. *But before they lay down, the men of the city, the men of Sodom, both young and old, all the people to the last man, surrounded the house.*

5. *And they called to Lot, "Where are the men who came to you tonight? Bring them out to us, that we may know them."*

Francis shuddered as the image of Finan barricaded in Lot's house, the lustful object of the men and boys of the city, burned in his imagination. He wanted what the men of Sodom had wanted. And he knew why the men of Sodom had wanted it. Most wanted to possess beauty, although a minority had wanted to defile it.

He felt a twitch in his groin. This happened with increasing frequency when he copied sections of the Bible that spoke of male friendships. He attempted to smother the enthusiasm of his body. The same enthusiasm he felt for Finan. "So help me God, I can no longer help myself."

Oh, how he wished God had not found it necessary to destroy Sodom. What had the men done, after all? And what sort of man was Lot? He offered his two daughters to the men of Sodom. What sort of father would do that? And this is the man God chose to save. God obviously had more lenient morals than the abbot. And then, after they had fled the fire and brimstone, the daughters had each slept with their father and produced children. Did God smite them? No, He did not.

Now, if Brother Francis had written the Bible, the outcome…

The heavy wooden door to the Scriptorium burst open. A gaggle of young monks, including Finan, were arguing volubly.

"We must flee!" one of them said.

"How? We have no means and the sea is too rough."

Voices were raised in disagreement.

"What is it, Finan?" Francis asked, laying his quill aside.

The hubbub subsided.

"The Norsemen!"

That was all he needed to say. The stories of Norse raids along the coast of Ireland had been spread like manure on a field among the monasteries and abbeys. Rathlin itself, decades before, had been the first to be attacked and the monks put to the sword. It had taken a long time to get the abbey back to the state it was in now.

"They're coming back?" Francis asked.

The group nodded.

"What can we do?" one of the young monks pleaded. "The abbot and the prior have taken the only sturdy boat."

"Put your faith in God," replied Francis, who never put his faith in anyone.

"Sod that," said another young monk known for his quick temper. "You can stay and be cut to ribbons, but I'm all for taking my chances with the sea."

"You'll drown," Finan said.

"That's as may be, but better the sea than the sword, and who knows what other filthy defilement. Anyone coming with me?"

The small group of absconders left hurriedly and the remainder looked about in bewilderment.

"Go to your cells and pray," instructed Francis, who felt the same panic they did. He had no desire to die either at the hands of the Norsemen or in the depths of the sea. "Stay awhile with me, Brother Finan."

Alone, the two men nervously gazed at each other, not daring to touch. Francis stood up and went to his hiding place and retrieved the parchment on which he had poured out his heart. "These are for you, Finan. They are unfinished but, under the circumstances, I think it best if you read them now. I may be prevented from completing them."

"Will we die, Francis?" Finan asked.

"It's a possibility," Francis said calmly. "But go now. Take these with you. Wait for me in your cell. I have something to do before I join you and then we will face this together." He leaned forward and kissed Finan on the lips.

"Please be quick, Francis," Finan said, and rushed out of the room.

Francis sharpened his quill and wrote with an intensity he had never known before. He began afresh. He manufactured an illustration of the angel who turned up at Sodom's city gate, and who bore a striking resemblance to Finan. Of course he was the most beautiful of God's angels. And Lot bore a striking resemblance to Francis himself.

4. He invited the beautiful angel to his house and there prepared for him a great feast. They conversed as brothers and Lot vowed never to be parted from his angel friend.

5. The men and boys of Sodom, having heard of the beauty of the angel, came to Lot's door to see for themselves the perfection that God had wrought. And they were in awe. But some merchants, more concerned with money and power, were impervious to beauty and called for the angel to be given to them.

Francis chuckled as he added a depiction of the head merchant who bore an amazing similarity to the abbot.

6. To the defilers he offered his wife and two daughters and they, bored and unhappy with life in Sodom, went freely to the homes of the merchants. The others filled the house of Lot to overflowing to hear the angel speak.

7. At the end of the night they departed to their houses in awe that God could create such a blessed creature.

8. Lot bid the stranger take his bed, saying that he would sleep on the floor, but the angel beckoned Lot to share the bed with him. Lot was ashamed for he was lowly and ill-born. "No one is ill-born in the sight of God," the angel said, and took Lot by the hand.

9. The blessed angel took Lot as his blood brother and companion for the night and Lot was filled with joy. After one week the angel told Lot that God had called him back and he had to leave.

10. "I have come to love you as no other creature," Lot said. "I cannot bear to part with you. I will end my life and join you in heaven." The angel was saddened to hear this. "If you take your own life," he said, "then you are damned, and I will never see you hereafter."

11. And Lot wept. And the angel wept. And God saw that their love was good and he opened his heart. He allowed the angel to stay with Lot until it was time to take him to his reward in heaven.

12. And for many years up to his passing, the love of Lot and the angel was talked about far and wide. For their love was stronger than father for son, mother for daughter, husband for wife, or subject for king.

Francis read the parchment quickly. His script was strong and bold. He placed it in a parchment copy of the Bible, replacing the original pages, and bound it carefully in oiled skins. He made the parcel waterproof. He would take it with him and cast it into the sea. He was satisfied it would wash ashore and that someone would find it and perhaps, with the help of God, it would be read.

Then he took all the other manuscripts in the library, with their tales of Lot's escape and incestuous relations with his daughters, and he poured bird fat over them. Then he set a sputtering candle atop the Bibles, short-wicked enough that it would burn down and set fire to the vile books he had had to copy all his life.

With much satisfaction he studied his handiwork before he shut and bolted the door to the Scriptorium. And with a joyful heart he made his way to the cell of Brother Finan, his angel.

Author's Note:

The topic, *Time Well Bent*, intrigued me and I immediately thought about great moments in history and great historical figures. While this was interesting, it struck me, however, that the deeds of little people, those not prominent on the world history stage, can have widespread ramifications.

Anonymous deeds can lead to great historical waves. Who, for example, first learned to boil an egg?

I hit upon the homophobically-interpreted passages in the Christian Bible as a starting point, especially the story of Sodom and Gomorrah, used to persecute gay peoples around the world for thousands of years. What if someone could change that story and put a positive spin on it? It was a short brain impulse to the creation of a same-sex attracted monk in a monastery on an island off the coast of Ireland during the Viking invasions. That he was the greatest of the scribe monks who created the illuminated manuscripts used in church services throughout the known world followed quickly. He would change the history of Christianity by the simple expedient of rewriting the story of Lot and the Angels in Sodom and send it out into the world. Fantasy, of course, as he was but one of many scribes across Europe, but from small ripples social tsunamis are created. Think of Stonewall.

MORISCA

Erin MacKay

M<small>Y NAME IS</small> G<small>ABRIELA</small>. P<small>ERHAPS</small> I should rather say, my name was Gabriela, at certain times. Gabriela is not what she called me, when she whispered my name in the dark.

It is dark now. I pretend it is so because she blew out the candles, and I pretend that it is cold because she has twisted the blanket around herself as she slept. Others who share the darkness with me, and who tomorrow will share my fate, whisper the name of God. I leave God alone, as He has left me. I lie wrapped in my happy illusions, and whisper her name instead.

When I was a child and living with my family in a pleasant house with a courtyard, my father called me Ghaliya. He told my mother and me that we were the most beautiful women in the kingdom of Castilla. But my father died, and the kingdom outside the walls of our house was Christian, and had been for some time. The people of Castilla did not like our dark eyes or our black hair, and they especially did not like our names. So we dressed like Christian women, covered our hair, and kept our eyes lowered, and in the city, my mother called me Gabriela.

To feed us, my mother became a laundress for people much richer than we were. She wept when her pretty hands turned red and rough, but I liked the work. It took me all over the city, to the river and the plaza and the market. At night I went home and put money in my mother's hands, ate a simple meal and slept well. I worked hard, I grew strong, and I laughed often.

The day came when we heard that King Enrique was bringing his half-brother, Prince Alfonso, home from exile in Arévalo, and his half-sister, too. Enrique expected little Infanta Isabel to live at court in the style of the princess that she was, and that meant there was work to be had. My mother and I stood in line at the castle with all the other men and women looking for jobs. My mother's references impressed the tired-looking man in the castle yard, but he shook his head. "We have washerwomen," he said. "Come back next spring, if you still want work then."

My mother pulled her veil over her face to hide her disappointment, and held out her hand for me. I looked at the tired man with a frown and he met my eyes for just a moment.

"Wait."

Washerwomen they had, but the King wanted strong young women of good character to serve in his pious sister's household, and there were few of those in line that morning. Moments later, I was Gabriela the chambermaid.

The castle was a wonderful place. It was built in the Gothic way, closed in and secure, not like our houses with their airy arches and courtyards and fragrant flowers. But in the castle there were twisting stairways and shadowed corridors and halls with high ceilings that bounced with echoes. I was given a dress and smock, of an ugly, sturdy fabric.

Mistress Teoda was the head housekeeper, and her job, as far as I could ever tell, was to scream at maids, often and loudly. My first day in the castle, I saw her beat another maid who sloshed dirty water onto the floor tiles. Poor Belita. It was not the last time she would be beaten for clumsiness, and though I tried to help her when I could, I had plenty of my own work to do.

If I had ever thought to see the King, I learned quickly that I was wrong. I was such a lowly little maid at first that my job was to clean the quarters of other servants, and I never had cause to venture out of that part of the large castle. Sometimes I glimpsed a bolt of imported fabric destined for a lush bedroom, or stole bits of heavenly fruits and spiced meats from the leftovers in the kitchen, but that was as close as I was allowed to get to the high courtiers of Valladolid.

The evening before the Infanta was to arrive, I went to my bed drooping with tiredness from all the preparations, yet I lay awake far into the night. Taresa, who shared my pallet, complained of my tossing and turning, but I knew she was just as excited as I. The corridors had hissed with whispers of the Infanta's beauty, intelligence and piety. Young as she was, already there were rumors of princes and lords lining up to ask the King for her hand in marriage. I thought it was a wonderful thing to be a princess, to wear lovely clothes and be surrounded by pretty ladies and brave knights, but whenever Mistress Teoda spoke of the Infanta, she shook her head as if in sorrow.

The city celebrated for days to welcome the little prince and princess to court, but I did not have much time to share in them. When the last feast ended, we servants discovered that the only change the arrival of the Infanta brought was more work. The King had given her two lady companions, a confessor, a governess and a tutor, and a few people whose place I did not know. They all had their own servants and valets and assistants—whose clean quarters were my responsibility. Some days I scurried from sunup to sundown without pausing for a moment.

One morning I finished my chores in the governess's room and she sent me on an errand to fetch a new quill for her. I liked the governess; her name was Mistress Costança and she was a small, tidy woman with a quiet voice. She often asked me to do small tasks that were not really my job, but I was happy that she entrusted them to me and so I did not complain.

I had just darted down the hallway in search of quills when I heard a crash, and a wail. Belita. The new strains of our jobs had not improved her; she had already pushed Mistress Teoda's patience to the breaking point. But, unlike me, she was the only person in her family who was working, and she desperately needed her job. Mistress Costança's quill would wait; I had to see if there was anything I could do to help Belita.

I followed the sound of her voice and found her on her hands and knees on the floor, her dress soaked through, staring in horror at a spreading river of greasy water. "Belita," I said, sighing. "What has happened this time?"

My voice brought her out of her shock. She sat back on her heels and began to sob. "Oh, Gabi, I stumbled over the bucket." She waved toward the overturned pail a few steps away. "It just—oh, it's gone everywhere! Mistress Teoda will sack me for certain this time."

I followed the trail of water to where it dripped down the stairs and into a hallway the courtiers sometimes used. "We have to clean it up before someone falls," I said. "Run back and change into dry clothes; I'll get some cloths to clean it up."

Belita ran as fast as her sopping skirts would let her. I went the other way, to the laundry where we got out cleaning cloths every morning. With a mound of them in my arms I hurried back down the hall. Mistress Teoda had already discovered the spill on the stairs; I could hear her exclaiming over it. So I walked faster, eager to get there before Belita and perhaps deflect some of Mistress Teoda's anger.

As I rounded the last corner, something hit me, hard. My feet went out from under me, the floor rose up to strike my bottom, the cloths flew in a dozen different directions. My head spinning, I had to blink a few times to make sense of the voices I suddenly heard around me, women's voices, squawking in dismay.

Only one sounded clear to me, pitched like a songbird above the fracas. "No, I'm fine, really."

I scrambled up to find a girl of about my own age being helped to her feet by two older women. As soon as I saw her, I knew I should fall to my knees and beg for the mercy of a swift death. But I could not move. I could not even breathe. She was the most beautiful thing I had ever seen in the world, lovelier than the sunrise, or a rose, or my father's smile. She was a sculpture of gold and ivory and crystal blue, dressed in fabrics so fine my worker's hand would have shredded them at a touch.

"Are you hurt?"

My heart stopped when I realized those gentle blue eyes were looking at me, that smooth voice was asking after *me*. Then Mistress Teoda appeared behind the women and my brain begin working again. My knees hit the floor so fast I had to swallow a cry of pain, but I bent over until my nose nearly touched the stone. "Your Highness," I gasped.

"Forgive me."

Her two attendants began scolding me, but their words flowed like a river over me and away. I could still feel the presence of the Infanta, a ray of sunlight warming the air around me. Somewhere over my bowed head, Mistress Teoda's insults and blows rained down, but I barely felt them.

The Infanta's voice cut through her ladies' remonstrations and brought a sudden silence.

"Here you are."

I did not realize my head cloth had fallen off until she held it out to me. I took it from her swiftly, appalled that such a rough garment should profane those soft, white fingers. "Thank you, Your Highness." I brushed strands of black hair from my eyes and set about covering my head as quickly as I could.

"What is your name?" she asked me.

"G… Gabriela, Your Highness."

There was a pause, and I think she might have been studying me. I had not yet gathered the courage to look any farther than her slippered feet. One of the women muttered, *"Morisca,"* just barely loud enough to hear. I did not move.

"Did you spill the water, Gabriela?"

I looked at Mistress Teoda's face, still red with anger and the effort of beating me. A few steps behind her, dressed in clean clothes, Belita peeked at me with wide eyes. I was miserable to have to lie to her, but I had no choice. "Yes, Your Highness."

The smallest breath escaped her. "I see."

Mistress Teoda stepped forward, her upper body bent into a servile bow. "Your Highness, allow me to remove this clumsy wretch from your sight. She will not trouble you again."

My eyes could see only the floor, but my heart could feel the Infanta moving away, down the hall toward the stairs. My head sank downward even further. The sunlight was leaving me, and I was about to be sacked.

"Get up," Mistress Teoda hissed.

I rose and began gathering the fallen cloths. Belita at last stepped forward to join me, her eyes full of fear and gratitude for what I was suffering for her. I gave her an encouraging smile, then a thought popped into my head. "Quill!" I cried.

Mistress Teoda narrowed her eyes at me, and my cheeks flamed. "I was on my way to get a new quill for Mistress Costança. I forgot."

"Someone else can get the quill," Mistress Teoda said. "You won't be here long enough to worry about it. You will clean up the mess you made and then it's back to the streets for you..." Mistress Teoda stopped, her eyes slowly moving upward. Her face showed such surprise that I dared look around to see.

The Infanta had appeared back around the corner, her lips curved in a smile of gentle amusement. "Mistress, I would like this girl to attend to my household. Lady Berta, take her back to our chambers. I want her to start immediately."

"But, Your Highness," one of the women said. "You already have a maid. Sancha came with you from Arévalo; surely you cannot dismiss her."

The Infanta smiled, and the sun shone again. "I am certain I can find it within me to be messy enough for two maids."

While I stared in lingering shock, the woman curtsied. "Yes, Your Highness." Belita, awed, moved to take the handful of cloths from me. The Infanta smiled approval and turned to continue on her way with her other lady companion. I stared after her for a moment, watching her gauzy veil flutter behind her, then realized Lady Berta was giving me a sharp look.

"Sorry, my lady," I murmured. I nodded to Mistress Teoda, who seemed just as dazed as I, then hurried to Lady Berta's side.

Sancha was a fair-haired Northern girl a little older than I. She smiled often and was glad of another person to share her chores and her cot. I spent the rest of the day learning how to behave, to walk quietly so the Infanta would hardly know I was there, to handle the delicate linens that furnished the room and the exotic silks of the Infanta's wardrobe. Sancha told me the habits of the lady companions, and what I could expect from each of them.

From my first night as a member of the Infanta's household, things were different than I expected they would be, different than everyone expected. Sancha and I had just settled in to sleep when the curtain that separated our tiny room from the rest of the suite parted. Lady Pascuala blinked in the darkness, and whispered, "Gabriela. Her Highness wishes to see you." She smiled and disappeared.

I rose and with shaking hands pulled my dress on over my chemise. Sancha braided my hair and helped me with my headcloth. With a nervous smile of thanks, I took a deep breath and darted out from behind the curtain. Lady Berta, Lady Pascuala, and the Infanta sat in the parlor sewing by the light of many candles. I curtsied to the Infanta, her beauty already sending me into a stupor. Lowering her embroidery to rest in her lap, she looked at me somberly. "Gabriela, I will ask you again: Did you spill the water?"

I had not expected that question. My mouth opened, then closed, as I tried to think what to say. Then I understood that she already knew the answer and was merely waiting for me to tell the truth. "No, Your Highness. I did not."

She did not reply immediately, and I fought the urge to look at her, to see her reaction.

"I wondered how a girl who had been sent to fetch a quill for Mistress Costança had managed to upset a bucket of water at the opposite end of the hall."

At the amusement in her tone, I could not help but raise my head. I found the Infanta smiling at me, and she held my gaze for a moment. "You are a good girl, Gabriela. The other little maid is very lucky to have such a brave friend."

My tongue lay numb in my mouth, so I could only lower my head in mute acceptance of her praise.

"No, look at me."

I did. She studied me so intently that I began to tremble beneath it. "Such black eyes," she murmured. "Berta, aren't they like obsidian?"

Berta sniffed. "Moorish eyes, Your Highness."

The Infanta's cheeks blushed pink. "Thank you, Gabriela," she said, her voice lower than before. "You may go."

I curtsied again and backed from the room, my eyes on the carpet.

"Your Highness, you cannot be thinking of keeping…" Berta began, but she stopped speaking abruptly. The curtain fell around me, enclosing me in darkness once more.

Attending the Infanta was a different life than the one I'd had before. She rose as early as the maids to take communion in her room. Sancha and I, along with the rest of the Infanta's household, joined her. Father Torquemada, the Infanta's confessor, greeted me kindly enough and I liked him. After mass, the Infanta filled her day with lessons and social visits, embroidery, reading, music, and games. Sometimes she was in her chambers and sometimes not.

Sancha and I spent the day quietly cleaning the rooms of the Infanta and her servants, emptying night soil, changing linens, dusting and scrubbing and seeing to the washing and mending of clothes. If the Infanta had a guest in her chambers while we worked, Sancha and I labored in silence, invisible to the point where—I swear—the courtiers could look through us and see to the other side. If she were alone with her ladies, though, I sometimes caught her blue eyes following me, watching me as if my chores interested her. At first, I didn't know what to do, and I would duck my head and pretend I hadn't seen. But once, in a playful mood, I summoned the boldness to smile at her. She blushed, but smiled back before she went back to her reading. The next time, I made a silly face, and she bit her lip to keep from laughing.

I saw Belita sometimes as I went about the castle, and Mistress Teoda. Belita curtsied to me now, and Mistress Teoda never raised her voice to me. The Infanta's ladies were different. Lady Berta had little use for me and was certain to find something in my work to criticize, or to send me scurrying off on some menial task whenever she got a chance. Lady Pascuala was kinder, but I think that came from good manners rather than from liking me. I found myself most comfortable with Mistress Costança, who treated me with the same polite distance she always had.

One morning, the Infanta and her ladies left early for an outing with Prince Alfonso and the courtiers who had grown close to them, and so I worked alone in the quiet of her empty chambers. I came upon the embroidery the Infanta had been working on the evening before. The pattern was Moorish, finely stitched on fabrics imported from the faraway lands of my forebears. I was afraid to touch it, but I stood close to the frame, admiring the work and imagining the slender fingers and the patient, creative mind that had done it.

"Do you like it?"

I jumped, surprised to see her back. "Yes, Your Highness. It's the loveliest I've ever seen."

"You flatter me," she complained. But she smiled, and came to stand beside me, so close I could smell the lavender scent of her dress. I thought she seemed uneasy, and I knew I should move away, but I didn't want to.

She ran a finger over the latest bit of stitching, then let her hand fall. "You don't have to be afraid of me."

"I…" I started to say I was not, but thought better of it. "I thought there was an outing today. Is Your Highness well?"

She waved a hand in dismissal of my concern, but her smile tightened. "Yes, thank you. Merely a bit annoyed."

She closed her mouth as if she were finished, but then more words came spilling out, and I thought perhaps she could not stop them. "An outing in this city is never just an outing. There are always friends and noblemen, and cousins of friends and noblemen, all hoping for favor with one of us. There is always someone to whom I should be betrothed, someone who secretly hopes I or my brother will rule after Enrique, or even rule now, instead of Enrique. Always people who want something. Every word, every glance, has three meanings and no one smiles without a reason. It's maddening."

As I stared, too stunned to reply, she realized how much she had said, and to whom she had said it. She drew herself up straight, but her eyes lowered as if to hide from me. "Forgive me, I should not have burdened you with all that."

Her stiff shame jerked me out of my reverie. "No, never be sorry," I said. Her eyebrows went up, and I remembered my place. "I mean… It sounds annoying, Your Highness. Miserable, actually." We both laughed softly at my honesty. "I'm just a maid, Your Highness. If you need to say those things, you can say them to me. Like pebbles thrown into a pond, Your Highness, they will sink down and never be seen again."

She looked at me, a wry smile spreading on her face. "Do I sound that desperate?"

"Desperate, Your Highness? Never. You just sound… Well, like a girl with too much to think about." I looked around me. "All I have to do is clean. I have enough room left in my head for both of us."

That made her laugh, and I was pleased to see that she seemed easier afterward.

"Gabriela." She said my name slowly. "Were you born with that name?"

"No, Your Highness. My father named me Ghaliya."

She frowned, tasting the word. "Ghaliya." She spoke the syllables too close to the front of her mouth, but still, it sounded lovely in her voice. "Are you baptized?"

"No, Your Highness."

That made her frown in earnest. "That won't do. I hate to think that you are damned. I'll have Father Torquemada arrange it immediately."

"No, thank you. I mean, I do not think you need fear for me, Your Highness."

Her eyes narrowed as if she were considering being annoyed with me. "I beg your pardon?"

I spoke because I had thought about the matter, and wanted her to know it was all right. "At mass, Father Torquemada speaks of a loving God, a God of infinite mercy who treasures all his creations. Surely, if I am a good girl, He would not send me to burn simply because my name is Ghaliya, and not Gabriela."

"But the Church teaches that infidels who do not love Christ are damned."

"The words of men," I replied. "But, forgive me for contradicting Your Highness. I will be baptized if that is your wish." And I meant it. I would not deliberately make her unhappy with me, not for anything. It was just water, after all.

"I do wish it. Besides, Berta and Pascuala will not countenance an unbaptized heathen in my service."

I had no doubt those ladies would cheerfully drown me in the fount, but I merely curtsied deeply. Three days later, with Mistress Costança by my side as my godmother, Father Torquemada spoke the words and anointed me with water. All I remembered of it, though, was the way the Infanta smiled as we became children of the same God.

My baptism, in her mind, gave her permission to be friends with me, because after that day, she spoke to me often. For a girl forced too soon to become a woman, I was a harmless pet, a little friend she could giggle and gossip with, and try to forget that she lay at the heart of a political storm. It humbled me to realize that she was seeking me out deliberately, when she knew we would be alone, because I was the only one she truly trusted. She spoke to me of tremulous hopes and looming fears, and even of anger for the dishonesty she had to breathe along with the air. I absorbed all of it, everything she shared with me, and gave her stillness and quiet in return. That simple exchange was our bond, our alliance lying silent and steadfast beneath all her other tangled relationships.

Matters with the King grew tense as the opposition grew bolder in their support of Prince Alfonso. Finally civil war broke out, and she was little more than a prisoner in the castle. The night her brother died, of what could only be poisoning, she sent everyone away but me. Until the sun rose, she let her grief and fears overflow their banks and consume her. By morning, she was as regal and composed as ever, but on that sobbing, shivering night, I gave her what comfort I could: the undemanding embrace of someone who only loved her, who wanted only her happiness.

So it was not witchcraft, you see, not the evil influence of my pagan soul that made a princess seek the friendship of a chambermaid. It was loneliness, and need.

Berta and Pascuala made a great show of affection for me when the Infanta was near. From where Isabel sat at her dressing table on this particular evening, her ladies appeared to be enjoying a toy puppet given by one of her many admirers. From where I stood, carefully brushing Isabel's golden hair, I could see that their squeals and laughter masked looks of iron resentment. As always, I made just as great a show of ignoring them.

Despite bitter bloodshed among the nobility, despite flights to a monastery, then to Ocaña and now to Madrigal, despite the endless skirmishes and negotiations that kept Enrique at bay, Isabel had grown only more beautiful as the years passed. It was not merely for political gain that suitors from France, Portugal and Aragon pressured Isabel and waited hopefully for Enrique's answer. I alone knew that the answer had already been given.

"I am tired, ladies," Isabel said suddenly. "I think I will retire." Berta and Pascuala silenced their merriment instantly. They had grown accustomed to Isabel's anxieties; she was in more danger here in Madrigal than she had ever been during the war that killed her brother. Enrique had declared Isabel his heir in the treaty that ended the war, but significant factions supported his daughter and so Isabel was not yet safe. The city of Ocaña had supported her, sworn its strength to protect her, but Madrigal was not nearly so staunch; we knew the nervous bishop under whose protection we now lived would buckle any day now. After months of this shaky existence, Isabel swung from poised determination to tears with little warning.

Pascuala and Berta exchanged looks as I began to blow out the candles. The first winter we had spent away from the castle, Isabel had taken me as her bedmate. While they had shared the Infanta's bed for practical purposes, chaperoning her person in Enrique's licentious court, and for warmth in the cold of winter, Isabel took me to her bed for other reasons entirely. I think they suspected it from the start.

In the face of their contempt and offended sensibilities, I chose my food carefully and drank nothing but water I had drawn myself. Their wrath was worth being able to comfort the Infanta when she needed it, to offer her the shelter of trusted arms and a devotion that had nothing to do with who would next wear the crown of Castilla and Leon.

It had been raining the night I finally understood that Isabel found me as lovely as I found her. That night, and the next, and the next, I learned her body by feel, every silky curve, and I learned where to touch her to make her shudder and gasp and whisper my name. So many nights she gazed into my eyes and whispered my name, Ghaliya, and when she begged me long enough, I at last whispered hers. In my heart, at that moment, she became Isabel. I never spoke her name aloud, in the sunlight. In the light of day, when I wore my maid's smock and she wore her armor of regal formality, she was only ever "Your Highness" to me, as I was "Gabriela" to her. In dim, secret candlelight, when I poured wine for the courtiers who conspired with her, I addressed her not at all, the better to be invisible to all those nervous eyes.

I only breathed it into darkness, muffled by velvet and silk and warm skin.

Berta and Pascuala retired sullenly to their own small chamber, leaving us alone. I braided Isabel's hair and we sat on the bed, fully dressed, waiting. After a time I blew out the last candle, to give the illusion that we were sleeping. Isabel sought my arms, trembling a little. "Sleep," I told her, pushing her to make her lean against the pillows. "I will stay awake."

"How can I sleep?" But she did, finally, after I had spent an hour stroking her hair and murmuring reassurances. As I had promised, I stayed awake, listening to her heart beat and resisting the urge to kiss her parted lips as she dreamed.

I listened, too, for hoof beats. The Archbishop of Toledo, one of Isabel's powerful allies, was sending men to escort us to Ocaña. Fernando of Aragon was making his way there, in secret, this very night, as we would soon be as well. The betrothal papers were signed, Enrique and his councilors were away in the south, and by the time they heard of Isabel's escape from Madrigal, she would be safely married to Fernando.

I had worried about Fernando. He was as pious as Isabel had once been, before she had dismissed Father Torquemada, and he was committed to the Reconquista. "How will a man who wants to kill Moors allow his wife a Moorish lady companion?" I had asked her.

She had put her hand to my cheek and smiled. "You are Lady Gabriela. That is all he needs to know. And while Aragon is strong, he can hardly carry on a war against the Moors without me." I had begun to feel a little sorry for Prince Fernando, and wondered if he understood what a formidable woman he was marrying.

"Ghaliya."

"Yes?"

"Have they arrived yet?"

"No, not yet. But they will soon. It is early, you must be patient. And sleep."

She whispered my name once more, there in the darkness, before she slept again. A few moments later, I heard the clatter of horses and men. I roused Isabel and put her cloak around her. Together we ran down the stairs and out into the chilly air of the courtyard.

It was not the Archbishop of Toledo.

I have plenty of darkness in which to whisper now. Father Torquemada has seen to that. Though I suppose he is merely an instrument, doing exactly what Berta expected him to do when she betrayed her princess and accused me. Pascuala retired to a nunnery to avoid the taint of scandal, but Berta enjoyed giving lurid testimony to the Inquisitors of the unspeakable acts I led the Infanta to commit, in whispers, in the dark. All the while Berta smirked at my shorn hair and my sackcloth. King Enrique will pay her well for her part in keeping the Infanta from marrying Fernando, but I think her jealousy was satisfied by the mere sight of me being led away in chains, and of the Infanta sobbing in the dust.

Isabel is betrothed to the King of Portugal now, at least until Enrique changes allegiances again. I fear for her after I am gone. Fernando of Aragon was her best hope for a husband who would protect her, and who would be her willing equal in intelligence and determination. Alfonso of Portugal wants her only for her inheritance and to curry favor with Enrique; she will wither beneath his indifferent domination. If circumstances shift, Enrique may yet match her with someone even worse, or give her a cup of her brother's poisoned fate.

I have heard that she is unwell, that she does not sleep and barely eats, but such news is weeks old and no one will give me any other. The Inquisitors think I am bewitching her from afar, with my dark Mohammedan arts, and they hope to break my supposed hold on her imperiled soul. Father Torquemada accused me of planting in her mind heretical notions of a God who loves heathen and Christian alike. Isabel will not deny this belief, no matter how many hours he spends instructing her in proper Catholic thought. It is for her defiance of him, I think, that I burn tomorrow. It is for her defiance that he will make her watch.

When she heard my sentence, he said, she wept for a day and a night, a sure sign of enthrallment. It sorrows me to think that she weeps for me. Even now, I know I should be praying to whatever God is out there for her welfare. But the only prayer that comes to my lips here in the darkness is her name.

Tomorrow, I will stand on the pyre and speak it aloud, in the sunlight, and if there is a loving God above, Isabel will know all I meant to say.

Author's Note:

The marriage of Ferdinand and Isabella not only united two powerful kingdoms, it brought two determined and shrewd leaders together in an equal co-regency. Their reign had a lasting impact on the history of Spain and the world.

History suggests that Isabella learned an early suspicion of non-Catholics, reinforced by the influence of Torquemada in the Spanish court. The co-regents' desire for Christian homogeneity drove the Reconquista, the expulsion of Muslims and Jews from Spain, and the institution of the Spanish Inquisition. Had Isabella encountered a different influence, perhaps tempering Ferdinand's zeal rather than compounding it, the history of the Catholic Church in Spain and its role in western history might be very different.

Had Ferdinand and Isabella not been in a strong enough political and economic position to take a chance on Christopher Columbus in 1492, he likely would have accepted England's offer to fund his voyage across the Atlantic. As much as Spanish culture and the Catholic mission system affected the colonization of South and Central America, the western hemisphere would be all but unrecognizable to us today had Columbus' voyage been an English venture.

GREAT RECKONINGS, LITTLE ROOMS

Catherine Lundoff

ACT 1, SCENE 1

The young man rubbed the sparse curling hairs on his chin as if their bristles pained him somewhat, and sighed as he put his quill back into the ink. The page before him was no less blank than it had been before the sigh, so the sound brought him nothing more than the not unwelcome attention of his companion.

She rose from the bed where she had reclined and walked toward him, her stride sinuous and seductive under layers of skirts and bodice. The light from the window fell on her face, not beautiful as beauty is commonly reckoned. No fair English rose here, pale of skin and blonde of hair. Instead, she was dark, her complexion the deep olive of the Mediterranean ports, her hair the thick course black curls of an Italian peasant. Her lips were full, even thick, and her nose suggested a trace of Jewish blood.

Yet she was beautiful if one had the wit to see it. Her eyes were large and dark and luminous with intelligence, her teeth good, and her figure fulsome, promising a glorious bounty to any lover who might strike her fancy. She reached his side before he had time to admire her further and leaned over to wrap her arms around his shoulders.

He closed his eyes and smiled as her lips caressed his neck lightly. His smile widened as her hand slipped down the front of his tunic but he stopped it before it could go further. She pouted at his gesture and snatched a book from the pile on the edge of the table, whirling away laughing.

97

A step on the stair cut short her merriment until a familiar knock sounded at the door. "It's Kit, come to lift your spirits, love!" The dark beauty smiled again as she swept the door open to admit their visitor.

The young man's frown was gone an instant before the man in the doorway might have seen it, but somehow he seemed to know it had been there. Christopher Marlowe swept into the room, a smile that barely reached his eyes twisting his lips. "Not pleased to see me, friend? But then," he caught the volume from the woman's hand, "you're hard at work on your Plautus, I see." He dropped into the chair in front of the table, his sharp gaze missing neither the pile of books nor the blank page.

"Come to spy on my progress, eh Kit?" The young man gave his friend a rueful smile that took the edge from his words.

"I had hoped to find you at work on another play. Another play writ anonymously that might catch Henslowe's eye perhaps. Some light fare like your *Comedy of Errors*. We are all a bit hungrier from the plague." Marlowe's lips twisted in a grimace. "And I myself have little touch for comedy."

"Ah, but your tragedies are for the ages, are they not? And we may all be a bit hungrier but you and Kyd and my brother, you mean. Would that I had the Lord Chamberlain's men speaking my words on stage for a fortnight!" The young man smiled up at the dark temptress at his side and kissed her hand.

The door swung open again, causing them all to start as another young man entered. This one's countenance was as like to the first's as two peas but for the ferocious scowl he wore, and a more fulsome beard. "Hello, Will," murmured the young man at the table.

Kit's smile turned darker, something malicious in it now. "The one and only Shake-scene himself," he murmured.

The scowling man's frown darkened and he responded with a string of oaths that made the playwright laugh. The woman, in contrast, slipped behind the young writer's chair. Will gave her a look of pure, frustrated longing before turning his furious glare on the others. "Still playing at being the man, Judith?" he snarled, his gaze locking with that of the seated writer.

The victim of his attack arched an eyebrow and stood with a graceful, catlike stretch. "Would you have me play whore to your poet instead, brother? Or mere muse? These are not roles that I desire."

Once the young man stood, the light caught his face. The contrast picked out the slight delicacy of his features but nothing more that suggested femininity, at least not before the other stepped forward so that their faces were closer. "Must it be whore then, sister? Surely you might have stayed at home and married a butcher or an innkeeper. Being in foal would look well on you." Will smiled maliciously as the blank page caught his eye. He glanced up to meet Judith's eyes, knowing how his words would sting, how unlikely it was that any man in Stratford-on-Avon would have her even if she wanted them.

"Careful, brother, or you'll turn out to be all that Master Chettle had to say of you, the foul as well as the fair." Judith's lips twisted as her gaze challenged his. How had they come to this, they who had once been as close friends as brother and sister could be? She forced the thought from her face. He must never know how his blows struck home.

Will turned away a moment, shoulders stiff. He turned back a breath or two later, stance switching from combatant to orator. Years of acting smoothed away all but the calmest and most pleasant of his expressions. He bowed as if entering the room for the first time. "I shall begin again. Good day, Master Marlowe, Mistress Emilia, sister. I came not to dispense strife, though it comes on my heels, but rather to invite you, one and all, to see my poor self appear in a new play of my own devising some days hence."

Kit raised an eyebrow and smiled. "Harlequin and Columbine, perhaps?"

Will gave a genuine laugh, hearty and deep. "It would please you to hear that, wouldn't it, Kit-cat? But no, I must disappoint here as elsewhere." His glance caught Emilia's for a moment. "I am to appear in a fine tragedy, that of *Titus Andronicus*. And it would please me if you were to attend, that afterward we might raise an ale to my new work. That is, if you can do so without being poisoned by jealousy." His lips curled in an ironic smile that took in both his sister and Marlowe.

"I...cannot, Will. But I hope that it may bring you glory." Emilia smiled, only her hands twisting together behind Judith's chair to suggest her agitation. She caught up her cloak and made for the door, but not before Will stepped in front of her and laid his hand on her arm.

"Though your eyes are nothing like the sun, Mistress, yet I would have them look on me kindly. In friendship for better times to come, at least, if the past is not enough." Emilia flinched as Judith surged to her feet and leapt forward only to be stayed by Marlowe's tight grip. Her eyes looked everywhere except at Will for a moment. Then she gave him a tremulous smile and the slightest of nods. A tear shone on her cheek. With a deft twist of her wrist, she broke free and vanished from the room.

Marlowe watched her leave, a strange look crossing his face. He whispered, "Was this the face that launched a thousand ships?" as the door closed, but the other two paid no attention to him.

Will stared at the closing door as Judith relaxed in Kit's grip. She spat her words. "Ill done, brother. She loves where her heart goes and you cannot force it elsewhere."

"Put the pretty words to verse, sister and we'll publish it abroad for a shilling or two in my own name. But for now say you will come to my play and see how it is done." He smiled mockingly, then, taking their silence for assent, turned on his heel and left without a word of farewell.

Judith slammed her open palm against the chair and bit off an oath before it could leave her lips. Would that she'd been born the man, not Will! The thought rankled her as it had since they were children.

Still, before there was Emilia, Will had been her friend for all that. They had sat together inventing tales and speaking lines for characters of their own invention since Will had taught her to read and write. Each had written poetry of their own but their first plays they had written together. Two minds as one. So of course, when they loved, they must needs love alike.

"I'd say give the girl up, but it's too late for that, isn't it?" Marlowe asked the question in an indifferent tone. He shrugged when she said nothing and gestured at the page. "Can you compose without your brother as muse? Or might another do as well?"

Judith bit her lip and was silent, wondering if Kit was suggesting himself as a replacement. The idea was very nearly too overwhelming to contemplate; the author of *Tamburlaine* offering his patronage to her! Or did he mean something else? No matter, she needed his help, in whatever guise it came. After a long moment, she nodded hesitantly, hoping with all her heart that she did not lie. With that fear uppermost, she pulled a page from beneath the pile of books and handed it to Kit.

He walked under the window and read it, frowning. He nodded once and handed it back. "We'll make a writer of you yet, little Jude. Only but finish it, and you'll hear the Chamberlain's Men speak your words as well as any other's."

Judith let out a breath she hadn't known she was holding. Marlowe did not give compliments lightly; the work was good. Perhaps she might succeed without Will's help as long as she could play the man.

Kit continued, "Now, I'm off to Deptford to meet with some that I know. A small errand for my other master, the one who is no muse. Come with me and we will raise a mug, there or in better company. You shall be Will as well as any other, at least for today. Nay, better, for you are not an angry man in love but a happy lad. Of a sort." Kit smiled, his eyes warming, his charm more than any mortal heart could withstand.

She hesitated, still wondering what Kit really wanted. He kept her secrets and praised her work, even stood her meals from time to time in the months since she had come to London, but asked little in return. Perhaps it was nothing more than a desire to be a thorn in Will's side, perhaps only the novelty of tricking the world around them. But if she did not trust him, she had no one else to play the part of brother, not as long as Emilia loved her and not Will. Whatever he wanted from her, she needed him.

Dismissing her misgivings, Judith smiled back as the playacting aspects of such an expedition began to appeal to her. Why should she not be Will for a few hours? She could imitate him so well as to be his shadow; she had done it enough since they were striplings, she should have no trouble doing it now. "Gentle Kit, I would not decline such an invitation were there twenty brothers betwixt us. Let us then away to Deptford and the Moor's net." She caught up her belt with its sheathed dagger and fastened it around her doublet. Marlowe bowed, his expression sardonic, as he ushered her out.

Act 1, Scene 2

Lincoln's Inn at Deptford was as like to any other house of its nature as might be; neither fish nor fowl, it was at once neither a public house nor yet merely a home. The innkeeper, one Mrs. Bull, let rooms to some who asked and served ale to many, yet she picked and chose her guests as carefully as she chose her ale, and those who drank there often served several masters.

The Queen's spymaster, Sir Francis Walsingham, called 'The Moor' for his dark complexion, had known many of the men who drank Mrs. Bull's ale. His ghostly hand lay heavy on the place, for all that he had been dead these three years past. The men who had served him as well as those who came after him worked in both light and shadow, their eyes missing little and their hands at once bloodstained and light-fingered.

This, then, was the company that young Judith Shakespeare encountered when she came to Deptford with her friend Kit Marlowe. But she was not as concerned with the men who watched her as she was with walking as Will would walk, meeting their stares as he would. A sharp-eyed, well dressed fellow hailed Kit from a corner table when they entered. "Marcade! Come here!"

Mercury? The nickname as well as the command made Judith raise an eyebrow despite her best intentions to keep her features still and impassive. But the fellow was handsome, near blindingly so, and Kit had an eye for handsome lads. She stifled a shrug as she trailed after him.

The seated man pulled the playwright down for a hearty kiss on the cheek before his cold, clear gaze fell on her. His expression shifted to something tigerish. "Did you bring your catamite here to parade him before me? Do you plan to govern me through my baser lusts, little Kit-cat?" The words were said softly but with an undertone of menace that sent a chill up her spine.

Kit laughed, the sound cutting through the dark layers in the other's words. He laid a hand on the man's shoulder and grinned back at Judith. "Nay, sweet Tom! I am not such a simpleton as that, though who loves not boys and tobacco is a fool, as I have said before. Yet I know what I have. I give you not my catamite but my rival, Will Shakespeare, whose words are all the talk of London."

"I thought Shakespeare to be older, more manly." The seated man, who Judith realized could be no other than Tom Walsingham, Marlowe's patron and lover and the Moor's own nephew, raked her with a sharp glance. "Not a stripling like this one. He seems as real as your Dutch coin, Kit."

"One man may play many parts on the stage as in the world, my lord." Judith stepped forward with a graceful gesture. "And be as real in one as in any of the others." She gave him one of Will's most charming smiles, the one he wore to soothe powerful men who might do him more harm than good.

Walsingham gave her another sharp glance, then nodded. "Well, he has a way with his words, like enough to the one you say he is. Here, make room for my friend Kit and his friend Will." This last command was delivered to the others at the table, one of whom gave Judith an evil look but moved aside nonetheless.

There was something in the fellow's ill-favored countenance, particularly the way he looked at Kit, which had her hand hovering above the dagger on her belt for a breath or two. His pockmarked face nearly burned green in jealous rage whenever Tom looked kindly upon the playwright. She wondered how Kit could bear it.

Yet the moment passed and soon she sat and spoke with Tom and Kit, raising a mug or two of ale until her spirits grew higher than they had in the last fortnight. But Tom's other companions, Poley and Frizer as they were called, cast a pall upon her spirits with their sidelong glances of ill will directed at Kit and, soon, at her as well.

Kit plainly thought little of them, the proof in his disdainful manner, and after a time Judith took her cue from him. At first, she mocked them lightly, teasing them about their scowls and their graces. But the atmosphere of ill will did not shift. Finally, the ale loosened her tongue more than she had intended and she met Frizer's eyes with a fierce glare of her own. "Fellow, your looks are foul enough to sour good ale. Your manners mark you as churlish a cur as I have ever met. Have you fair wit or words to balance them?"

Tom laughed and Kit's lips curled in an amused grimace, though his frown sent her a quick warning. By then, it was too late. Frizer lurched to his feet, hand on his knife, and Poley caught his arm. He shook Poley off as he hissed, "Codpiece sniffing sodomite! Are you a heretic as well?" He jerked his chin at Kit. "Don't be in such a hurry to welcome your master below." With that, he turned on his heel and left.

This time it was Kit who laughed. "Am I heretic now? Such is the price of loyal service!" He glanced at Tom, his expression angry and wary all at once, yet Tom was silent. His expression told Judith nothing but Kit found some comfort in his face and his posture relaxed somewhat.

Poley stood and announced that he must leave for other errands. He slipped away so quietly the others scarcely noticed his departure. Judith gave Kit a worried frown. A charge of sodomy was ill enough; to add heresy to it meant a trip to the executioner's block if it were proven. Or if you had no protection. She wondered if Tom would stand by him if the worst happened.

But no more was said. They drank more ale, debating the best of the new plays until Kit and Tom began to discuss philosophy and Judith fell silent. Her education had been slipshod, gleaned from the pickings of her brother's learning since their father saw no need for a girl to know such things. Still, it was fascinating and she absorbed all she could, Frizer and Poley forgotten in the flow of words until it was time for them to return to their rooms.

Act 2, Scene 1

Judith didn't see the bill posted on the church wall until three days after her night in Deptford. She was coming from the printer's office where she had pled her case for the publishing of a new play, not yet finished, when it caught her eye. The first few lines were a spiteful piece of venom accusing the Dutch of treachery and cowardice in their war with Spain, causing brave English soldiers to die in their stead. She might have ignored it but for the signature: Tamburlaine.

That was enough to make her stop and read it through. The play had been Kit's masterwork, the one that her brother and Kyd and all the other playwrights sought to emulate. It could be no accident that the name appeared on this document.

But had Kit written it himself? She scanned the verses; it seemed too clumsy for his hand, despite a few touches that suggested his skill. And what had he to do with the Dutch? There was no connection as far as she knew, save what Tom had said of 'Dutch coin.' But she could make no sense of that so perhaps it was nothing, the words some private jest between the two. She turned away, trying to convince herself of that.

The words nagged at her though, filling her thoughts until she found herself at Kit's rooms some hours later. He should know of this, even if it had naught to do with him. At least he might be on his guard if something more lay beyond the verses than simple malice.

But he was not to be found at his room and the landlord sent her on to Tom Walsingham's lodgings. They too were deserted; there, a servant said that his master had gone to the country and that Master Marlowe might have gone with him. He would say no more and Judith had no coin with which to press her case. She turned reluctantly from the house and walked home.

Emilia was waiting for her there, having stolen a few hours from her husband's side. Judith forgot the poem and Kit and even her brother in her lover's body.

The next few days passed quickly. Judith wrote and read what she had written to Emilia. She saw Will's new play and found the words to praise it.

He glowed a bit, almost as he had before Emilia came between them. She wondered if he would find that glow of goodwill sufficient to read her new play, but decided to wait. She would show it to Kit first. Whenever he reappeared.

Act 2, Scene 2

When two more days passed without word, Judith could stand it no longer. She left her room that afternoon to walk to Deptford. It took some time to make the journey, which gave her ample time for thought.

She could not have said why she went, except that now there were rumors about the flyers that she'd seen, rumors that mentioned Kit. And Thomas Kyd had been arrested and charged with heresy, or so the whispers said. True, Kyd was no friend of hers and she liked his stiff prose little enough. But he was also a friend of Kit's and if the charge fell on one, it might well fall on another. The thought chilled her.

For this expedition she had added more hair to her chin with an actor's art, forcing her face into a near mirror of Will's. It might give her extra protection on the street or in the inn if she appeared older, fiercer. She remembered Frizer's rage and shivered with no ale to warm her against it. Still, she must know what had happened to Kit; surely he could not have moved permanently to the country. It would prove too dull for such as he.

The inn was where she remembered it and the men at the tables were much the same. But this time she entered cautiously, searching for Mrs. Bull and whatever information she could provide, and meeting few men's eyes. The common room was near to empty in any case so there were few enough to see her. She crept to the kitchen, then waited while the kitchen boy fetched the landlady.

When Mrs. Bull finally appeared, her sharp black eyes studied Judith as if she were some new specimen, an exotic creature wafted in from far off lands. Judith stammered her questions and Mrs. Bull merely looked at her for a few moments. When at last she spoke, her voice was thick with unvoiced amusement. "One of Master Marlowe's friends, are you? Odd that he'd not have told you where he might be going if he was leaving London."

That lent steel to Judith's backbone. "I'm merely here to deliver a message and his landlord said I might find him here. It's all the same to me whether he drinks your ale or another's." She drew herself up and gave the other woman her haughtiest look.

Mrs. Bull made a dry sound like bones rattling that might have been a chuckle. "I'll not be telling tales of Master Marlowe, but if he's to come here, it will be with Master Walsingham after sunset. Spend your coin here or elsewhere until then." The innkeeper shrugged and turned back to the kitchen, leaving Judith in the doorway.

She accepted her dismissal reluctantly, turning away to peer out the window at the murky sky outside. It was hard to tell when darkness would fall but it could not be much longer, surely. She groped in her pouch for coin and found a scant few shillings. Just enough to buy her an ale and a bowl of stew, even here.

Taking a deep breath, Judith slipped onto an empty bench in a dark corner and beckoned a servant. Food and drink arrived soon after and Judith bent her head to the task of eating, only looking up when the door swung open for those entering and leaving. It seemed like an eternity, though the food was good. Men came and went but none were Kit or his friend.

At last she was done eating and drinking and had no more coin to allow her to linger. She stood slowly and made her way to the door in time for it to swing open, leaving her face to face with Frizer. He recognized her instantly, despite the extra beard she had carefully applied. The scent of beer hung over him like a cloud. "It's another sodomite heretic! 'Tis our lucky day, Poley. The Privy Council will pay well for this one too, I think." He herded Judith back into the room with an evil smile.

Poley and another man followed at his heels, the former giving her a glance of pure contempt. There would be little help from that quarter, she realized. Her brain spun with ideas for escape at the same time that she wrestled with his words. The Privy Council? Was Kit in the Tower?

Frizer's grip on her shoulder tightened, driving her fears for Kit from her head for the moment. He fumbled for the knife at his belt, eyes glowing with drunken bloodlust. She summoned anger as a shield. "Devil take thee, cur! What do you mean by laying your hands on me?" She twisted sharply and jumped back a pace or two, causing her assailant to stumble into the room, releasing her. Her hand was on her own knife but she didn't unsheathe it yet. There might yet be time to end this with words, before her clumsiness with a blade was revealed.

Frizer's unknown companion caught him as he staggered sideways and shoved him toward a table. Poley stepped close to Judith, overwhelming her with the stale scent of his breath. "Begone, little whoreson. Your protector is going to burn and Ingram will sink his knife in your belly if you stay. And that would be a waste of good steel." He shoved her roughly toward the door as Frizer lurched to his feet, bellowing.

Judith fled, raucous laughter pursuing her onto the streets of Deptford. She ran as if pursued by demons, fleet-footed and unassailed, for the safety of her room. Once there, she slammed the door behind her, heart racing as she gasped for air and locked the night out. She berated herself for cowardice until she could stay awake no longer, then collapsed on the bed, falling eventually into a night of ill dreams haunted by fearful visions of Kit on the block and her own shamefaced return to her father's home, or worse.

Act 3, Scene 1

The next two nights she passed playing a lad on stage in one of the plays that Lord Strange's company was staging. There was still no word from Kit and she began to fear that he was already dead.

On the third day, Will came to see her just before she left for the theater. "I bring you joy of the play, sister. You are as fine a lad as ever tread the boards, myself excepted." He bowed with a flourish and Judith laughed despite her worries.

"Thank you for your kindness, brother. You have been many a fine lad so this is praise indeed. On another point before I must leave, have you had word of Kit?"

Will gave her an impish grin and flourished a grubby bit of paper at her. "Not from Kit but from one close to him."

She took the note, reading and rereading it in increasing bewilderment. "What does this mean?"

Will snorted at her slow wit. "It is an invitation to dine with a powerful man whose patronage can only advance my plays. Surely your foolish jealousy cannot blind you to the advantages of such a relationship?"

"But Will, Tom is Kit's patron and…"

"Perhaps he seeks a better playwright. No, say no more, little sister. I understand that you would stand a friend to Kit but I cannot, nay will not, decline such an opportunity."

Judith remembered Tom's cold face when the words "sodomite" and "heretic" were spoken and shivered. He would let Kit go to the block or the flames and acquire a new protégé. She tried what she could to dissuade Will, but it was no use and she had to leave for the theater. On returning, she longed for Emilia to come, but her beloved remained as absent as Kit. She passed a restless night in frightening dreams, filled with the premonition of ills to come.

The next morning Judith was awakened by a familiar knock at the door shortly after dawn. Heart pounding, she rose, tugging on a doublet and picking up her knife as she moved to unbar the door. Hand on the heavy oak, she asked, "Kit?"

"Open the door, little one. I'm here alone." Kit's voice, certainly, but in tones that seemed broken.

Judith hesitated a moment, then unbarred the door. Kit stood on the other side, covered in blood, his eyes red and his hands trembling. She recoiled backward, giving him room to enter.

He lurched inside, sinking onto the bed with a quiet groan. Now that he was out of the darkened hall, she could see the marks of torture on him: bruises and cuts too systematic to be natural. It wrung her heart and she fetched a pitcher of water to wash him clean. He said nothing while she ministered to his wounds, only the hiss of his breath to tell her when something hurt more that it should.

At last, she held a mug of flat beer to his lips and let him lie back on her bed. He closed his eyes and his body went slowly limp as he fell asleep. She looked down at him, frowning for a long moment. But it seemed cruel to wake him merely to satisfy her curiosity; any danger he brought to her door might have found her by other means anyway.

Instead she moved to her chair and table, taking up her quill as she gnawed on a piece of bread. She had been thinking of a play that revolved around twin brothers, not unlike Will and herself. The point scratched busily on the page before her as the plot took shape.

Act 3, Scene 2

She had written nearly an entire act when Kit finally sat up with a groan and dropped his head into his hands. Judith stood and stretched, back and hands stiff from her labors, before she spoke. "What happened, Kit? I looked for you everywhere, even in Deptford."

Kit looked up, eyes sharp in his alarmed face. "You went back there looking for me? Did anyone see you?"

Judith shuddered at the memory of Frizer's furious eyes. "That cur who drank with us when we went there, Frizer. And Poley. Frizer tried to draw his blade on me but was too far in his cups. I ran…ran as fast as I could from the place." She hung her head, cheeks burning under her beard. A real man would have stayed to fight. She waited for Marlowe's scorn.

Kit swore, a string of colorful oaths falling from his cut lips. Then he laughed quietly. "They say that he stumbles who runs fastest, yet I'm glad to hear that you eluded the blade so that you might stand friend to me today. As to Frizer, he is a dangerous dog. I advise you to run swiftly away whenever you may see him next." He closed his eyes again.

"Were you in the Tower, Kit? I heard tales of the Privy Council, of charges of heresy." Judith waited but Kit was silent, his face turned toward the floor. When she could stand it no longer, she spoke again. "Will told me yesterday that he intended to steal your patron away but since you are here and free, I can see that this is not so." She attempted to laugh lightly but the sound died away when she saw Kit's face. "What is it?"

Kit stood, swaying a little, and walked to her table, murmuring softly, "What further mischief is this? What did he say?" He frowned, his face darkening until Judith was well and truly frightened.

"It was an invitation to dine with…Tom in Deptford. But the note did not seem as if he had written such a thing. I tried to persuade Will but he would hear nothing of it. Is Will in some danger, Kit?" She caught his sleeve. "Is it the Privy Council or something else?"

Kit's eyes were wild and he pulled a scrap of a note from his doublet. "A note like this one?"

Judith stared and nodded. "Whence came this to you, Kit?"

"My jailor gave it to me as he opened the door of my cell. I think we must go and find Will. I do not like this, little Jude; it is not Tom's way to commit more to the page than he must." He paused, seeming to gather his thoughts. "But first, we must disguise me. My looks are not popular on the streets today. Have you still your skirts and maiden's garb, little Jude?"

Act 3, Scene 3

It was but the work of a short hour to make Kit into a plain but believable maid. Judith laughed a bit to see him in her old gown and even he began to smile a bit at last. When all was complete, they left to go in search of Will.

But he was not to be found at any of his usual haunts and Judith was struck with a terrible fear. She ached inside, empty of the weight of her brother in her heart for the first time in many years. Kit stumbled at her side, cutting into her thoughts, and she reached out to steady him as if he were a maid in truth. He was exhausted, the dark circles under his eyes making them glitter feverishly in contrast to his white face.

She caught his arm and turned them back to her room just as a coach rattled across the street before them and stopped. Tom Walsingham's sharp-featured face met her gaze impassively from the window before he swung the door open without a word.

Judith looked to Kit for guidance but found none; he was spent, his complexion grey with pain and effort. She wrapped her arm around his waist and hauled him forward, pulling him into the coach with Tom's help. She followed and Tom rapped on the outside of the door to start the driver up again. He studied Kit in his skirts for a long moment, lips curled in an odd smile. But his expression still held a ghost of tenderness, which helped to reassure her; he might save Kit yet.

Finally he turned to her. "I am astonished to find you here, Master Shakespeare. I had had other news of you that suggested I might not find you in this life again." Judith stiffened, but he continued before she could say anything else. "I am glad to see that it is otherwise with you."

"What is it you know, my lord? Do you have some word of my broth…" She caught herself a moment too late.

"A brother? Faith! That would explain it then. I fear I have ill news for you, Master Shakespeare, but let us only reach the inn and see what is to be done before we speak more."

Judith stared at him, her mind awhirl with horror and misgiving. Then Kit moaned as the wheels hit a hole and they both turned to him, Tom pulling the cape from his shoulders and tucking it around him. "Poor boy. I would that I could have taken this hurt from you," he murmured. He pulled Kit's head to his shoulder but would say no more until the coach began to lurch its way into Deptford.

The Lincoln Inn looked much the way it had when Judith had fled it last. This time however, Frizer and Poley emerged to meet the coach. Frizer's eyes shifted guiltily under Walsingham's hard stare and he stammered his words a bit. "We thought it a game, my lord. We thought to teach the young gamecock a lesson while we carried out your other orders...my lord, he drew his blade first. We wrestled for it..." He stopped as Judith threw herself out of the coach, his jaw agape as though he were seeing a ghost.

She shoved her way past him and dashed into the inn. Mrs. Bull caught her eye and pointed silently upstairs. She reached the landing as if she had wings. There she tried each door until she found the one she sought. Tom and Kit followed on her heels until all three stood over a corpse that might have been Judith's own, but for some thickness of the frame, some weight about the jaws.

Judith dropped to her knees, sobbing hysterically, and Tom closed the door as she wailed, "It was meant to be me. I insulted them, me, not Will!"

"I believe that it was meant to be me, was it not, sweet Tom?" Kit's voice was like cold water on her grief and she sat up, tears still pouring down her face. "You feared that I might speak under the Council's caresses and betray you, did you not? Your curs without were to lure me here and slay me alone but they thought to rid themselves of another annoyance as well. Is it not so, sweet Tom?"

Kit and Tom faced each other over Will's bloody body, staring as though no corpse lay between them. Kit's face was nearly as pale as Will's, but his eyes were steady. In the end, it was Tom who dropped his gaze first. "I cannot stand against a heresy charge, Marcade. Not that and...the other. I would be sent to the block."

"And if it were merely my own life?" Kit spoke swiftly, his pain touching each word.

Tom flinched, looking at Judith for the first time since he entered. "Know that I am sorry. He was never meant to die." Judith glared back at him, shaking with fury and reaction. "Still," he continued, as if there were no more to be said, "this may yet be put to good account."

"I have lost my truest friend!" Judith shouted, lurching to her feet, right hand fumbling for the hilt of her blade. Kit stepped between her and Tom, placing his hands on her shoulders. She struggled with him a moment and he pressed her to him in a tight embrace, holding her until she went limp, body shuddering.

Then Kit turned back to Tom. "You have killed me as well as Will. I cannot stay here with a price on my head. England's theaters may never recover from it. What good account can you make of slaying the future?"

Tom frowned. "Hear my thoughts, gentle sirs. Kit must die, either here or on the block. The Queen's justice demands his blood for his crimes against God and nature. Therefore, Christopher known as Marlowe dies here this day in Deptford." He gestured at Will's body. "The plays may be written in France or Italy as well as here. Will yet stands before us and he has his brother's way with words. He can be your voice in England, Marcade."

Judith slumped against Kit's shoulder, knowing it was the only way to save him. Then it was left only for coin to cross a few palms, enough to say that one Christopher Marlowe, atheist and blaspheming heretic, poet and playwright, had died that day. The witnesses were called, their testimony taken. And by then, Judith and Kit had been dismissed, sent home where her despair would not confuse the telling of the tale.

Act 4, Scene 1

Kit stood staring out the window, a small sack of his goods packed for a journey at his feet. "Well, little Judith, it seems there are just two of us left now to make one good playwright," he said at last. "And I think I must call you Will to grow accustomed to the name in my mouth." He stared out onto the surrounding roofs for a long moment before he turned back to face her.

She sniffled once or twice more, then rubbed her face with the back of her hand. She found her voice with an effort. "But I have no gift for tragedy."

"Nor I for comedy."

"And the poems? What of those?"

Kit reached over and caught up a page from the pile on the table. He studied it a moment and his lips quirked in a wry smile. "I think that together we might manage. The new play?" He reached out a hand to accept the handful of pages she held out.

"But what of your own plays, your own poems, Kit?"

"I am dead, little Will who was Judith. What use have dead men for such things?"

"I can sell them for you. Only give me a letter dated before this week, saying that you left them to me. I will deliver them for you and send you the coin." Judith spoke eagerly. "Think of how they will fight to publish them now that you are...dead." She faltered over the word.

Kit nodded. "And I will send you new tragedies from France, Italy, Spain and whatever other Popish hells I may visit ere I can return to England once more." He looked away from her to the pages in his hands. Like quicksilver, he flipped through them, even laughing aloud once or twice. "Twins, mistaken identities and the lovers reunited at the end of it all. You are in truth the one and only comic Shakespeare." He gave her a deep bow.

Judith shook her head, taking the pages back. "Merely half, Kit. And never quite whole again I think." She wiped her cheek again, picked up her quill and began to write.

Author's Note:

In her essay "A Room of One's Own," Virginia Woolf wrote, "Let me imagine, since the facts are so hard to come by, what would have happened had Shakespeare had a wonderfully gifted sister, called Judith, let us say..."

And why not? Such a woman might have met the fate that Woolf suggests in her essay if she tried to live in London as a woman. But what if she had been able to pass as a man? And what if she had been taken under the wing of Christopher Marlowe, the great gay playwright of the Elizabethan Age? Who then might have been the author of the plays whose authorship is still being debated centuries later? And who killed by the assassin's knife in a tavern in Deptford?

The truth may never be known...

BARBARIC SPLENDOR

Simon Sheppard

23 March, 1640

DE VRIES IS DEAD NOW. KOOPMAN is dead. And van Duyn. All dead. The journey to Cathay, which had set sail from Amsterdam amidst a heady mix of anticipation and fear, has been smashed brutally upon the rocks, the ship gone, the crewmen, most of them, dead. The rest of us, thirteen in all, now are guests in the fabled Palace of the Khan. And I, as Captain of the doomed expedition, am, I suppose, the most esteemed guest of all.

And in this log, which I providentially rescued from the wreck, I shall keep a faithful account of our strange sojourn.

It has been a day and a night now since the VOC ship *Verlossing* was dashed upon the dark rocks of this place. We had been so close to our goal, so near to dropping anchor at the shores of Xanadu, but a brutal gale descended from the heavens and laid waste to our plans. The wretched peasants who had found us washed up on the storm-wracked shore, our bodies bloody and broken, soon brought us to a shabby village, and thence a band of soldiers escorted us into the hills, following the winding course of the River Alph. The journey was no more than eight or ten miles, yet over exceedingly mountainous ground, and several of the most grievously wounded of us, most notably Schouten and Bol, did not survive the arduous day's march. But van Zeeland, my boon companion, though suffering mightily, lived to see journey's end, and for that I humbly thank our Lord and Savior Jesus Christ.

113

Oh, what a sight it was, our first vision of the Palace of the Khan! For the darkness of the storm had given way to the bright last rays of day, which shone upon the walls and spires of Xanadu. Indeed, the light of the setting sun, reflected from the gilded hulk of Kubla Khan's great pleasure dome, was so bright as to nearly blind our bedazzled eyes. And so we marched through groves of fragrant trees and riotous flowers, to a great wooden gate, its immense lintel carved with a beast of the most hideous mien. But we, glad to still be upon this green Earth, took little note of that portent as we were led ever onward.

Truly, here was Magnificence beyond even the wildest rumors that had reached the burghers of Amsterdam. Dusk had descended upon the palace gardens, and everywhere slender youths with torches rushed through the heavy, perfumed air, lighting lanterns, many of silk, some of stone, until it seemed that the strange blooms that surrounded us were lit by the light of day itself.

The soldiers who had brought us were relieved by a phalanx of palace guards, each one young and handsome, each attired in a uniform of rich crimson silk and brocade which barely concealed his muscular body. And presently we came to the walls of the palace itself, and were led though a doorway writhing with carved images of dragons and encrusted with precious stones. We were taken through a maze of corridors, past a succession of rooms, each larger and more sumptuous than the one before, till we came to a large torchlit chamber draped in curtains of gold, with great cushions scattered about the marble floor.

Lieutenant Kindt, our expedition's translator, had urgently informed me that the language spoken in this land, though having certain similarities with the barbarian tongues in which he was schooled, was largely unfamiliar. But the half-naked men who had brought us to this place made it clear with signs and gestures that this was the room in which we were to make our rest. And so with great relief we shed our outer garments and lay upon the great cushions that were, in fact, the chamber's only furniture.

No sooner had we done so than a retinue of young, lithe, near-naked male servants appeared, each bearing a large silver serving-platter of food. They wordlessly laid this strange feast before us on the floor, then disappeared. Much of the food tasted surpassingly odd, nearly repulsive in its foreignness. But we were famished from the terrible rigors of the day, and set to with a hearty appetite, all except van Zeeland, who lay groaning in a sort of stupor.

When we had eaten what we could, the same silent boys came in and spirited out the platters, and then returned with piles of richly woven blankets. As the torches guttered and died, we arranged ourselves for sleep. Poor van Zeeland had begun to tremble and cry out most piteously, so I myself lay down upon his pillow and warmed his shaking body with my own; in this way we were to spend the night. Despite the shock of the wreck and the surpassing strangeness of the place in which we found ourselves, exhaustion had overtaken me. I said a silent prayer for the safety of my wife and sons, so far away in Amsterdam, and sank into a dreamless sleep.

24 March, 1640

We have spent our first full day here in isolation, with only the interruption of servants bringing us food to break the awful, uncertain silence of our situation. Poor van Zeeland's condition was getting even worse, and when the servants noticed this, they shortly returned with four well-proportioned men bearing a gilded litter of Oriental design. They placed our ailing shipmate upon this and carried him off through one of the three doors of our chamber. Now and again, I would attempt to pass through these doors, but always they were stoutly locked. I came to realize with a growing sense of dread that we might be not so much guests as prisoners, captives in a golden, dreadful dungeon. And so transpired our first full day in Xanadu, until the light from the windows high above our heads had faded into dusk.

It was then that the servants reappeared and gestured to us that we should arise and follow them. One of the boys drew back a heavy drape and revealed a fourth, smaller door to our room. It was through this unlocked door that they led us into a bath chamber. In the center of the room was a sunken stone tub; several servants were filling it with water being heated over a stove in a corner of the room. As we stood there awkwardly, not knowing what to do, the boys attempted to disrobe us, pulling and tugging at our, to them, unfamiliar garments. As you might well imagine, many of us most heartily resisted this presumption, and swatted the effeminate boys away, but the prospect of a hot bath held sway, and shortly, most of us were naked and allowed ourselves to be led into the enormous basin. Once we were immersed, several of the servant boys poured sweet-smelling oils into the water and then attempted to join us, indicating that they were to assist us with our baths. Only mighty howls of protest prevented this. By the time we emerged from the tub to discover that our clothing had disappeared, and that all we now possessed to mask our nakedness were loose silken robes, we had developed a strong distaste for the degenerate luxury of the court of Kubla Khan. Surely he is a most debased descendant of that former Khan, his namesake, extolled in the journals of Signor Marco Polo four centuries past.

25 March, 1640

Had I known, as I was led through the thousand gates of Xanadu, what would await us here, I might even then have wished that I had never seen the doorway carved with dragons, but had perished, with my mates, upon the rocks.

It was not until the following morning that we were allowed from our room, which by then seemed less a lodging than a cage. An elderly man in sea-green robes entered the room, expostulated in an unknown tongue, and with guttural words and crude gestures led us to understand that we were to pass through one of the doors that until then had been kept locked. As we walked into the corridor we were surrounded by a detachment of muscular guardsmen, who escorted us down a maze of twisting corridors. At first the distant din we heard was faint, but as we walked on the noise grew louder, a horrible clashing of cymbals and strange whinings, something that must pass for music in this barbaric place.

Finally, one last golden curtain was drawn aside and we found ourselves in the great domed hall of the Palace. In size this room rivaled even the enormous nave of the half-destroyed church at Utrecht. The floor was strewn with carpets of jewel-like intricacy, the walls draped in tapestries shot with threads of silver and gold. In the far reaches of the hall, a throne stood before a great carven doorway, a throne carved out of precious jade and surmounted by an elaborately carved dragon, its eyes agleam with the fire of rubies. Far above our heads, the great domed ceiling was painted in black like the nighttime sky, and representations of the stars and planets pierced the dome and glowed with light.

Torches completed the illumination, each blazing brand held by an utterly naked boy, his gilded body glinting with an unnatural glow. In all its voluptuous savagery and wonder, this was a place that could rival Hell itself. And yet, the ultimate horror came with the realization that what I at first glance took to be animal carcasses oddly arrayed around the room were in fact the tortured bodies of men, their eyes gouged out, their bellies slit, genitals severed, each corpse hung by its ankles against the wall of the Great Hall. Beneath each, a dark pool of blood coagulated upon the marble floor. I could not contain my revulsion at this savage sight, a fate infinitely more horrible than that suffered by the condemned of Amsterdam in the gallowsfield north of the River IJ.

At that moment the din of the musicians (for such they must fancy themselves) grew faster and louder still, and from a great doorway strode the massive form of the ruler of this strange and Godless place.

Kubla Khan was bedecked in robes of untold magnificence, and wore over his face a bejeweled golden mask. Yet, for all his finery, he moved with manly vigor. He clapped his hands once and the din ceased. In the sudden silence, his cruel, guttural voice rang out to us, though surely he fully realized that we comprehended not a word. Finishing his harangue, he clapped his hands once again, and four oiled and well-muscled men brought a splendid litter and conveyed him the several paces to his throne. All the men of Xanadu fell to the floor as one. The guards gestured that we do the same; it seemed unwise to resist. Only then did the great ruler sit upon the dragon throne. Only then did the horrid ceremony begin.

From one of the many doorways, an Asiatic captive was led in, a thick iron collar around his wretched throat. And yet, though he must surely have known that his doom awaited him, he exhibited no fear, no panic, but moved slowly, deliberately, as though walking through a dream. The two men who held his arms led him to the center of the hall. When they released their grip he stood stock-still, arms still outstretched before him. The two guards then pulled back a circular hatch in the floor, several feet across. From somewhere beneath the floor a roaring sound was heard, the sound of tumultuous water against rock. And, faint at first, but growing louder, another sound, like the growl of some great beast, most likely a hideous dragon such as that carved upon the royal throne.

The Khan himself arose, took up a gleaming scimitar, and strode over to the captive. When he reached the prisoner's side, the masked ruler raised the sword above his head and brought it down with one swift stroke, neatly severing the man's hands from his wrists. The hands dropped into the abyss, from which the animal roar, having already grown loud, now became frenzied. The captive blinked, and for a moment dazedly stared at the bleeding stumps of his arms, as though not able to comprehend his loss. He then swayed, lost his footing, and pitched headmost downwards through the hole. At the very last, a horrid scream was torn from his throat. It blended with the savage roar, and then both subsided into an awful silence, leaving only the sound of rushing water.

Of what came after, when the hatch was once again shut and Kubla Khan returned to his throne, of those repugnant celebrations I will say no more. For their unmanly, lascivious nature, their vile lusts and unnatural copulations, were enough to sicken even the hardiest of us. At the last, I could only shut my eyes and take succor from the One Who Died for Our Sins.

14 April, 1940

It is now many days since we came to this hellish place, and many of my shipmates, I fear, are being lost to the temptations of Luxury and Vice.

Fortunately, Lieutenant Kindt has progressed greatly in his understanding of the heathens' language. Through him I have learned that the Great Khan's Palace is under siege from a band of rebels, in the pay, it is said, of a neighboring warlord. The eviscerated corpses we saw arrayed around the Pleasure Dome were those of captured rebels, and the man whose death we witnessed was apparently some sort of rebel commander. All this makes the savagery of the place somewhat easier to bear, but the Sodomitical vices of Xanadu are unimaginably foul, and to that I shall never be reconciled.

Kindt has also learned that we are indeed not the first Civilized Men to make our way to this place at the edge of the world. The Khan was visited by several earlier expeditions, including a company of men who were apparently Spaniards, as far as can be ascertained from their few mementos which were shown to Kindt. But what became of these papists was not vouchsafed to him. This knowledge was a mixed blessing at best; knowing that other white men had come this way and were now nowhere to be seen scarce provided comfort.

A week or so after he was taken from our midst, van Zeeland was returned to us, looking fully restored and in fact healthier than he had been when we left Amsterdam. But he was far from the shipmate we'd known. There was a wild, dreamy look in his eyes, and he had adopted the dress of the slave boys here, wearing but a flimsy loincloth that barely provided modesty. I inquired of him as to his recovery, but he would only say that he had been administered many doses of an elixir called, in Kindt's translation, "the Milk of Paradise."

In the days following van Zeeland's return, he was frequently absent from us. One or another of the burly palace guards would enter and signal to van Zeeland, who would rise and follow him out through a curtained passageway. In an hour or two, van Zeeland would return alone, his eyes glazed from the effects of the cursed potion, and stinking of debauched lust. Nieuwenhuis in particular, being the strictest Calvinist amongst us, was most strongly disturbed by van Zeeland's downfall, refusing to so much as look at my erstwhile close friend, or even to join us at meals when van Zeeland was amongst us.

The constant tension among my men is taking its toll. Arguments are frequent, and sometimes come to blows. Indeed, it has been many nights since I have slept at all well. For as I attempt to sink into sleep, I can hear the far-off roar of that beast beneath the palace. And its hideous roar is not so much a warning as an invitation, beckoning me on to I know not what, toward something I fear to even think upon.

17 April, 1640

The most terrible thing has happened. Two nights ago, we were awakened from fitful sleep by Nieuwenhuis's outraged shout. And in the faint light we could see van Zeeland still lying between the thighs of handsome young Heyn, in the midst of performing the most abominable vice upon Heyn's person; sad to state, such was the insistence of the assault that poor Heyn's manhood stood boldly upward, an unholy column of flesh. Several of the men leapt upon van Zeeland, dragged him off the poor fellow, and began to beat him most fiercely. It took all my powers of persuasion to convince them that in his damnation van

Zeeland was already suffering sufficiently, and that further punishment should better to be left to Our Heavenly Father. I am not indeed certain that this is my true belief, but I do know that those of us who remain as prisoners of the Khan must not turn one upon another, as we are suffering a common fate. As we are all and each of us damned.

18 April, 1640

This morning we awoke to a most awful sight. Van Zeeland, exiled by the rest of us to sleeping in a far corner of our chamber, lay upon his pillow dead, bulging eyes staring blankly, face already turning black, marks of strangulation round his throat. And most hideous of all, his manhood had been ripped, with something approaching superhuman strength, from his now-bloody belly, and stuffed into his mouth.

God forgive me, but my suspicions initially fell upon Nieuwenhuis, whose hatred of van Zeeland was undisguised. He, however, protested his innocence, and cried that it must be the evil magic of the Khan's sorcerers, or perhaps the depraved work of a palace guard. When challenged as to the traces of blood on his garments, he surmised they had been stained whilst he examined the corpse, though none of us recalled his being near van Zeeland's remains.

The tumult had roused the servants, who then called for the guards. The burly guards unflinchingly picked up van Zeeland's mutilated corpse and carried it from the room. None of us had much appetite for breakfast, excepting Nieuwenhuis, who ate most heartily.

Later we were escorted at sword's point into the Pleasure Dome. Most gratefully, there was none of the clashing music of occasions past, only the strange, soft wailing of a young boy. We lay on the marble floor like the miserable wretches we have become. The great Khan then entered and wordlessly took his place upon the Dragon Throne. As before, two muscular guards with gleaming, oiled flesh dragged the hatch from the great opening in the center of the floor. And as before, the roar of a rushing, watery tumult was soon joined by the higher-pitched bellow of the unknown beast. (This creature I with increasing certainty believe to indeed be a dragon, of an aspect like that of Babylon, the Great Whore of Revelations.)

It was then that the unfortunate van Zeeland was brought in, borne on some sort of litter by four impassive guards. They made their way to the center of the room, and, without a word of prayer, let fall our departed shipmate's corpse into the hellish abyss. The roaring grew louder for a moment, but shortly subsided into a contented silence. I cannot be sure, but I believe I heard the gnashing of great teeth, even as the young boy's strange song continued.

The Khan soon took his leave, and we were led back to our chamber, to our prison of luxury. But in the hours since, I cannot expunge from my mind the image of my friend's naked body falling, limbs flailing, through the darkness, to be dashed upon the rocks, where some horrid, unknown beast finds him, grabs him in its steaming-hot jaws, and tears at his body, chewing the remains of what once was a man, gulping down great chunks of brutalized human flesh.

13 May, 1640

Since van Zeeland's death, life here has become even more dreadful, so dreadful that for near a month I could not bring myself to make any record in this log. It now seems less than likely that my words will ever be read. Still, it is my duty to chronicle these horrible events.

Of the twelve of us left, several have been dragged down into a life of unspeakable vice. Heyn in particular has become a favorite of the guards, and has begun to imbibe the vile "Milk of Paradise." Several nights ago, I awoke to the sound of him sobbing, crying out for home. As he seemed to be overcome by shame and regret, I went to his bed to comfort him. But when I put my arm about him, his crying abruptly ceased and he grabbed me in the roughest, most obscene manner. I pushed him away, and he made no further attempt upon me, but since then my mind has been in a fury of disquiet, wondering which among us will be the next to be corrupted.

And, even worse, the purest man of our crew is among us no more. The day after van Zeeland's death Nieuwenhuis, whose Calvinism was rigid and unbending, but whose unswerving virtue was a model for the other men, was led away in chains. Through Lieutenant Kindt's translation, we were told he had been accused of van Zeeland's murder, and all our protests to the contrary did not halt the proceedings. (And yet, truth be told, even had Nieuwenhuis been guilty of the crime, van Zeeland's fate had something of the justice of divine retribution about it.) Placed in leg irons, his arms bound behind him with rough ropes, Nieuwenhuis was led away, maintaining a dignified mien to the last. Since then, near a month has passed and we have heard nothing more of his fate. Perhaps he, too, has perished in the jaws of the beast.

From what little we can glean, the Court is in a state of disarray. There are rumors that the rebels have made steady progress, occupying new territory in Xanadu, even coming as close as the mountains surrounding the Pleasure Dome itself. Should the rebels succeed, I wonder: would they prove to be our saviors, or captors still more terrible then those in whose Decadent Grip we now are being held?

During these most awful days, my thoughts oft return to home, to the canals and fields of Holland, and to my beloved wife. And at these times the burden of my sorrows seems too much to bear. What a dark fate is mine! What an unholy place is this! With fervency and hope I daily pray to Our Lord Christ Jesus for deliverance, but my pleas are met only with silence.

20 May, 1640

It now appears that the rebel forces are at the very gates of Kubla Khan's palace. The executions of traitors, which we are oft required to attend, have increased to a sickening frequency. Blood flows over the marble floors, and the dragon is regularly fed. And it lately seems we can sometimes discern the faint sounds of battle; the guards attending us seem fewer, and more distracted.

Meanwhile, I and several of the men, those most to be trusted—Kindt, Bakker, and de Bont—have contrived something of a plan. Kindt has made the acquaintance of a guard, and has learned that the ground upon which the Palace stands is honeycombed by a maze of caverns and passages, and that it may be possible to thereby safely make one's way all the way to the sea. Indeed, one of the entrances to these tunnelways may be reached, albeit circuitously, from a passage which gives onto the ornate garden where, under guard, we are now each day after dinner permitted an hour's exercise out-of-doors. Just how and why Kindt was told of this I know not, but with such knowledge we may someday make an attempt for our freedom. May that day come soon.

25 May, 1640

Much has happened in the last several days, of a horror so great that I tremble from the effort to write it down.

Two evenings ago, whilst we were outside in the torchlit garden, the walls of the Palace were breached by the enemies of the realm. Amid great tumult, our guards rushed away to defend their Khan, and we were left on our own. I rejoiced at this great stroke of fortune. We four conspirators, Bakker, Kindt, de Bont, and myself, quickly detailed the possibility of escape to the remainder of my crew. To my shocked surprise, only Heyn seemed interested in joining in the attempt. Bakker, in particular, objected to Heyn's joining us, as he had lately been so involved in foul, unmanly deeds. But when Bakker challenged Heyn to convince us that we should tolerate his presence, Heyn replied that he had managed to obtain a copy of the key to the door that gave onto the underground passages, and that without his help, we would never succeed.

This news astonished me greatly. But each second brought us closer to capture, either by the rebels or by the guards of Kubla Khan. Indeed, the clashing of swords and the screams of the injured and the dying grew ever louder. As the leader of the group, I told Heyn that he might join us in our flight. The remaining crewmen, our shipmates and comrades, decided to a man that our plan was so fraught with danger that remaining behind, as perilous as it was, seemed the most prudent course. Though five of us would attempt to gain our freedom, an equal number would stay behind. At the time, this seemed pure cowardice. It is only now that their decision looks like a sort of wisdom.

Each of us would-be escapees grabbed a torch from the walls and, with Kindt leading the way, we hastened through a gateway, then a maze of corridors, and down a flight of stairs. At the bottom of these stairs stood a great wooden door which, indeed, was locked. Had Heyn not joined us, we would never have made our way past the obstacle, but he removed a cord from around his neck, and with the brass key on this cord, opened the door with ease.

As we descended into the gloom, the sounds of battle dwindled to nothing, shortly to be replaced by a silence so complete I could hear my own thoughts as if spoken aloud. The passage we followed went steeply downhill, turning this way and that until we had lost all sense of direction. Yet we pressed ever onward.

Presently, the passageway leveled out and the walls of the corridor gave way to a rocky cavern, and through this cavern ran the River Alph. Kindt had been told that it should be possible to follow the river all the way to the sea, and in this slim chance lay our sole hope of escape. But as we followed the course of the river the cavern grew narrower and smaller, till it was no cavern at all but a small tunnel, and we had to wade, half crouching, in the cold torrent. De Bont and Heyn both spoke of going back, but Kindt, Bakker and I, refusing to admit defeat, persisted in our flight, and soon enough a dim light appeared before us. We hurried on.

The passageway again broadened, so that we no longer had to make our way upon the slippery rocks of the treacherous riverbed, but on a pathway beside the cavern's moist wall. But relief soon was replaced by frustration as our progress was utterly blocked by an iron fence. For a moment, we were stymied. But the light of the torches revealed a gateway that, although locked, providentially was opened by the key which Heyn carried.

The rock-cut room in which we now found ourselves stretched away on every side, its immensity beyond the reach of our torches. Bakker and de Bont agreed to forge the roaring torrent and explore what lay on the far bank, whilst I led Heyn and Kindt forward in the gloom. Of a sudden I tripped over something lying in my path. To my great horror, the torchlight revealed what seemed to be the remains of a human arm, and feasting upon it a host of worms, each dead-white and as large as my thumb. Indeed, all around us lay human offal, crawling with parasites that made the rocky floor seem alive with white, wriggling motion. It was then that I realized that we must be passing through the precinct of the dragon. I drew breath to shout a warning to Bakker and de Bont, who had reached the river's far shore and were nearly lost from view.

But before I could say a word, I heard it: the awful high-pitched roar of the dragon, growing louder by the second.

De Bont and Bakker turned and hurried toward us, their voices raised in terror. But de Bont stumbled, his foot wedged in a rocky crevice, and fell to the ground. Bakker struggled to free him while the roaring grew louder.

"Save yourself," cried de Bont, and it was then that the Ultimate Horror appeared. The light of their fallen torches shone upon, not a great dragon, but a band of white men, perhaps two dozen in all, emaciated, clothes filthy and in rags, their eyes wild and staring. A great, unearthly howl issued from their throats. They descended upon the unfortunate de Bont and fell upon him like dogs upon their prey. With teeth and claws and knives, they tore at him, at his very flesh, and ripped away bleeding chunks from his still-living form. Bakker, who had been forced to surrender our shipmate to the ravening beasts, was fleeing toward the river when he was himself hit in the back by a large rock hurled by one of the ghastly crew.

Kindt and I stood transfixed by this Awful Sight, but Heyn plunged into the river in an attempt to rescue Bakker. Too late! For before Heyn could reach the far bank, half-a-dozen of the white savages were upon Bakker's prostrate form, tearing chunks of flesh from his body. Wisely, Heyn turned back, for naught more could be done for our unfortunate friends.

Yet more of the beasts had emerged from the shadows, most joining their mates in the unholy feast. But several of them looked in our direction; it would be a matter of moments before they were upon us as well.

Heyn had nearly rejoined me and Kindt, and still I could not tear my gaze from the horror. And then one of the foul beasts devouring Bakker looked up, stared into my eyes, his beard dripping with blood, a look of wild joy on his face.

It was Nieuwenhuis.

We fled then, the three of us, back the way we'd come, white worms bursting beneath our feet, never looking back till we reached the iron gate. We slammed it shut, and Heyn locked it with his key just as half a dozen of the Man-beasts reached the fence. We left them pounding at the gate and screaming in that awful way of theirs. We had no other choice but to retrace our steps, back to the Pleasure Dome.

When we emerged at last, the garden was a shambles. The smell of burning lay heavy in the air. The route back to our chamber was littered with the dead and dying.

But, as we soon found out, the ultimate battle had been fought, the rebellion fully crushed. Kubla Khan still sat, omnipotent, upon the Dragon Throne.

And, to our relief, four of the five Dutchmen we'd left behind had survived, only Mesdag having perished in the chaos.

After order was restored, Kindt's inquiries brought the expected, horrid response: the beasts we had seen underground were the remnants of previous expeditions to Xanadu, many of them the Spaniards who had come bearing their flag, their swords, and the Cross Triumphant.

That was yesterday. This evening we were led into the throne room once more. The floor was littered with corpses, piled high like so much wood or grain. The round hatch was already open. The beasts will eat well tonight.

And now I can write no more. Words fail me, and all hope is gone. My shipmates and I are all truly Doomed. I conclude this journal in the forlorn hope that somehow it will eventually find its way back to Amsterdam, so that our story will one day become known. I send my love to my wife and children, and my prayers to Christ Jesus, ruler of Heaven and Earth. God save our unhappy souls.

Editor's Note:

The above journal was eventually brought back to Holland by the den Bosch expedition of 1648. Den Bosch's men reported being shocked to find seven of their countrymen living a life of great luxury at the court of Kubla Kahn, "reveling in unseemly decadence, drinking strong intoxicants of an unknown nature, and disporting themselves with Asiatic catamites." Before departing the court at Xanadu, den Bosch, with the permission of Kubla Khan, offered to take any of the men of the Verlossing *back with him on the return trip to Amsterdam. All of them, including the author of these diaries, refused.*

Author's Note:

Ever since I discovered Coleridge's "Kubla Khan" in college—it was great to read whilst tripping on acid—I've been enraptured by the dreamy "barbaric splendor" of the piece. And spending time in Amsterdam got me interested in the voyages of the Dutch explorers, as well as the rise of Calvinism. So it was an enjoyable challenge to cook up a clash of civilizations: mercantile, quasi-religious imperialism encountering a "pagan" Oriental autocracy. I set out to portray the Calvinists as puritanical but repressed, and the court of the Khan as an unholy-but-hot blend of high civilization, overwhelming luxury, and bloodthirstiness toward foreigners. Fortunately, the world has now progressed far past such things.

OPENING NIGHT

Lisabet Sarai

19 January 1887
London

Blast! Rehearsals had been going so well. The director turned his eyes to the tableau on the stage. Durward Lely lay sprawled on the boards, his right leg twisted underneath his body. Jessie, Leonora and the female members of the chorus flitted around him, offering more sympathy than assistance. The tenor's face was sickly white and distorted with pain.

"Don't touch him! Don't move him! The doctor's on his way." Gilbert pushed through the cast, took a flask out of his coat pocket and held it to Durward's lips. "Here, this might help. How are you holding up?"

Durward groaned.

"Hang on, old man, shouldn't be more than a few minutes. I told the messenger that Doctor Marsh should bring plenty of morphine."

"Gilbert! What's going on? I can't even leave for a quarter of an hour..." Sullivan strode down the center aisle of the theater, still wearing his overcoat and hat. "I ran into young Jack racing along Fleet Street and he said something about an accident."

Gilbert gestured toward the crumpled actor. "He slipped while he was practicing the hornpipe. Can't be sure, but I wouldn't be surprised if his leg is broken."

"Broken! But we're opening in three days!"

"Do you think that I'm not aware of that fact, Arthur? Our first responsibility, though, is to try and make Durward more comfortable. Ah, Doctor Marsh! Thank you for coming on such short notice, and in such abominable weather, too."

"Never mind that, Mr. Gilbert. Where's the injured man?" As if in answer, Durward let out another dramatic groan.

The doctor hurried to the actor's side. He gently prodded the leg, eliciting a whole chorus of moans and cries. The cast members hovered around, holding their collective breath.

"His fibula is snapped, in two places I think. We'll set it here, then move him to hospital." The doctor retrieved a sealed glass flask and a syringe from his bag. "Ladies, you might want to leave. This won't be pretty."

He turned to the patient, who was now only half conscious. "Mr. Lely, this is going to hurt, but I've got some laudanum here to dull the pain." As the needle entered Durward's arm, he seemed to relax a bit.

"Mr. Gilbert, send your boy back to my clinic for splints and plaster. Meanwhile, I want you to hold his shoulders to keep him from moving while I try to straighten the limb."

"When will he be able to dance again?" Sullivan still stood in the aisle, nervously mangling his hat brim.

"Dance? He'll be lucky if he's walking in two months." Lely sobbed at the doctor's words. "Don't worry, man, I doubt there will be any permanent effects. But you are going to have to be patient and follow my instructions. Now, hold him, Mr. Gilbert."

A melodious tenor scream rang through the theater.

Sullivan shuddered. "I'll see you in the office, Gilbert. When you're finished here." Durward screamed again as Sullivan hurried backstage.

"This is what happens when you encourage a thirty-five year old man to dance the hornpipe."

"I didn't encourage him; it was his own idea. In any case, your music was perfect. The scene worked brilliantly."

"I should never have listened to you." Sullivan sighed wearily. "How many times have I said that, Gilbert?"

"Too many for me to count. You realize, however, that I am usually right."

"I don't want to get entangled in that argument again. The question now is, what are we going to do? Should we postpone the opening?"

"We've got three weeks worth of advance bookings. We've already spent the proceeds on salaries. I don't think we can afford to postpone."

"Well, then, does Lely have an understudy?"

"Of course." Gilbert flipped through his memorandum book. "Frank Wilson. Blond chap, quite the dandy. He helps with the sets."

"Can he sing? Can he act?"

Gilbert rose, slipping his notebook into his pocket. "I bloody well hope so."

Gilbert found Wilson down by the Embankment, smoking and staring at the river. The sleet had stopped but the sky was still piled with leaden clouds. He watched the young man for a few moments before calling out.

The understudy had a distinct grace about him as he lounged against the rail. He wore a gray worsted overcoat and felt bowler with a hatband of green silk. He half turned, revealing an elegant profile, and Gilbert noticed the matching cravat. Gilbert wondered how the young man could afford such snappy clothing on an actor's wages.

"Mr. Wilson!"

Frank faced Gilbert. His face was alight, glowing like a misplaced sun in the grimy dusk. Gilbert took a deep breath. Yes, the lad was handsome, with classic features, a cleft chin, and dimples that spoke of mischief. It was more than that, though. Despite his youth, this man had presence, a powerful attractiveness that drew the eye and the heart. Charisma, that was the word.

"Mr. Gilbert." Wilson deliberately mashed his cigarette out against the iron rail. "What's wrong, sir?"

"Are you up on the Dick Dauntless part? The lines? The songs?"

The light in the young man's face became more focused. "Yes, of course. Why? Is poor Mr. Lely ill? How unfortunate!"

Gilbert was not deceived by the concerned words. Wilson was burning to take over the injured tenor's role.

"He has suffered an accident and is effectively incapacitated as far as the play is concerned. However, we cannot afford to delay the opening. We resume rehearsals at four o'clock."

Frank Wilson beamed. "I'll be there." He climbed the steps to Gilbert's side, and took his arm. The director caught a whiff of scent, lilac with some sharper undertone. "May I accompany you, sir?"

Gilbert swore that he could feel the heat of the other man's flesh, even through the heavy wool coat. He swayed on his feet, suddenly woozy. Damn, Kitty was right, he was coming down with the grippe, if not something worse.

Frank steadied him. Gilbert had an impression of great strength. He felt a momentary impulse to give in, to do nothing but lean against the solid young man and be supported, succored. He was so very tired of all the tension, the conflicts, the bickering of the cast, the acrimonious exchanges with Sullivan. How easy it would be, to yield to this handsome young man…

A few chill drops of rain on his face woke him from his reverie. He extricated himself from Wilson's arm and strode back up the slope to the theater. "Come on," he called, "the cast is waiting." He didn't need to look back to know that Frank Wilson was scrambling after him.

"All right, let's take it from the start of the *Parlez Vous* number."

The chorus regrouped around Frank Wilson, who was now dressed in a common seaman's uniform. Frank launched into the satirical ditty, capering around the stage in a manner that could easily convince you that he'd spent his life climbing the shrouds and manning the gunwales. His voice was a bit higher than Lely's. It didn't have the same darker resonance, but it was clear and strong. And he didn't miss a single note, nor drop a word. His elocution was perfect.

Gilbert had to admit to himself that with his energy, youth and self-confidence, Wilson was actually better suited to the part of the aggressively self-promoting sailor than middle-aged Durward could ever be.

> *"And I'll wager in their joy they kissed*
> *each other's cheek,*
> *(which is what them furriners do)..."*

All at once Wilson was staring right at him, an odd smile twisting his full lips. Gilbert felt something twist inside his own chest in response. Palpitations, or some such symptom. He didn't feel ill, though. Instead there was a strange, buoyant excitement that filled his lungs like hydrogen.

> *"And they blessed their lucky stars*
> *We were hearty British tars,*
> *Who had pity on a poor Parley-voo,*
> *D'ye see,*
> *Who had pity on a poor Parley-voo."*

Frank flung himself straight into the hornpipe, his steps so quick that his nimble feet were a blur. All the while he grinned, lighting up the stage. The chorus began to clap the major beats, sucked into the momentum. The orchestra picked up the pace, but Frank matched it, marking the figures precisely, barely, it seemed, touching the boards. All the while, his eyes were fixed on Gilbert. Despite the frenzy of the dance, he never lost control.

He was brilliant.

By the end of the number, Gilbert could see that Frank was winded, but the director didn't call a break. Let's push him, Gilbert thought. Test his limits.

Frank continued to give a flawless performance. He was a jocular confidant to his beloved foster brother Robin Oakapple, volunteering to speak to the fair Rose Maybud on the behalf of the shy Robin. He was absurd and yet sincere as he "listened to his heart's dictates" and claimed Rose as his own instead of pleading Robin's case, praising her as a "tight little craft" and "the loveliest gal I've ever set eyes on." He was deliciously smarmy and despicable when revealing Robin's true identity as the delinquent heir to the house of Ruddygore and its attendant curse. Frank played masterfully against George Grossmith as Robin, and George rose to the occasion, displaying the quirky humor that had endeared him to D'Oyly Carte audiences for a more than a decade.

A new star. Gilbert recognized the signs. Perhaps there was a silver lining to the cloud that had enveloped the production when Lely had tripped over his own feet and landed in a crumpled heap on the stage.

Sullivan brought the first act finale to a close with a flourish. He looked decidedly more cheerful than he had earlier in the afternoon.

"Take a break," Gilbert called to the cast. "We'll start Act Two, in full costume, in half an hour."

Gilbert found that Wilson had already installed himself in Lely's dressing room. The young man sprawled in a chair, legs carelessly apart, breathing heavily. Sweat beaded his forehead. Gilbert was perversely pleased to see that the apparently effortless performance had, in fact, cost Wilson something.

"Well, Mr. Wilson. That was well done, especially for the first time."

Frank grinned. "It was, rather." He leaned forward like a conspirator. "I could tell that you, at least, enjoyed it."

Gilbert cleared his throat. He smelled acrid perspiration, laced with lilac. "I could appreciate your talent, certainly."

"Come on now, admit it. You loved it. You couldn't take your eyes off me."

Gilbert's dizziness returned briefly. The intensity of Frank's gaze unnerved him.

"Tell me that you enjoyed it, William." Wilson grabbed both of Gilbert's hands and pulled him closer. Gilbert didn't have the wit to pull himself away. "Tell me how you didn't dare blink for fear you'd miss something. How hard your heart beat as you watched me, performing for you." The arrogance suddenly melted from Frank's face, to be replaced by raw need. "I've been trying for so very long now to get you to notice me."

"Mr. Wilson, please." Gilbert tried without success to release himself from the younger man's powerful grip.

"Frank. Call me Frank. I want to hear you say my Christian name." He drew Gilbert's hand to his chest. "Feel *my* heart, William. Feel how it's beating, for you."

Sure enough, Gilbert felt the strong, even rhythm through the damp cotton of Wilson's costume, which rose and fell beneath his palm. His own breathing was ragged and labored. Of their own accord, his fingertips wandered across the young man's chest, tracing the ridges of muscle down to the abdomen. There was something about this brash youth, some kind of perfection that was almost painful.

Frank sat completely still under Gilbert's touch, his eyes moist, his lips parted. A flush climbed up his fair cheeks. Sweat-soaked blond curls clung to his brow. "Yes," he whispered. "Oh yes!"

Gilbert started, as if waking from some dream. Deliberately, he drew his hand away, trying to recover his dignity. "Mr. Wilson. You're embarrassing me, and I should think you'd feel embarrassed as well."

"I'm not embarrassed, or ashamed, William. I want you, and I don't care who knows it. You're a comic genius, unappreciated by ordinary stiffs like Sullivan and D'Oyly Carte. And what's more, with your bearish body and your wild whiskers and that brusque manner you adopt to camouflage your soft heart, you're as attractive as hell."

Frank cupped his swelling groin in one hand, daring Gilbert to look away. He pointed at the noticeable bulge in the director's trousers. "You may pretend to be shocked or horrified, but the truth is pretty obvious."

"I…you…" A knock interrupted Gilbert's sputtering attempts at self-justification. Grossmith stuck his head into the dressing room.

"Rehearsal in five minutes, Frank. Better be on time if you don't want the old Mustachio to get into a tizzy. Oh! Mr. Gilbert, sir, I didn't realize you were here."

Gilbert rose hastily. "I was just discussing some of the nuances of the character with Mr. Wilson. Meanwhile, you should be more aware of your audience, Mr. Grossmith, before you deliver your lines."

"Yes, sir. I'm sorry, sir."

"Never mind. Let's get the rehearsal started." Halfway out the door, Gilbert glanced back at the understudy. "On stage, Mr. Wilson."

Frank's tone flirted with insolence. "Of course, Mr. Gilbert. Right away, sir."

Rehearsals continued to progress well. Wilson polished and elaborated his portrayal of Richard Dauntless, wringing appreciative laughs and groans from the rest of the cast. Word came from Lely's house that he was recovering as well as could be expected, and that he wished the cast good luck.

Everyone was in an expansive mood, except Gilbert. A persistent sense of foreboding hung over him. His slumber teemed with incoherent but terrible dreams that woke him, screaming. He tossed and turned so much that Kitty finally insisted he go sleep in the guest room.

During the day, he tried to avoid Frank Wilson as much as possible. Outside of rehearsal periods, he closeted himself in his office, smoking his pipe and reworking some of the lyrics that still didn't satisfy him. He stayed late at the theater, knowing that sleep would only torture him if he returned home.

Opening night was tomorrow, and everyone seemed to be eager and ready. So why did he feel so weighed down, so anxious and exhausted?

It was past ten when a knock woke him from a doze that must have crept up on him despite the fear of nightmares. "Yes, who is it?"

His visitor didn't wait to be invited in. "It's me, William. It's Frank."

Gilbert bolted upright, anger providing him with sudden energy. Red boiled behind his eyelids. "What are you doing here? I can't have you here. Get out, this instant."

The younger man shut the door. He sidled over in Gilbert's direction. Gilbert backed away. "I needed to see you, William. To talk to you, about the other afternoon. I'm sorry, I shouldn't have pushed you so hard."

"Never mind. Just go away now. Please, go away."

"I apologize for being so rude, so insensitive. I've been wanting you so long, it just seemed natural to say it. To show you. I should have realized how new this would be for you, how shocking." With theatrical grace, Wilson glided to his knees in front of Gilbert, his head bowed. "Forgive me, please."

Gilbert gazed down at Frank's golden curls, gleaming in the harsh electric light. He smelled the man's floral cologne. Damn, his heart was beating like thunder, and there was an uncomfortable tightness in his crotch. Damn, damn, damn.

"Get up," he said gruffly. "Show a bit of self-respect, Wilson."

"Not until I hear you say that I'm forgiven."

"Fine, fine, I forgive you, now get up and go."

Gilbert didn't understand how he did it, but all at once Frank was standing in front of him, face to face, close, much too close. He was taller than Gilbert and had to bend to whisper.

"Thank you, William." Then Gilbert felt the man's mouth on his own. He felt Frank's tongue toying with his mustache, tickling, probing, tentative at first, then bold and confident as Gilbert opened his lips.

Gilbert's resistance melted. Frank's arms encircled him, and Gilbert reciprocated, stirred by the sensation of strength in those young limbs. Frank tasted of horehound and tobacco, masculine and yet sweet. Frank kissed him eagerly, passionately, and from some place he had not known existed, Gilbert responded with equal passion.

He felt the hard, hot lump that he knew was Frank's cock, grinding against his thigh. Somehow this did not terrify or appall him. He welcomed it, exquisitely aware that his own cock was swollen and sensitive.

The dark clouds that had haunted him for the past two days dissolved in the brilliance of Frank's kiss. Gilbert did not think, did not worry or reason or judge. For the first time in a very long time, he simply allowed himself to feel.

Frank brought his hand down to fondle Gilbert's erection. For the briefest instant, Gilbert rejoiced at the touch. Then the weight of reality, the burden of thought, came crashing down upon him.

"No!" Gilbert hissed. "No! Stop. We must stop."

"But, William..." Frank aimed a kiss at him; Gilbert twisted away.

"We cannot do this. I cannot."

Frank dusted a finger lightly over Gilbert's groin. "Oh, I think you can, and quite well, too."

Gilbert moved as quickly as his bulk would allow to put the desk between himself and his nemesis.

"You realize that we could be imprisoned? We could even be hanged!"

"No one will know. Why should anyone care about our private pleasures? Our special kind of love?"

Gilbert groaned. "Love? Wilson, I'm a married man. I'm a respectable man with a very public career, and a whole company depending on him for their livelihood. You must try to understand, Frank, why this is so impossible."

"But you do want me, don't you?" Wilson's face shone with that same eerie light Gilbert had seen on the first day by the Embankment. With those blue eyes, that alabaster complexion, those silky curls, he looked like an angel. Gilbert ached inside. Of course he wanted the man, brilliant, devious devil that he was.

"What does it matter?" Gilbert sank into his chair, his head in his hands. "It can never be."

Wilson pulled himself to his full height. "If you won't have me, then I'll leave. I'll quit the play."

Gilbert gave a chuckle that was almost indistinguishable from a sob. "No, you won't. Because there's one thing that you love more than me, more than anything."

Wilson's face grew momentarily dark. Then he deliberately erased the grimace, affecting a conspiratorial tone.

"You're right. I won't leave, at least not until you've found someone to replace me. I wouldn't do that to you, William. But I believe that I can safely say you will be sorry that you refused me.

I'll go now, and let you think. Perhaps something will happen to change your mind."

Wilson slipped out without waiting for Gilbert's reply. Gilbert slumped down onto his desk, his mouth full of horehound and tobacco, bitterness and despair.

22 January 1887
London

"Five minutes to curtain!" Smithson scurried through the wings, delivering the message to the bridesmaids and villagers who milled about backstage, gossiping, warming up, or practicing a dance figure one last time. Gilbert sat on his stool behind the prompt desk, painfully aware of a huge gulf between himself and the other members of the company. He could just make out the susurration of the audience beyond the velvet drapes.

Sullivan swept by on his way to the orchestra pit, resplendent in black satin tails and brocade waistcoat. He smiled amiably at his partner.

"It looks like a good house, William. Even the Prince of Wales is in his box."

"They're all expecting another *Mikado*. I sincerely hope that they won't be disappointed."

"It's a fine play, don't worry. The ghost scene will have them shivering delightfully. And I'm certain that Mr. Wilson will be a huge hit."

At mention of Wilson's name, Gilbert felt a chill, then a fever. An abyss seemed to open at his feet. He teetered precariously on the edge. His mouth turned so dry he could hardly speak.

"Yes," he finally managed to croak. "I'm sure you're right."

He gestured to the chorus to take their places on stage. His heart slammed fiercely against his ribs, and his head ached. He wondered if he were going to have a stroke. He heard the first notes of the overture, and then before he realized it, the last notes. He nodded to Smithson, and the curtain rose on the charming Cornish fishing village of Rederring and the dulcet harmonies of the chorus.

"Fair is Rose as the bright May-day;
Soft is Rose as the warm west-wind;
Sweet is Rose as the new-mown hay—
Rose is the queen of maiden-kind!"

The chorus of professional bridesmaids serenades the fair Rose Maybud, considering the thorny question of why such a fair flower remains unmarried though she has been of age for more than six months. Soon they reveal the quandary. Rose is too polite to ever speak of her affections to a possible suitor. Meanwhile, all the young men in the village, most notably the eminently eligible Robin Oakapple, are so intimidated by her beauty and goodness that they dare not propose. Robin encounters Rose and tries to speak, but is utterly foiled by Rose's perverse interpretations of her book of etiquette.

The audience was applauding each song, and laughing at all the right places. Gilbert felt his spirits rise by just a hair.

Then Frank Wilson joined him in the wings, waiting for his cue.

They did not speak. Wilson stared fiercely at Gilbert as if to consume him with this gaze. Gilbert, flustered and miserable, still could not look away. Something compelled him to look upon the youth, with all his terrible beauty.

> *"From the briny sea,*
> *Comes young Richard, all victorious!*
> *Valorous is he—*
> *His achievements are all glorious..."*

Frank half-smiled. He blew Gilbert a kiss, and stepped on stage.

The *Parlez Vous* song and the hornpipe were a triumph. The audience roared and called for two encores.

He's a natural, thought Gilbert, truly gifted. He has a long and successful career ahead of him, if he can just forget this infatuation he has for me.

He turned his attention to the scene on stage, allowing himself the momentary luxury of admiring Wilson's talent.

"Robin, do you call to mind how, years ago, we swore that, come what might, we would always act upon our hearts' dictates?"

"Aye, Dick, and I've always kept that oath. In doubt, difficulty, and danger I've always asked my heart what I should do, and it has never failed me."

"Right! Let your heart be your compass, with a clear conscience for your binnacle light, and you'll sail ten knots on a bowline, clear of shoals, rocks, and quicksands! Well, now, what does my heart say in this here difficult situation? Why it says, 'Dick,' it says— (it calls me Dick acos it's known me from a babby)—'Dick,' it says, 'you ain't shy—you ain't modest—you got to tell your brother Robin the truth about how you feel.'"

The audience chuckled appreciatively. But a sudden bolt of worry sent Gilbert to his script. He knew that line wasn't quite right.

"Robin, I can't stand by and watch you throw yourself away on some simpering maid, not when I loves you like I do."

Why was Frank ad-libbing? Grossmith looked confused; desperately, he fell back to an earlier line. "Alas, Dick, I love Rose Maybud, and love in vain!"

Nervous laughter filled the theater. What a strange joke!

"And I'm telling you, I can give you all the love you ever need. Give her up and come away with me. We'll sail the high seas together, have adventures like you'd never imagine, Robin. And at night, I'll lay you alongside, becalmed under my lee, and then I'll show you what love really is."

Members of the audience looked at each other, aghast. A murmuring grew, swelled louder as George once again tried to get the scene on track.

"Will you do this thing for me? Can you, do you think? Yes, there's no false modesty about you—"

Frank interrupted, threw himself at Grossmith's feet, grabbing the other man's hands with convincing passion. "I'll do anything for you, my brother, my darling, my love. Let me take you away from her, away from this piddling little village." He gripped George's fingers tightly as the baritone tried to pull them away. "Let me show you how my heart burns for you. And oh, how my body yearns for you—William."

Frank put his hands on Grossmith's face and drew him into a long kiss.

A woman in the balcony screamed and fainted. The audience erupted in a storm of protest. "Fie!" "For shame!" "Call the police!" "Boo!" Gilbert watched in horror as spectators shook their fists and cursed at the players.

Someone threw some kind of vegetable at the stage. It hit Frank on the back of his head, streaking his blond hair with red pulp as he prolonged the kiss. He turned to the audience, stood, and bowed, an angelic smile on his lips.

"Curtain!" yelled Gilbert. "Drop the curtain!" While some playgoers had already flounced out of the theater in a huff, a remnant of the audience was rapidly coalescing into an angry mob and was headed for the stage.

The orchestra struck up a lively rendition of the *Parlez Vous* song, trying to drown out the shouts and slurs. Meanwhile Sullivan rushed backstage.

"Get out, Gilbert. I'll handle the situation. You're the one they're going to try and crucify."

"But—I had nothing to do with this! You know very well that Wilson was ad-libbing."

"But why, Gilbert? Why did he use the name 'William'? Your name?"

"I—I don't have any idea. He must be deluded, crazy. Why else would he do such a thing?"

Sullivan gave an exasperated sigh. "In any case, it doesn't matter what the truth is. The public adores a scandal. They'll interpret this in the worst way possible. You had better lie low. And I'd advise you to tell Wilson to do the same, if you should see him."

There was a tight knot in Gilbert's chest, a pain that threatened to overwhelm him. "I doubt very much," he said gruffly, "that I shall see him."

13 February 1887
Covent Garden

Gilbert lay on his back on the bed, staring at the cherubs decorating the ceiling. He wore only his undershirt and braces. Soprano moans and baritone grunts filtered through the wall from the room next door. It was long past the supper hour; he supposed that he should order something to be brought up, but he did not have the energy.

Why bother, anyway? His trousers were already baggy, and his waistcoat hung on him like a scarecrow. Why not just stop eating altogether, and allow himself to waste away?

Don't be so melodramatic, William. He heard the inner admonishment in Kitty's voice, that sweet, sensible voice that had so often kept him on an even keel when his tempers and moods threatened to swamp him.

Kitty. She was lost to him now. She had tearfully asked him to leave, after he confessed his brief lapse with Frank. "I know that you couldn't help yourself, William, but look at it from my perspective. I'll always love you, but I'll never be able to trust you."

He was starting to cry again. Damn, he shouldn't be so soft. Somehow he seemed to have lost control completely.

Yesterday, he'd had a visit from Sullivan's solicitor. The partnership was officially dissolved, due to "irreconcilable artistic differences." Gilbert imagined Richard D'Oyly Carte rubbing his hands together with glee, to finally be rid of the gadfly who was always snooping into his accounts. Well, at least Sullivan had the decency not to accuse Gilbert of moral turpitude.

Ruddygore, or "Ruddigore" as Sullivan had retitled it in the face of public disapproval, ran for a mere ten performances before it folded. The first few nights it played to full houses, curiosity seekers and scandalmongers drawn by the lurid reports about the opening night. Before long, though, the sensation lost its thrill. Critics began to complain that having ghosts come back to life and marry was inappropriate material for family entertainment. Meanwhile, Gilbert had heard that Richard Temple, who replaced Frank Wilson as Dick Dauntless, was a pale shadow of his predecessor.

There was a soft knock. Gilbert didn't even bother to sit up. "Come in." It might, he supposed, be the police, but after two weeks he had more or less stopped worrying about them. There was, after all, no proof of anything improper, only a suggestion, and no matter what people said of him, the law still required proof. Probably it was one of Mrs. Thorne's girls, bringing him a bite even though he hadn't bothered to order.

"William. It's me."

Gilbert had thought never to hear that melodious voice again. Still he lay there, immobile, waiting to see what happened next.

Frank came to sit by the bed. He took in Gilbert's gaunt and disheveled appearance in one glance. "My poor William. You look awful."

"All thanks to you, I might mention." Gilbert propped himself up on one elbow and surveyed the younger man. Frank looked as fresh and dapper as ever. Clearly the public outcry hadn't touched him at all. "How did you find me?"

"Lucky guess. Where would a disgraced man, rejected by his wife, abandoned by his friends and abhorred by society, go to hide out? Among outcasts like himself, of course."

"Mrs. Thorne is an old friend of mine, from long before I married. She has been kind enough to offer me asylum."

"And have you taken advantage of the other comforts that she is in a position to offer?"

Gilbert had conflicting urges: to slap the provocative grin off Frank's face, and to kiss it away. Instead, he turned his back on the younger man and stared at the wall. Please, he thought, just let him go away. Leave me in my misery. Don't tempt me.

"William, I'm sorry." A warm hand, gentle on Gilbert's shoulder. "I had to do it. There was no other way that we could be together."

"No way other than ruining me?" Gilbert's voice was bitter.

"I had to set you free. Free from your other life, from your fears and your prejudices. Then, I knew, you would turn to me." As he spoke, Frank rolled Gilbert onto his back again, leaned down, and kissed him.

Gilbert didn't want to respond, but his body betrayed him. Once again Frank's scent made him dizzy, dizzy with desire. He allowed himself to float for a few heady moments in the hot, wet currents of the kiss, before he pushed Frank away.

"Leave me alone. We can't be together. Disgraced or not, I'm still well known. If we were to be seen in each other's company, I'd be in prison in a trice."

Frank reached inside his coat and extracted a cardboard folio. "We can be together. Just not here in England." Gilbert recognized the insignia of one of the top steamship lines. "In America, they're not nearly so particular about such things. Life, liberty and the pursuit of happiness, you know."

"Frank, my plays have been mounted in New York, in Boston, in Philadelphia. I'm a public figure. Maybe I wouldn't be jailed, but you may be sure that I'd be snubbed by polite society."

"Polite society? Very much over-rated, I can tell you. I was expelled from polite society years ago. Now my family pays me very well to stay out."

Frank smoothed Gilbert's mustache with his fingertip. The familiar little gesture made Gilbert ache inside. "Anyway, I wasn't thinking about any of those proper Eastern cities. I thought we should head west—wide open spaces and all that. I've heard that San Francisco has become quite civilized."

Gilbert allowed the younger man to stroke his arm. The touch was gentle, chaste, yet it inflamed him. For the first time in weeks, he felt alive. Perhaps this could work. After all, what was there to keep him here in England? But this man—this rogue? "How can I possibly trust you? After what you did?"

All the urbanity and arrogance vanished from Frank's face. There was only youth, and desire. "Please, I didn't know how else I could make you mine. I want you so badly. You can't possibly know or believe how much I want you."

Gilbert reached up and pulled Frank down onto the bed with him. "Perhaps I do, after all."

30 May 2007
San Francisco

"Charlie, can you help me with these buttons? No matter how hard I try, I can't reach them."

"There you go, Chet. Turn around. Yes, indeed, you do make a very charming Rose Maybud."

"Well, I appreciate your compliments, Sir. But the question is, is it meet that an utter stranger should thus express himself? Let me consult my book of etiquette—"

"Damn etiquette, Chet. Give me a kiss."

"Well, when you put it that way..."

Their embrace was interrupted by Lew, the director. "Hey, save that for the cast party! We've got a show to do first!"

"How's the audience?"

"A bit rowdy, but that's to be expected at the maiden performance of the Castro Savoyards. Anyway, curtain's in ten minutes. Break a leg."

"Ooh, I hope not. I've got a marathon on Sunday."

"Ha ha. Okay, then, have fun."

Charlie slipped a hand under the voluminous skirt of Chet's costume and gave his lover's cock an affectionate squeeze. "I'm having fun already."

Lew was on stage, making introductory remarks. Lew did like to talk.

"Ruddigore was the last collaboration of William Gilbert and Arthur Sullivan. Although the pair had many conflicts during their successful but tempestuous relationship, their sudden final break after Ruddigore has never been officially explained. The unofficial story, though, is that the conventional, married Gilbert fell in love and ran off with a young actor from the company."

The murmuring of the audience stilled to appreciative silence.

"Given his genius, I'm more than happy to claim William S. Gilbert as one of our own." The crowd broke into wild applause. "Friends, I give you Gilbert and Sullivan's *Ruddigore: or The Witch's Curse.*"

The orchestra—keyboard, guitar, flute and drums—began a thin version of the overture while the "bridesmaids" stumbled over each other's feet getting in position outside Rose Maybud's cottage.

Charlie glanced out the window. A crescent moon climbed above the silhouettes of Victorian houses.

Wherever he was, Charlie hoped Gilbert was watching.

Note: Lyrics and dialogue are taken from *The Complete Plays Of Gilbert And Sullivan*, The Modern Library, published by Bennett A. Cerf and Donald S. Klopper. (No copyright date but most likely from 1938)

Author's Note:

I've been a Gilbert and Sullivan afficionado since I was five and my parents took me to a Martyn Green concert on the Boston Common. "Ruddigore" is perhaps my favorite G&S operetta, followed by "Iolanthe" as a close second.

When I became an adult, I noticed that the dialogue and relationship between Dick Dauntless and Robin Oakapple was a bit peculiar and suggestive—lots of talk about eternal bonds and being closer than brothers and so on. This observation, and the speculation that it inspired, provided the initial spark for "Opening Night."

My fascination with the Victorian era, when public morality and private behavior were so at odds, fanned the flames. Add to this the fact that so many gay men that I know love musicals, including G&S. If a straight, and straight-laced William Gilbert could inspire such enthusiasm in the gay community, how would he have been worshiped if he actually had loved another man, at a time when this would have been social suicide at best and an excuse for incarceration as a criminal at worst?

A HAPPIER YEAR

Emily Salter

IN THE END, HE FOUND FORSTER by chance.

In the few years since the war ended, Henry had sometimes dreamt, secretly, of searching for Forster, perhaps tracking him down to India in the home of some elegant Maharajah. But in truth he had no idea where Forster was, or even if he was still alive. They were only ever dreams that flittered across his mind at idle moments. Such a reality would belong to a man with far greater inclinations for adventure than Henry could claim, not to mention to one who could walk without the aid of a cane. A Jerry bullet piercing his knee in 1917 had seen to that.

Henry wasn't the sort for adventure, whatever he told his mother. The year he had spent traveling down through France and into Italy wasn't about adventure, it was to avoid the lure of the "suitable" girls his mother was no doubt lining up back in Hertfordshire. When he had left England last spring she seemed keen on one of their neighbour's cousins—a pretty, delicate girl with cornflower blue eyes and red hair that reminded him of Laurence. She'd have made a good wife, he supposed, but a few months after he had arrived in Paris his mother had written to say the girl was to marry some promising young barrister.

The group he was traveling with were a misfit band, or at least Henry liked to think they were.

Geoffrey was from the lower echelons of the middle class and not the sort of chap Henry would have associated with back home, but when they met a few hundred miles away in Paris in the early summer of 1921, they had latched onto each other immediately.

They journeyed to Montpellier a few months later, after admitting that the bohemian Parisian lifestyle terrified them. That was where they met Philip, an American who wanted to be a dandy but was too brash to really carry it off. The three of them had traveled across the border and into Italy where they found Piero. At first he had fooled them all into believing he grew up picking olives, but when they started wondering whether a farm boy would speak quite such good English or be quite so literate, they discovered he was actually from a rather wealthy family in Florence.

And of course they all recognised in each other the very thing they tried so hard to keep hidden from the rest of the world.

In the early autumn of 1922 they were staying in a guest house, a two hour train ride away from Naples, where the Signora seemed so grateful to have regular guests as the summer died that she was also willing to feign ignorance on the occasions when Philip or Geoffrey didn't return to their own room. What they liked, what they were, may not have put them in any danger of being arrested as in England, but that still didn't mean they could flaunt themselves.

There, in the idyll of the blissfully unravaged Italian countryside, the four of them could sit and drink wine and smoke and talk about books and, maybe for a moment, almost pretend there had never been a war.

Piero's rambunctious, accented voice cut across the rest of them.

"No, I don't like that one," he said one night when Henry mentioned *Maurice*. "It's too depression."

"Depressing," Philip corrected him.

"What on earth are you talking about?" Henry said. "It has a wonderfully happy ending!"

"It does?" Piero laughed. "Maybe. I didn't reach the end. I couldn't. Too much complaining. He was too miserable." He reached over and tucked his thumb under Henry's chin. "Too *English*."

Piero was the youngest and they called him a boy even though he was probably, if not already past twenty, very close to it. He wasn't truly beautiful like some of the men Henry had seen in Italy. His nose was most definitely hooked rather than aquiline and the freckle above his lip was on the verge of being a mole. But the dark eyes that peered out from under his shaggy fringe were bright and piercing and when he laughed, which was often, it seemed to be in harmony with the fountain in the town square.

Henry jerked away. "If you haven't read the entire book then clearly your opinion is ill informed so perhaps you should refrain from such inane discussion."

A moment passed and awkward looks were exchanged before Geoffrey said, "It's just a book, old boy."

And Henry knew it was silly to take an insult to *Maurice* as a personal affront, but he couldn't help it.

The scandalous *Maurice*; the dirty little book E.M. Forster had published eight years ago, to much public dismay. The newspapers had called it "obscene" and "perverted."

It is a sordid tale of sexual deviancy, one had written. *And it is made worse by the fact this man is supposedly a gentleman and Cambridge educated. It is not just a disgrace, it is an insult.*

For a while Forster's shame had been in the newspapers and rumours about him had been in people's minds, but then Gavrilo Princip had shot the Archduke and his Sophie. Suddenly the exploits of an author weren't so important and when Forster was arrested, charged with gross indecency and eventually convicted and sentenced to two years imprisonment (without hard labour; the Judge was lenient), the news was barely afforded a few inches.

Henry had been seventeen when the book was published and Laurence not even a year older.

They had been Henry and Laurence to their parents, Sutton and Wainwright to their masters, and Harry and Larry when their friends were in a jovial mood. But to each other, in diaries, in letters, in notes scrawled on the inside covers of books, they were just H and L. Nothing more. Nothing else needed.

It was Laurence who had initiated it. Laurence who had first brought up the subject of Forster.

"The gall of the man, to write such a thing," he'd said. "It's shocking, really."

Henry had nodded his vehement agreement. "Absolutely."

"I'm sure no-one would think it half so bad if it didn't have a happy ending."

"Does it? How do you know that?"

He'd paused for a moment and it had seemed to Henry that he was gathering his courage.

"I've read it."

The words had seemed to hesitate in the air before penetrating Henry's mind. His chest felt suddenly empty. It was a confession, he knew, of so much more.

He'd glanced sideways to where Laurence had apparently become very interested in his fingernails, the freckles dusting his face standing harshly against his skin, which had turned milky pale.

Then, in a voice smaller than Henry had ever heard, he'd asked, "Would you like to read it?"

Henry's empty chest had suddenly pounded back into life and he'd had to wait until the blood stopped rushing furiously through his ears before nodding, slowly, once.

Henry didn't dare tell his family he had read the book. His mother was so appalled with Forster that she had made Henry's sister Lydia throw away her copy of *A Room With A View*, lest it corrupt her.

No, none of them could know he had read it. They couldn't know Laurence had slipped him his copy when he came for tea over the summer vac, or that Henry had stuffed it inside his shirt to sneak it upstairs. They couldn't know he had devoured it in one night or that he had emerged from it in the morning, his head filled with images of the lovers embracing in the boathouse and dreams of escaping into the greenwood.

"It's a nice thought, isn't it?" Laurence had said. "Being friends first, then falling in love."

"*They* broke each other's hearts," Henry pointed out. "It was the gamekeeper he fell in love with in the end."

"Of course," he'd said. The tips of his ears had turned pink and clashed with his auburn curls, Henry remembered. "But he still loved his friend first."

When war was declared, Laurence had signed up immediately. Henry had had to wait until he was old enough and it was the winter of 1915 before he was allowed on a French battlefield.

His mother wrote him letters full of news about Aunt Ruth's chrysanthemum disasters and requests from Lydia to move Henry's pianola into her room, though she would probably have already done so by the time he got the letter. And Henry would write back that he hoped the rabbits stayed away and that of course Lydia could move the pianola if she hadn't done so already.

He kept his news light and brief and didn't trouble them with tales of wading through waist-deep water in the trenches or rats gorging themselves on human remains.

He wrote to Laurence of such things though, and of fears that the war wouldn't be over by this Christmas nor even the next, and of how he yearned for them both to be home again, sleeping in his rickety bed, with their legs entwined.

When he was finished he always signed off, *Love for now and always, H.* Then he burnt the letter, sitting by the fire until he was sure the last of the embers had turned to ash.

"And will we break each other's hearts?" Henry had asked, eight years and a lifetime ago.

Laurence hadn't said anything; he just reached out and laid his fingertips over the back of Henry's hand. It was the first time they had touched.

Piero was one of the most demonstrative fellows Henry had ever known, and when they first met, Piero had touched his hands and arms and face and even his bottom once. But he didn't realise the boy wasn't just being continental until Philip said, "Don't even bother trying, kid. You're wasting your time. Henry here is pure and chaste."

He'd felt his cheeks burn and he knew he must have been blushing furiously, especially when Philip and Piero started guffawing. Geoffrey's round face had simply turned pink in sympathetic embarrassment and for a moment Henry hated them all. He didn't need sympathy from the likes of Geoffrey, nor would he tolerate ridicule from anyone.

He'd stormed off that day just as he did the day Piero insulted *Maurice*, though less laughter followed him on the latter occasion.

Night came and Henry was still awake which wasn't unusual. He rarely slept. Usually he was able to sit and read by lamplight and perhaps be granted a few hours' sleep, but not tonight.

He sat in a high-backed chair in his room, gazing out over the view, such as it was—a small copse of trees and a dirty river just visible beyond.

Propping his bad leg up on a threadbare footstool, he had *Maurice* open in his lap. The pages were yellowing and the text was obscured on many pages by the scores of notes in the margins and between the lines. Some of them were in Laurence's handwriting, others answering in Henry's hand. It was their final conversation, taking place over years, separated by miles, and buried somewhere within it was the love story which had started it all.

He was reading one of his favourite chapters again, his eyes glazing over, not really following the words, while his memory filled in the gaps.

A gentle knock made him tumble out of his reverie just as the door opened and Piero walked in without waiting for an invitation.

"You don't like sleeping, do you?" he'd said by way of greeting. "Not many men your age do."

"How old were you when the war ended?" Henry said, shifting in his seat and trying to get up.

Piero waved him down, then took another step into the room and walked towards him. "Not old enough. Thank God."

He held out his cigarette case and, after a moment, Henry accepted one gratefully. For a moment they were both still, Henry sitting, bound by the pain in his leg, Piero standing with his arm resting against the windowsill.

Piero held up his hand as blew the smoke out, undulating his fingers gently as he watched the grey swirls rising and curling and fading away.

"Why do you love this book so much?" he asked after a moment, tapping the cover of the book that still sat in Henry's lap. "It's not good."

"The book or my love for it?"

"The book. The love is strange but love is always good." He took another drag on his cigarette and then, when Henry still hadn't answered him, he said, "So how does it end?"

"Did you read as far as his meeting with the gamekeeper?"

"What gamekeeper?"

Henry sighed. "His friend's gamekeeper. He falls in love with him at the end. They, er…"

"Fuck?"

"No!" Henry said quickly. "Well, yes, they do," he amended. He shook his head. "They're together at the end. They… they give up everything for each other. They disappear together, just go off into some remote corner of the forest where no-one will ever find them."

"So they run away?" Piero said. "Hmm." He blew out a long stream of smoke and waited for it all to disperse. "Perhaps your book is not so stupid after all."

The first time Henry and Laurence made love, the strangest thing about it was how normal it felt.

Henry had met Laurence when he was twelve, the same age at which he realised his newly formed thoughts were improper and his emerging desires perverted. For so long he'd surmised that the Devil must have put these wicked thoughts into his head and that it was just desires of the body, which he mustn't ever let overcome him.

It had given him unimaginable pleasure to lie beneath Laurence, squeezing his thighs together as tightly as he could, while Laurence thrust in and out of the tiny space. The rough, auburn hair at Laurence's groin rubbing against his cock, Laurence's cock sliding against his balls, both of them clutching at each other, bodies rising and parting and pushing, and Laurence's lips mapping a trail across his neck and shoulders; and Henry fighting to keep his eyes open because this was *Laurence*—Laurence who had fuelled his fantasies for so long, Laurence whom he loved, and he was there, *just there*, and Henry didn't want to miss a single moment.

 But it was afterwards, lying with his head on Laurence's chest, brushing his fingers through the dusting of strawberry blond hair, that Henry felt, for the first time in his life, utter contentment. Whatever had come before, whatever was to come in the future, he knew he would always have this moment.

He lay there and he knew this couldn't be the Devil. Wickedness could never feel this perfect.

Henry kept a photograph of his mother with him wherever he traveled, more out of habit than by reason of missing her.

Piero left him looking out of the window and picked up the frame in which the image sat.

"Will you go home soon?" he asked. "Marry? Make children?"

"Perhaps."

"Is that what you want to do?"

"Not particularly." He took a deep drag on his cigarette, then turned to look at Piero. "Won't you do the same one day?"

"Never," he said, with such conviction that Henry almost believed him. "I will never go home, never become a politician. That's what my father says I should do. Things are changing, he says. But I won't do it."

"Easy to say now."

Piero snorted. "Don't you want to be like the men in your precious book?"

"That's just a story. It's a fairytale, really. It couldn't happen."

Piero came and crouched down by Henry's chair. He reached up and laid the palm of his hand over Henry's fingers, then gently, almost gingerly, curled his own fingers round. When Henry tried to pull away, Piero gripped him tightly.

"Are all you Englishmen such cowards?"

Henry snatched his hand away. "You have no right to call anyone a coward."

For a brief moment a look of shame flickered across Piero's face, but it was soon gone and frustration and anger took its place. "You will end up alone, you know that?" Piero said. "Even if you marry some little girl you don't even like, you will be alone. Alone and sad and old. Like the man who wrote your stupid book!"

"Oh, really? And what do you know about him?"

"I've seen him. Grey and thin and *ugly*," he spat.

"What…what do you mean, you've seen him?"

Piero frowned and took another drag on his cigarette, which seemed to calm him slightly. "The man who wrote your book. He lives in a town…ah, perhaps thirty miles away. Or he lived there a few months ago. I was there before I met you. Didn't you know he was in Italy?"

Henry stared for a moment and didn't speak until Piero raised an expectant eyebrow at him.

"I had no idea. I knew he'd left England when he was released from prison but…I had no idea."

"You should talk to people more then." He laughed, his anger of moments before gone. "Look at you! You're like an excited schoolboy! He's just an old man."

Laurence had been dead for a week before Henry was shot in the knee, though Henry didn't learn of it until he'd been in hospital for a fortnight.

It was an unremarkable death, the same sort which befell thousands like him. When Henry was discharged and sent home, he made sure to visit Laurence's mother to offer his condolences and assure her that every man who died on the battlefield was a hero and he had no doubt Laurence died proudly and bravely. As he spoke, he tried to make his own words drown out the memory of shells and rifles and the bodies of the unlucky many falling in No Man's Land and staying there, buried in the rain and mud.

Laurence's mother smiled and thanked him and said he was always such a good friend to Laurence and that he would have to promise to stay in touch. Then she asked Kitty, the maid, to fetch the parcel from Laurence's room. In it was a collection of books—Latin and Greek texts from school, a selection of sonnets and, underneath the rest, a heavily annotated *Maurice*.

"I have no use for any of these," she said, not meeting Henry's eyes. "I'm sure Laurence would want you to have them."

Piero was laughing at him even as he guided Henry to the right train which would take him to the town where Forster had once—and hopefully still—lived. As Henry boarded, he heard Piero muttering something about a "crazy Englishman" before calling out that he would wait for Henry.

As Henry traveled, he tried to think of all the things he would want to say to Forster if he saw him, but then he realised he would never remember it all, so he wrote it down. He wrote of Laurence, of course, and of the pangs he had felt when Forster was sent down, and how horribly unfair it all was.

Forster sat in the piazza most afternoons, Piero had told him, so that's where Henry headed as soon as he got off the train.

It was a warm day and the town, though small, was busy. When he reached the piazza, holding *Maurice* tight in his left hand, he hobbled round the edges for what must have been nearly half an hour until his knee was aching and he was leaning all his weight on his cane. Just as he felt he was about to collapse, a man on a bicycle nearly collided with him. As he rode past, it was as though he drew a veil with him, and behind it, not even twenty feet away, sat a man, alone, younger than his frailty made him look.

Henry had only seen the photographs of Forster that ran in the paper when the scandal first broke. This was a hollow, grey imitation of that man. His skin had a sheen of sun-brown but underneath it was dull. His moustache was white with just a few strands of black left and though he wore a wide-brimmed hat, the few wisps of hair that escaped were also white.

Henry stopped, and for a moment it seemed the world stopped with him. All the noise of the piazza faded away and the people melted into the background. All he could see was the man in the distance, oblivious to Henry's presence.

Piero thought he knew what kept Henry awake, but he was wrong—it wasn't nightmares of the trenches, it was beautiful, cruel dreams of Laurence. He would wake in the dark, his skin tingling with the ghostly touch of Laurence's fingers, and for just a moment he could feel Laurence's breath on his skin and hear Laurence's voice whispering against his ear. But only for a moment, before he remembered and had to mourn all over again.

In spite of it all, he knew he wouldn't change a thing.

He looked down at the book clutched in his hands. Such a small thing, fragile and flimsy. The pages were all curling at the edges and the spine was cracked. This little story, this little fantasy that could never really be but that had been so much to him.

He looked at Forster again, his withered face turned towards the sun, old and damaged but with such a look of peace as Henry had never seen. For a moment, he saw his life as it might have been—married to a girl with blue eyes and hair that reminded him of the man he would never have been able to love.

But he *had* loved him. For a moment, just a moment, he had been complete and content. It was more than many men ever had, he knew, and so much more than he would ever have known without this silly little book.

Behind him the fountain streams danced in the sunlight. He took the letter to Forster out of his breast pocket and, after a moment, tossed the pages into the fountain and watched as they curled up and the ink seeped out, swirling in the water for an instant before fading away. Then he turned and shuffled out of the piazza, ready for his journey home, where Piero would be waiting for him at the train station.

Author's Note:

E.M. Forster wrote Maurice *between 1913 and 1914, before anything like the concept of "gay fiction" we have today existed. Ending as it does with the two lovers, Maurice and Alec, happy and about to start a life together, Forster didn't dare publish it in his lifetime, in an England where homosexuality was still a crime.*

Forster died in 1970, three years after the decriminalisation of homosexual sex, and Maurice *was finally published in 1971. Though generally not as highly thought of as* Howards End *or* A Passage to India*, it is nonetheless an extremely personal, romantic and hopeful novel.*

"A Happier Year" (the title is taken from Forster's dedication to the novel) looks at the effect the book has on two young men, on the eve of the First World War, in a world where Forster actually published the book in 1914. It's a small alteration of history but one which has a huge impact on the characters and, I hope, shows the power fiction has to inspire us and change us.

THE HEART OF THE STORM

Connie Wilkins

THE NIGHT SKY ARCHED AWAY TO infinity. The stars in their unfathomable distance seemed more real to Rowan than the earth three thousand feet below. She swayed in the harness, heart pounding, lungs beginning to pump again now that the parachute had safely deployed. Elation coursed through mind and body like freedom, like power, like—like sex. Not that sex was anything but a faint memory these days.

Time and gravity seemed to loosen their hold, and for a long moment she could imagine that the world she drifted toward was not the war-torn one she'd left.

Concentrate! Look down, check the terrain, anticipate your landing! Rowan wrenched her thoughts back to reality, but it was too dark below to make out many features on the ground. In the east, clouds edged with silver by the hidden moon towered in sublime indifference to the affairs of men.

She twisted slowly toward the southwest. There, along the Breton coast, dull flashes illuminated a smoky mist. *Same old world, same war.* The Allied bombers were making a run at the battleships and U-boats in St-Nazaire's harbor, a frequent enough assault that the Germans might not suspect a diversion. Rowan wasn't the only agent being dropped over Brittany tonight. She breathed an uncharacteristic prayer for safe passage of the plane and soft landings for those who had jumped farther north.

Worry about your own landing! The breeze was freshening into a light wind. The terrain below blinked into visibility as the moon emerged from behind the clouds, illuminating Rowan's dangling form as well as the mushroom billow of the parachute.

Landmarks began to match the map in her head. Two streams converging at a certain angle; the spire of a distant, isolated church; a deserted road. The wind was taking her to the east, too fast! But better east than west, where the great marsh of Le Briere spread across 99,000 acres between the Vilaine estuary to the north and the mouth of the Loire to the south.

There should be a signal fire somewhere in the angle between the streams. No sign of it yet. She tugged on the lines, warping the shape of the 'chute, altering direction just slightly. Yes, there, a spark…gone…there again, a steady glow, not bright, but enough. They would have been watching and listening for the drop plane, and feeding the native peat into the fire in anticipation of her landing.

Or anticipation, at least, of someone's landing. They had not been informed that the explosives expert being sent from London was a woman.

Nature might not have suited Rowan for the roles of wife, mother, nurturer; but fate, she thought, had prepared her for a mission at least as vital. With a university degree in chemistry and post-graduate training as a pharmacist, she was well qualified to teach the resistance fighters of the Maquis how to make explosives with materials available at any apothecary. And, while she had been born in Cornwall, not France, her Breton grandmother had sent her to a convent school in Quimper in the vain hope of teaching her a proper level of feminine docility. Certainly she knew more about Brittany and the Bretons than someone from Paris or Marseilles.

It had not been easy to persuade the British SOE and de Gaulle's Comite National Francaise to let her volunteer for the Free French. Obtaining additional training in demolitions had been even harder, but there had been no one better suited. She had worked tirelessly, persistant when necessary, steeling herself to feign docility when there was no other course, avoiding the least hint of scandal. The desires of the flesh had been reined in, painfully, by the fierce grip of her determination. What if she were a woman? All the better to deceive the Germans. If the men of the Maquis didn't like it—and, from her year at school in Brittany, she was sure they wouldn't—it was too late now.

Oh hell! Too late? Time and gravity reclaimed her suddenly, brutally. The ground hurtled upward. A gust of wind—the flash of upturned faces, and then pale mounds of haystacks looming beyond the circle of the fire's glow— Rowan drew up her legs, curled into a ball, and tried to propel herself toward the nearest stack by force of will.

The world, abruptly, was a maelstrom of choking dust and prickling straw. Her left ankle twisted beneath her. *No time for pain!* Reflexes from training kicked in. She freed her knife and slashed at the 'chute's lines. No point now in hauling at the mass of fabric to conceal it in the hay. If German voices approached, rather than Breton, there was nothing to be done but stand and face them. *If I can stand at all!*

At first there were no voices, only feet running through the stubble of the field. A flaring torch stopped a few feet away, its circle of light overlapping her. Rowan stood—yes, she could stand, just barely, painfully—and pulled the leather helmet from her head, brushing back a dark forelock as it fell across her brow. She could feel the eyes behind the light surveying her.

"Those London fools have sent us a woman!" The male voice was brusque with annoyance, but the words were unmistakably Breton.

So much for chopping my hair short! I knew I couldn't deceive them for long, but—not even for a moment? Relief overrode Rowan's irritation. She took a step away from the hay, staggered, and only just kept from falling.

"Hold up the torch, Joachim." This voice was authoritative, musical, and unmistakable female. Rowan, startled, staggered again, and would have fallen if not for the quick support of a pair of strong, slender arms. The scent of a woman teased her nostrils. Long strands of flame-gold hair—or did they merely reflect the torchlight?—brushed against her face, their silken stroke sending shivers of delight throughout her body. She felt dizzy.

Am I hallucinating? Have I hit my head and don't remember it? Other arms moved her back to sit on the hay, and she felt a man's woolen shirt rough against her cheek. A low voice rumbled from his body into hers.

"Your ways won't work on a woman, Sylvie!"

The Brieron dialect would have been impenetrable to Rowan if Sister Amalie at the convent school had not been a native of the marshland. The language they had spoken together had had far less to do with words, though, than with touch, and Rowan had taught as much as she'd learned, which explained why she'd been made to leave after only one year. She doubted that Sister had ever taken her final vows.

"Oh, yes, my ways will work on this one." Sylvie's laugh was low and amused. "And if they did not, what of it? You are too suspicious of strangers, Joachim. There is no need to bind by charms those already bound by a common enemy."

Rowan looked up into eyes the deep brown of peat water, flecked with amber in the torchlight. She had understood enough to brace herself to be on guard. Breton folklore had been denounced at the convent school as mere peasant superstition, and Rowan had paid very little attention to such stories; still, hadn't there had been something about blonde *fee* women whose unearthly beauty ensnared mortal men? Only fairy tales, of course. But what strange folk had she landed among? If they themselves believed in charms, how was she to teach them the science of explosives?

There was nothing unearthly about the face laughing down at her, framed by bright waves of hair escaping from a loosely tied kerchief. Rowan's heart, or something not far from it, lurched at the sight of freckles sprinkled across a snub nose and a merry, curving mouth meant for joy. A queenly or angelic sort of beauty Rowan could have easily withstood, but this... A tingle spread across her skin, then worked its way deeper, piercing layers of repression, stirring up barely-banked embers.

"Are you hurt?" Sylvie asked, in perfect cosmopolitan French, and then repeated the question in English. "Your ankle?" She knelt, throwing back the dark cloak covering her white skirt and smock, then ran her hands down Rowan's calf. Even through heavy leather flight trousers her touch burned like brandy, searing Rowan's leg all the way up to her crotch.

Sylvie gripped the injured ankle lightly, then released it. "Is this painful?"

"Only when you stop," Rowan thought dazedly, and then realized that she had spoken aloud, and in the Brieron dialect. Hadn't Sister Amalie used those very words once, when they were... Well. Now, like a randy dolt, she'd revealed what might have been a useful secret, along with something else that she knew already was no secret to this woman.

"Ah," Sylvie said, quirking an eyebrow. "Such pleasant surprises can be found in the oddest circumstances! But perhaps we shall keep some of this to ourselves." She made the merest gesture toward Joachim and a younger man who were busy hauling in the parachute. There would doubtless be some black-market dealer who would pay well for the silk fabric, with no questions asked.

"Of course, as you wish," Rowan answered in formal French, and then spoiled the effect by yelping as Sylvie's grip on her ankle tightened sharply, then eased. Rowan stepped reflexively backward. The ankle bore her weight now without the least complaint. Ripples of heat ran up her calf, then dissipated as the imprint of Sylvie's fingers faded. Rowan very nearly whimpered with the sense of loss.

"Well," Joachim said crossly as he returned, "is she our bomb-maker, or is she not? And what are we to call her?"

"Could you speak more slowly? I'm not familiar with your dialect," Rowan lied cooly.

"Can you show us how make bombs?" he repeated impatiently in servicable French. "And what is your name?"

"Rowan," she said shortly. "And yes, if you can get me the materials I need, and follow my instructions to the letter, we will make explosive devices." She was suddenly very tired. "But not tonight."

"Of course not," Sylvie said firmly. "Jacques," she called to the younger man, who was hanging back, "slide the *chaland* into the water, please. We will meet you at the landing."

Jacques cast her a look of abject devotion, then hurried off into the darkness. "Come," Sylvie said, putting an arm around Rowan and urging her in the direction Jacques had taken. "We will soon be on the water, and then you may rest for a few hours until we are deeply and safely into the marsh."

The landing was merely a cleared space on the edge of a stream so narrow that the *chaland*, a flat-bottomed Brieron punt with its stern nearly as tapered as its prow, barely fit between the banks. The torches were extinguished, hissing, in the black water. "You will see well enough by moonlight once your eyes adjust," Sylvie assured her, brushing a finger light as a dragonfly's wing across her eyelids; and it was true, Rowan realized, as her night vision became clearer than she had ever noticed before.

Jacques poled the boat along the winding channel overhung by low trees. The two women sat pressed together toward the stern, sharing Sylvie's cloak, an arrangement that provided Rowan with more warmth than could be attributed to the woolen cloth alone. She wanted to relax into the moment, savor the feel of Sylvie's skin separated from her own by only a few layers of cloth, watch the play of moonlight over the ripples on the water and the curves of Sylvie's face. *If this be enchantment, which I do not believe, what of it? We all work for the same cause.*

But Joachim, sitting facing them, resumed his testy questioning. "How soon, then, *Mlle.* Rowan? How long must we wait?"

Rowan was too tired, or too distracted, to think clearly. Sylvie's feminine perfume seemed to evoke the spirit of some rare, night-blooming flower. "Soon enough," she told him, thinking that he wanted details of the coming Allied invasion. "But they would scarcely tell me the time and place and then drop me so nearly into the lap of the enemy. We will have at least a month, I think, to prepare."

He shook his head vigorously and waved a dismissive hand. "No, no, how soon can you make the explosives?"

"As soon as I have the components. There must be apothecaries in some of the villages, and surely several if you go as far as St.-Nazaire or La Roche-Bernard. I will make a list, and you can gather the materials in amounts small enough to attract no attention."

Sylvie's hand had been resting lightly on Rowan's thigh. Now her grip tightened. "You know of the bridge at La Roche-Bernard?"

"I have heard of it," Rowan said, becoming more distracted by the moment. "The longest suspension bridge in the world, spanning the Vilaine Gorge. The town is far beneath, downstream along the river. I studied the maps in detail while I was in London."

"And do they know in London," Joachim said caustically, "that the Germans are stockpiling ammunition at their headquarters near the base of the bridge? And that they plan to begin transporting it in five days to the northern coast to fight off the expected invasion?"

"They know," Rowan said, although, in fact, she had not realized that the danger was quite so imminent. Five days! "So I am here, and we will be ready." *That great high bridge? And Maquis operatives to train who still believe in charms!*

"Yes, you are here," Sylvie said firmly, "at exactly the right time. And you will find that we have not been idle. There will be little or no chance for rest, though, in the days ahead, so we must take all we may as we travel."

Rowan's mind was roiling. Rest seemed impossible. The stream merged with another, and then others, swelling into a small river, and the punt moved faster and more smoothly with the flow. Sylvie tucked the cloak close around them, leaned her red-gold head against Rowan's dark hair, humming an almost inaudible tune; and suddenly, it seemed, Rowan was waking from a long, deep sleep.

Ripples of coral clouds streaked the brightening sky. Strong arms helped her from the boat. Not Joachim; the wide breast she leaned against was unmistakably that of a woman. Through the mist of waking Rowan looked up into a face faintly lined by time and weather, topped by cropped steel-gray hair.

"Where..." but Rowan's voice felt rusty. She drew in a deep breath and recognized Sylvie's scent clinging strongly to the older woman, blending with notes of sun-warmed herbs. Had she been helped, too, from the boat? Or had they shared a deeper embrace? And whatever made her imagine such a thing, or care?

But she knew. Memories teased at her, of a discreet club in London where she had ventured once with a friend from University. Short-haired women in tweeds or loose trousers and waistcoats had come and gone with with pretty girls clinging to their arms. In the last two years she had not dared to return, determined to remain above reproach, but only watched once or twice from a distance and then gone home with fuel enough for imagination that by midnight her narrow bed was warm and her tangled sheets damp.

"You are on an island of safety," came the response, in a contralto voice edged with humor. Rowan, even through a haze of sleep, did not doubt that for an instant.

A girl of about nine or ten took Rowan's hand shyly and led her to a sprawling cottage with thatched roof and reed-strewn floors. She was shown a room where she could wash and tidy herself, and another where an assortment of shirts and trousers were laid out across a pallet stuffed with goose feathers. Rowan gratefully stripped off her flight suit and harness and found clothing that fit well enough. *At least I am tall enough for men's clothes!*

The child poked her head shyly around the edge of the door. "Corrie says to come and have your breakfast. We are to have crepes today!»

«Is Sylvie there?»

«No, of course not!» It clearly seemed to her a foolish question. «Sylvie goes about her own business, and one must not ask.»

Oh? Well, I will ask, if the mission requires it!

Rowan followed the child out past a chicken coop into a tiny garden fenced by boards, their gently curving lines attesting to a former existence as the sides of *chalands*. The gray-haired woman sitting at a wooden table must be Corrie. In this brighter light she did not appear so much old as poised comfortably between youth and age, dressed for practicality in the same sort of homespun shirt and trousers worn by Joachim. She looked up at Rowan, surveying her calmly for a moment as though to assess her now that the sunlight had strengthened, and then waved her to a bench.

I'll wager she *knows everything there is to know about Sylvie, or is not afraid to ask!*

The coffee was hot and strong, augmented by some herb Rowan did not recognize, but far more palatable than any she had tasted in London since rationing began. "No, thank you," she said when Corrie offered milk and honey. "This is too good to need sweetening."

Corrie nodded approval. "Here comes Claudette with our sweets, in any case, although you must try the honey sometime while you are with us. The wild bees of the Briere guard their gold well, but we still find it." The child set a tray of crepes on warm plates before them. Blackberry jam oozed from between the lightly browned layers. A dish of some darker strips with a slight resemblance to kippers was included, and when Corrie offered it, Rowan, feeling suddenly starved, decided not to ask, just eat.

"I should warn you that not everyone appreciates the virtues of smoked eel," Corrie said, a smile twitching at the corners of her wide mouth.

Rowan, feeling challenged, took a mouthful and chewed, undeterred by the crunching of small bones. The smoky tang made an odd but satisfying contrast to the sweet crepes. "You can't imagine what I've been obliged to eat in London. This is a different world, in so many ways." She gestured across the table, then on toward the panorama of reeds and meadows and blue channels stretching languidly to the horizon, recalling the sense of being isolated from time, from reality, as she had drifted downward under the parachute. The tranquility of the marsh seemed unworldly, the only motion a rippling of water and faint shivering of rushes stirred by an otherwise imperceptible breeze. One could rest here forever... *Like the lotus-eaters of Lethe...*

The sudden honk of a goose broke the silence. On the far bank of the stream fluffy brown goslings scattered among the thickest reeds as two predatory herons soared overhead.

"Different from London, yes," Corrie said. "But even we cannot escape the world." Her jaw seemed suddenly squarer and the lines beside her mouth no longer suggested smiles and hearty laughter. "The foot soldiers and tanks of the invaders will not penetrate here, but their planes still fly overhead. And while they could not starve us out, for the marshland supports its own, we are bound by ties of blood and friendship to all of Brittany. And all of France as well," she added as an afterthought.

Rowan's relief must have shown on her face. Corrie chuckled. "Did you think we had lured you into this watery maze to keep you from your mission?"

Something about the older woman inspired frankness. "I did feel a certain sense of being...lured. And Sylvie spoke of binding by charms." Rowan spoke lightly, but watched closely for Corrie's reaction.

"Did she? How careless of her! It's bad enough that the Germans think her a witch." Corrie seemed to be savoring some private joke. "Well, one who bears the name of the Rowan tree need fear no evil charms. And even if there are such things, they are clearly not sufficient to fight our battles for us. We need your bombs." She pushed back her chair and stood up. "Come along now, if you are quite finished, and I will show you what we have done to prepare. I'm afraid there will be little rest for any of us for many days and nights to come."

Rowan had known that Corrie was tall, but she was just beginning to appreciate her commanding presence. Sylvie was flame and grace and seduction; Corrie, she thought, was a weathered, sheltering rock who might transform into a raging lioness at need. *Where on earth is all that coming from? But oh, if I could only be singed by whatever sparks they may strike from each other!*

Corrie's broad form was well along a trail leading through a clump of alders by the time Rowan, ducking her face to hide its warm flush, caught up. The path led to a small cove on the far side of the island, nearly filled by a barge supporting a large tin-roofed structure. Several *chalands* were squeezed in on either side, and men were unloading bundles onto the deck.

"Where better to assemble explosives than afloat in the heart of a marshland?" Corrie said cheerily. "And our factory is movable, as well, although not too quickly nor too far. We had to haul the barge here in segments." She trotted lightly up the plank. Rowan followed, feeling curious eyes surveying her.

Inside the building four women were opening feed sacks and splitting hay bales to reveal a wide assortment of pharmaceuticals, most containing acids and nitrates and chlorides in one combination or another. They clearly had at least a half-formed notion of what she would need. Shelves bearing more materials were built along two walls, while a large worktable occupied the center. Pots and kettles of various types hung on racks next to a black iron stove. "There is plenty of peat for fuel," Corrie said, "but we have brought in coal, as well, if hotter fires are needed."

"This will be excellent!" Rowan said, nodding in greeting toward the women. "I had expected to make do with far less. Given time, I could have made explosives with little more than droppings from the hen yard. With what you have here, and whatever more you can get me quickly...well, it will be a long four days, but we can do it, if you will follow my directions in every detail."

"Write me a list of whatever else you require, and we will send for it," Corrie said. "Do it quickly, though; a storm is on its way, but I think it can be held off until nightfall."

Be held off? Rowan knew by Corrie's sidelong glance that she was watching for a reaction. Let her wait. Rowan would do some watching of her own.

She made a quick survey of what was on hand, and jotted down a list of requirements, emphasizing especially the need for glass or ceramic containers. Then she turned to the instruction of her assistants. Their grasp of procedures was impressive; she had the notion that their experience went well beyond daily cooking chores when it came to measuring, mixing, testing, and isolating incompatible materials. One elderly woman in a starched white cap asked her what words to say over a mixture, then laughed and shook her head after an admonitory look from Corrie.

By late afternoon more punts arrived with materials from Rowan's list. There were a few roads through the marshes, she was told, but the Germans had commandeered most vehicles, even horses and donkeys, so everything must be transported by bicycle from the more distant towns and villages to the landings where the boats waited.

Gray storm clouds were heaped on the western horizon, looming nearer as the day wore on. Corrie spent more and more time on the deck watching the sky. Finally she disappeared for so long that Rowan would have gone ashore to look for her, except that one of the women blocked her way, asking trivial questions that had been dealt with hours ago. Rowan suspected deliberate obstruction.

One more boat arrived, just past sunset, after most of the other punters had departed. In the distraction of unloading Rowan slipped away, intending to follow the path back to the house to look for Corrie on the pretext of asking whether dinner would be brought to those still working. When the track she took led instead slightly upward, she kept on, hoping for a wider view.

The sky grew suddenly much darker. Thunder rumbled in the distance. Rowan nearly turned back, but not far ahead she could see a gleam of light through willow branches. Hurrying on, almost certain Corrie would be there, she passed into the grove of trees and halted in surprise. A slender figure in white stood gazing into the waters of a spring-fed pool. A small fire in a circle of rocks behind her illuminated the red-gold highlights in her hair.

"Sylvie?"

Without glancing up, Sylvie beckoned her forward. "Look," she said softly. Rowan gazed into the pool and saw, not the reflection of willow branches arching densely above them, but a scene of dark towering clouds edged with vermilion, like embers from the fire of the departed sun.

Sylvie took Rowan's hand, turning toward her. The touch stirred Rowan's flesh, even as her mind whirled with the impossibility of what she had seen.

"Believe, or do not believe," Sylvie said gently. "It makes no difference. I cannot understand your magic of molecules and atoms, but I must still believe in its power, and make use of it."

"I thought Corrie would be here, holding back the storm," Rowan said, only now admitting this to herself, and refusing to examine the thought. Belief or its lack seemed irrelevant. Sylvie's closeness, the curve of her lips, the rise and fall of her breasts beneath her white gown, projected a magnetism owing nothing to the physics taught in schools.

"And so she was," Sylvie said, "but that is a wearing task, and she is not as young as she once was. I sent her to rest."

To rest? But Corrie is not that old. And she said there would be little rest for any of us. Clearly Corrie too went about her own business, and one must not ask. Safer, of course, not to trust Rowan with secrets when she might yet be taken by the Germans; but still she felt a pang.

Sylvie's hand tightened on hers. "Are you disappointed to find me here instead?" The amusement in her smile told Rowan that she had no doubt as to the answer.

"No, of course not!" Rowan's hand was still in Sylvie's; she reached out boldly to take the other. *Why not show some initiative? Shouldn't being charmed include some benefits?* She gazed into Sylvie's amber-flecked eyes, aching to lean forward until her mouth was touching those full, tempting lips. Instead, she heard her own voice ask, as though from a great distance, "Are you and Corrie...close?"

Sylvie smiled again. "Oh yes. Very close."

"As close as this?" Now Rowan dared to put her arms around Sylvie, who did not resist but rather pressed her body closer into the embrace. Rowan touched her mouth gently to cheek and lips. Sylvie responded with an urgency that sparked a jolt of desire, and with mounting hunger Rowan kissed her all along the curve from chin to throat, and below, nudging downward the gathered neckline of her dress. The very air sparked and tingled, charged with erotic energy. Heat flared in Rowan's depths, tension swelled...

A sudden crash of thunder drilled right through to their bones. "Quickly!" Sylvie shouted, and with scarcely a pause for breath they were racing together down the hill, dodging great raindrops, until there were too many to evade. Sylvie's white dress glowed as though phosphorescent, leading Rowan safely through the growing dark.

They burst into the cottage with water streaming from their hair and clothing plastered to their bodies. Sylvie's lush curves glowed pink through fabric made translucent by the soaking, a temptation Rowan, still highly aroused, could never have resisted if the house had not been swarming with all those who had remained on the island.

Sylvie greeted everyone cheerfully, playing hostess once she had put on dry clothes. The women produced a meal in easy cooperation. Rowan answered questions about explosives and asked some of her own about the bridge at La Roche-Bernard, finding herself spending the rest of the evening bent over charts with Joachim as he drew diagrams detailing the bridge's construction and just how and where the Germans stored their munitions.

Corrie didn't reappear. Everyone went to bed early, wherever they could find a likely corner. The child Claudette and the oldest of the assisting women shared Rowan's goose feather pallet, but she tossed and turned so, waking often from interrupted dreams of Sylvie in her arms—or, disturbingly, in Corrie's arms—that she moved finally to the reed-covered floor for the sake of her bed-mates.

There was little rest for anyone in the next three days. Rowan tried to be everywhere, overseeing the rough refinement of chemicals and the preparation of fuses, charting blast vectors and bridge stress points with Joachim and the other men who would be helping to handle the final detonation, and emphasizing safety precautions over and over again.

Whenever her strength wavered, Corrie was beside her, smoothing misunderstandings, bringing order out of chaos, building confidence in those who needed it. She had a towering presence, at once commanding and kind, along with some further aura that made Rowan struggle to suppress a thrill of something between awe and longing. *Like a roe deer in the presence of a great elk! But I'm no bleating doe!* She mustered her own powers of science and of will, and maintained the authority that no one, least of all Corrie, seemed to question. *Dare I ask her to go with me to help when, inevitably, I move on to train Maquis groups in other areas? How immovably is Corrie bound to this place, by blood, by nurture, by...magic?*

Late every afternoon, just before sunset, Corrie disappeared into some private retreat. Sylvie would arrive in the early evening, often wearied by her own secret pursuits, but still managing to inject some degree of merriment into the brief time between work and what little sleep could be managed.

Rowan lay on her crowded pallet each night imagining Sylvie creeping at last into Corrie's bed, laying her bright head against the weary gray one and feeling those strong arms wrap around her, giving comfort, giving...but by then she would be asleep.

Corrie, Rowan suspected, was working on plans of her own. There had been mutterings about the certainty of reprisals for the bombing. The Germans were known to punish at random, with no regard to proof of guilt. Corrie had asked whether there would be unmistakable traces of fuses and their rough-made explosives after a successful detonation; Rowan had assured her that if the ammunition dump went up and the bridge came down, there would be no way to prove that God and all his Angels had not ignited the blast with their fiery trumpets, but the Germans would certainly have few doubts as to who was responsible.

"Would it be possible, however unlikely, for a lightning strike to do the job?"

Rowan stared, speechless. "If you can command the lightning," she said at last, "what need do you have of me?"

"What need? Let me think." The first smile in two days softened Corrie's stern features. "No, I cannot command the lightning." She put a hand on Rowan's shoulder and gave it a brief squeeze that left a lingering heat. "That detail I must trust to you." And then she was off across the room to help a short woman lift down a canister from an upper shelf.

The band of saboteurs embarked in two *chalands* while the sky was still dark, the gently rippling channels lit only by the waning moon. Rowan did not question the feather-touch of Sylvie's hand across her eyelids, giving her the night-sight of an owl, nor did she hesitate to return the warm pressure of Sylvie's full lips on her own as they parted.

Corrie did not appear. *I can't believe she wouldn't come to see me off!* Some half-formed notion had begun to stir at the back of Rowan's mind, though she was not yet prepared to examine it closely.

By mid-morning Rowan rode in a farmer's cart filled with peat blocks and onions, pulled by a mule so old the Germans could think of no better use for him. Joachim and the others proceeded toward La Roche-Bernard at seemingly random intervals, on bicycles with panniers of garden produce. The concealed components for the explosives were divided into several sections. Only when all had met at a farmhouse, near the town but well off the main road, was Rowan ready to mix the components and bundle them into a long burlap sack well wrapped with twine. Just past sunset she climbed into the cart again, holding the infernal bundle on her lap like a suckling pig destined for a general's table.

A line of storm clouds had loomed in the west all day. Now, from the high bridge, they seemed to fill most of the sky. "We can't wait for full night," Rowan muttered to Joachim, and he nodded. They had planned to reconnoiter on the northern side, and then re-cross to the southern side after dark, but it could be pouring rain by then. *Is Corrie straining to hold back the storm? Or is it Sylvie's job by now?*

There was no other traffic, since most travelers knew enough to find shelter. Lightning flashed in the approaching clouds. Returning to the southern end of the bridge, the cart tipped suddenly, as though an axle had broken. While the farmer unhitched the mule and led it away, the twine-tied bundle slid between bridge and railing, to be lowered by rope down, down, far into the gorge, until it dangled just above a cluster of tin-roofed warehouses on the river's bank.

"Go!" Rowan ordered fiercely. "Get off the bridge, all of you!" No one dared to challenge the blaze of command in her eyes. When they were clear, she struck a sulfur match, lit the long wire fuse, and watched to be sure the spark continued downward. Then, as thunder cracked and the first drops of rain began to fall, she leapt onto the waiting bicycle and pedaled for her life.

Ninety seconds and half a kilometer later, she huddled with the others behind a hillock, watching lightning slice across the clouds. Suddenly a flash so close it seemed brighter than any lightning bolt ripped the sky. The earth lurched beneath them, again and again, as pile after pile of munitions ignited, until a mighty creak and crash sounded through the smoke and rain and steam. The southern end of the bridge had split away from the land to crumble into the fiery gorge.

They tried to persuade her to stay through the night in a safe house at the edge of the marsh, but she would not be held.

"No," she told Joachim when he became too overbearing. "I *will* go back tonight. If no one can take me, I will pole the boat myself. How can I lose my way when such a powerful charm binds and draws me?" She stared him in the face until he had to look away, remembering his own words the night she had landed.

"Then I will take you," he muttered. "But," looking up again with the ghost of a smile, "the Corrigan never had need of any charm to bind you!"

The early sun sparkled on reeds and grasses still wet from the evening rain as they neared the island. Rowan sprang from the *chaland* when there were still two feet of water between prow and landing.

She barely paused at the cottage, where only a few were stirring. The path to the hilltop showed signs of passage since the rain; she had no doubt that Corrie knew she was coming, and the scent of strong coffee as she entered the willow grove made her even more certain. A glance showed a flask and two mugs and a napkin-covered basket set out on a flat stone beside the fire circle.

The cloaked figure sitting against a willow trunk started to rise.

"We did it," Rowan said simply. "The bridge is down, the munitions are blown sky high, and in years to come there will be legends told of how lightning smote the invaders' stockpiled weapons."

"How does it feel to be a legend?" Hoarseness marred the attempted humor in Corrie's tone. Her eyes held a gleam of laughter, but her faced showed great strain and her shoulders slumped with weariness as she stood. She had never seemed so...human.

"I'm still puzzling that out." Rowan went forward without hesitation and slipped her hands under the wool cloak, stretching her arms around Corrie's warm body. "Tell me how it works," she murmured, resting her head against the homespun shirt pulsing with the beat of the heart beneath. "Is it true that if the Corrigan's lover will still desire her in her daylight form, as well as in the seductive nighttime guise, they may live happily together?"

"So they say." Corrie's arms were around her now, but lightly, and her lips just brushed Rowan's dark cropped hair.

"But if I dare to love you now, must I lose you?" Rowan moved her hands along Corrie's strong back and worked her mouth slowly across her shirtfront, making it clear that carnal love was definitely part of the package. Corrie stood quite still, barely breathing, although her heartbeat quickened. "Don't the legends say that the younger form becomes the true one, both night and day?" Rowan went on.

"Who would ever choose otherwise?" Corrie's tone was light, but Rowan sensed her tension.

"I would," she said firmly. "Sylvie is lovely, enchanting, and I would miss her, but if I had to choose, I would choose you." Her hands lowered to pull their bodies even closer together.

Corrie's arms tightened until Rowan could scarcely breathe. "Who believes the old legends? If there is love enough, I think, we can choose to be either, at will, though I have never seen it tested."

"You had better be right." Rowan felt her own heart pound and her blood race. "Because it's going to be tested now."

"Wait." But Corrie's moving hands didn't seem to be aware of her own instructions. "This is wartime. You know that once you have taught us to manage on our own, you must move on to other Maquis cells."

"Are you bound to this place? Could you come with me, to organize, teach, use your special skills, if they can be invoked elsewhere?"

"There are three more spring-fed pools across Brittany where the power is strong enough. But I could not stay away too long, while you..."

"There is nowhere I would rather be. Afterward, win or lose, we would come back to the heart of the Briere."

"If there is an afterward." But Corrie's mouth had moved to Rowan's cheek and was inching toward her lips.

"We had better not waste what time we have, then," Rowan said; and she didn't. Questions would come, but for now they faded in the flare of desire. Only hunger needed answering.

The destruction of the bridge seemed to pale, for the moment, beside this blaze of magic older and earthier than legend. An achingly short moment; there was still work to be done, and already little Claudette was calling from below; but when night came again, after more hours laboring side by side on the necessary contrivances of war, Rowan's dark head rested against Corrie's, still gray, on the goose-feather pillow, while they found comfort and joy, if very little sleep, in each other's arms.

Author's Note:

WWII has always held a great fascination for me, probably because I was born in the midst of it. I've written other stories set in that period, and done far more research than I've yet used in fiction. When, in the course of research for something else, I came across the information that a female pharmacist was, in fact, dropped by parachute into Brittany to train the Maquis in making explosives, I knew I had to use such a character sometime. When I later read in a guidebook that the bridge at La Roche-Bernard (and the German munitions stored beneath it) had been destroyed by lightning, I knew that the time had come.

There's nothing like keeping a soup pot of random facts simmering on your creative stove.

AT READING STATION, CHANGING TRAINS

C.A. Gardner

W HEN T.E. OPENED THE DOOR, HE forgot for a moment where he was. She stood facing him as she had in the desert, calm, grave, her red hair streaked with gray: Gertrude Bell, "Al Khatun," the "uncrowned queen of Iraq." They'd first met in Carchemish, both protégés of David Hogarth; she'd joined the Arab Bureau in 1915, and her reports from behind the lines had helped with his campaigns. The two of them had fought together in Cairo in 1921 to convince Churchill that Feisal ibn Hussein, removed by French forces from the throne he'd won in Syria, should be offered the crown of Iraq.

Just four years ago: it was impossible that she should look so much older, with lines about her eyes and mouth as crinkled as a well-read letter. He had never expected to see her here, at Clouds Hill, his cottage refuge. In a few days he might not have been here at all. Trenchard had promised him his life back: reinstatement in the R.A.F., where he could once more bury his fame among the ranks. It had been that or a more permanent retirement. He was so weary with life, with fame—with secrets—that sometimes that final darkness seemed a better choice.

The evening sun cupped her cheeks: one with gold, the other with blue shadow. "It's me, Ned," she said, as if he wouldn't know her. She'd grown so thin; the sand had etched her away to her essential lines. As a faint smile played about her lips, that other world receded—just Gertrude, not Arabia beyond that door. He stood aside to let her in.

"Can I get you something to drink? Tea?" He led her up the stairs and to the left, into the Music Room. She took the leather settee near the gramophone.

"If you don't have anything stronger."

"There's water."

"I'll have the tea."

Getting out the China tea and setting the spring water to boil on the fire, he watched his hands as though they belonged to someone else. The silence stretched. He loved the quiet of the cottage, secluded from the press and the boisterous, intensely masculine confinement at Bovington Camp. "No one calls me Ned anymore," he said conversationally. "Except my brother. It's T.E. Shaw now. Some of the servicemen call me Ted. God knows why."

"Ted, then," she said, as he handed her the cup. He sat on the edge of a chair, sipping water. So few people in England appreciated it: if one didn't dilute the palate, there was far more flavor in water than in wine.

"What brings you to Clouds Hill? It's a long way from Iraq. Still getting along with Feisal, I hope?"

Her face colored to match her coiled hair. "It's not easy, giving advice to kings. But he says I'll always have a place there. And I've got the museum to look after." She added softly, "I don't think a day goes by that he doesn't wish his friend was beside him."

For a moment, he could not tell what he felt—still as far from his body as ever. Then feeling rushed back like fire: longing for his friend, for an understanding that went beyond words. He was aware of his shallow breath in the little room. Distantly, he heard himself say, "I wanted to be there."   He couldn't tell her why he had not gone back.

"Feisal's at 10 Princes Gate in London, if you care to see him. He was hoping you'd want to come regardless, but anyway," she fumbled with her bag, "he wanted me to give you this."

She drew out a rectangular package, wrapped carefully in white silk. What looked at first like ties were the edges of a gold border, like that of the wedding costume Feisal had given him when he took up their cause.

That weight on his knees was too familiar. Even before he pulled back the silk, he knew what it was. He hadn't seen it since November 1919, at Reading Station, changing trains. When he'd lost it, he'd thought for a moment he'd sloughed off that weight forever. Instead, it had settled more keenly on his shoulders, and nothing he could do would shake it off.

Seven Pillars of Wisdom. The labor of his soul. Guilt and penance. In that first draft, he had bared himself completely, with an honesty so devastating he hadn't the courage to replicate it. Writing the book again had nearly broken him, even with the worst secret left out. He'd struggled feverishly to remember, rushing through 400,000 words in two months with scarcely any food or sleep, pushing harder as the memory faded, till one morning he woke and the words were gone like the diaries and notes he'd burned the first time through.

Now they sprang at him again—those familiar, damning lines. It had taken almost three years to get permission to reenlist in the R.A.F.; he'd been ousted after reporters exposed his assumed name in December 1922. He'd pulled several strings to get in that first time, as John Hume Ross, without the medical exam; it had taken even more favors to convince them to take him back as T.E. Shaw. On August 18, he was due to report back at Uxbridge; but if this text got out, the scandal would kill his Air Force career for good—the only thing that had brought him any measure of peace since the war.

He propped each sheet on his chest as he looked at the next one, and the next. It was all there. The ghost of Dahoum, the youth Salim Ahmed, whom he'd loved—the boy he'd brought home to visit Mother in England once, and immortalized in limestone on the roof at Carchemish, naked as a Greek god. Stranded in enemy territory, Dahoum had died of typhus before Lawrence reached Damascus. A day seldom passed that he did not think of Dahoum dying without him.

All for nothing. His hopes for Feisal, who'd given his heart to a traitor— Lawrence's promises turned lies, to fill his mouth with sand. His own secret, and the way it had been wrested from him at Deraa, until there was no place to hide from the stark truth of a body he'd rather die than acknowledge. In his agony over how he'd failed, he'd confessed it all.

Losing the book had been like losing his soul. But when he'd tried to tell Hogarth what it meant, the absurdity of his agony choked him—it was just a few sheets of paper, of value to no one. It was all finished, one way or another. And so he had laughed, and said it didn't matter, while every moment, every hour he was hoping, sweating that someone would find the manuscript and recognize what it was. Whoever had stolen the bag might have expected loot, and tossed out the papers as meaningless trash. But as six years passed and nothing surfaced, one possibility loomed large: that someone from the government, following him, had taken it. He was the thorn in their side. There had always been a sense of threat behind their pressure for him to break with Feisal, to back down from his demands for Arabia. His going mum in the R.A.F. was as much to their advantage as his own.

But now it had come back to him, from Feisal's hands.

It took all his control to look up at her again. "Did he tell you how he got this?"

"It was during one of his trips to London in 1922. It wasn't long after you joined the Air Force. Feisal used to tell me about how you'd ride up madly on that motorbike, dressed in your dingy blue uniform, and the doormen would try to deny you entrance."

T.E. brushed his hand over the manuscript. Behind the margins, he could see those days again: Feisal, tall and slender in silk robes, his headcloth tied with scarlet that set off the jet of his beard. Despite the treachery of nations, in the face of his own sorrow, he'd tried to cheer T.E., to persuade him to leave stultifying England for the desert, where his life meant something. Feisal's dark eyes had flashed as he'd tried to jolt T.E. out of his misery, to force him to stand, to throw off his shackles. But T.E. had forged those chains himself. The government suggestions had come so quickly after he'd lost the book, he couldn't doubt who'd found it. Rather than betray Feisal further, he'd retired from the field.

T.E. expelled a heavy breath. "How did he find it? Surely he wasn't at Reading Station?"

"A man said he had something to sell, and there was almost no price too high for what he was offering. I gather he knew you had no money, and there might have been other reasons why he didn't want to go to you himself."

T.E. sat very still.

"Feisal says he threatened to sell the book to Lowell Thomas, or the papers. He seemed to think Feisal would pay because he was your friend—but there was some hint he hoped the book would poison him against you. Feisal paid, but only with the guarantee that the man wouldn't harm you further. Feisal made him understand he'd never escape if he did. Of course, the seller had his own demand in return. The manuscript was expressly never to go to you."

T.E.'s voice was gruff. "And what made Feisal change his mind?"

"I thought it might—do you some good to have it. While there's still time. Please, Ted—don't wait until there's nothing but regret."

He thought she might be speaking for herself. There was such weary sadness in her eyes. He recognized the shadow there. It was the same one that loomed behind the mirror. He knew how deadening it could be, working in the political sphere, even for those you loved. And Gertrude had led a man's life, without the benefits of being a man; it had cost her the chance at a family. "Are you happy there, with Feisal? So far from home?"

"I was never happy anywhere else. Come see. You're still a hero to a lot of people."

"And a villain to some. To all, if the truth were known."

"Only in your own eyes," she said. "Feisal would always welcome you."

He nodded tightly. "Did you read it? Did you translate it for him?"

She didn't answer. She didn't need to. He could see it there, in the compassion of her worn face—she saw him, through the clothes, the scarring, the starvation. The spare parts. He stood before her as naked as he'd been in Deraa, all protection stripped, the ugly truth exposed even before rape forced him to recognize the reality of the body. By the pity in those green eyes, she saw him as a sister in suffering: all that she'd faced as a woman, she thought now that he shared.

He hated it.

She reached out a hand to him. He jumped up from his chair. The manuscript scattered.

"I'm sorry—I didn't mean—"

The silence stretched between them, untouched as the hand he'd shied from.

She tried again. "We need you, Ted. Now more than ever. Everything's so unstable. Feisal's father was forced to abdicate from the throne of Hejaz in favor of Ali, but I don't think even Ali can hold it much longer. That would only leave Feisal in Iraq and Abdulla in Transjordan, and without the Hashemites, most of our hope for unity is gone. You could always ignite fires in cold rooms. I can't believe that spark has gone out."

He couldn't answer. Nothing had the meaning he'd thought it had.

"I should be off," she said at last.

He nerved himself and gave her shoulder one quick, fleeting touch—silent apology—as he showed her out the door.

T.E. squared up the manuscript and set it on the desk. Ross would be here soon. They'd been friends for so long—since Oxford High School, where they'd nearly been expelled, though for what they did, T.E. had never taken off his clothes—at least not when there was light enough to see. Ross hadn't minded. He took his friend's eccentricities cheerfully—all but the command, when T.E. got back from Arabia, that they not touch that way again: "It's for your own good as much as mine. I'm too much of a public figure and it would ruin your reputation." The explanation hadn't satisfied, but it was better than the truth. Dahoum, Deraa: the days when he could allow himself such pleasures, even vicariously, were long gone. Still, T.E. had taken Ross's name when he joined the ranks—appeasement and homage to young love.

They'd spent so many pleasant hours here with friends from the Tank Corps, part of the camaraderie he'd found in the ranks, in the desert. T.E.'s literary friends joined him here as well: E.M. Forster, Thomas and Florence Hardy, sometimes even Charlotte and Bernard Shaw. Among such company, he could almost forget what sometimes lay on that desk instead—letters from the Old Man, his fictitious uncle. Reading them made T.E.'s skin crawl, as if the vengeful man was real, watching with his mother's angry eyes—though she'd been fiercely glad, as soon as he could talk, to find she had not a daughter, but another son.

On sunny Sunday afternoons, bent over the bed as he endured his punishment, T.E.'s eye would rove past the storage cupboard, the wood-paneled walls, the spines of his books as he strove for distance, for control—to feel only the ridges of the bedspread against his face, the cool breeze from the window on his back. Each time, he flew so far he forgot to notice how his body floundered, and had to ask Ross by letter how disgusting he'd become.

Mortification of the flesh in the name of preserving family secrets. One friend to whip him and another to watch to be sure things only went so far. They did not know this reenactment of T.E.'s torture at Deraa was more than the expiation of his Arabian guilt; it was also his chance to master the body at last, to spurn the flesh that had failed him since birth—to beat down desire before it could betray him again. He was a small man, and what little food he needed was scant enough to keep certain bloody signs from appearing, most of the time. What chest he had had been further deflated after the war, when transfusions made the amputation little risk. The surgeon was a friend, and T.E. had endured worse pain. He'd already known he was going into the ranks—it would be one less thing to worry about, in the rough company of fellow men. Before he'd enlisted, he'd had three months of solitude to recover while he shaped the counterfeit *Seven Pillars*—one lie to hide another.

He had enlisted to escape the need for such lies, to experience the simple world of masculine solidarity where he could be himself without the complications, the expectations. He was still chained by human weakness like any man: but buried in the R.A.F., he'd found his soul again, or at least enough of it to fill the breast of 352087 A/c Ross—a number and a name that no one cared about but his friends.

In the silent house, he heard the lock turn, then the familiar sound of stairs. T.E. was painfully aware of his body, the edge of the desk biting one hand, paper sharp under the other. The heaviness of a lifetime pressed on him like the dead weight of a fallen friend.

T.E. called, "Ross, do you recognize this?"

Ross froze. There was no mistaking that look. He didn't ask what it was

"So you did take it, then. I wasn't sure at first."

Ross reached toward the manuscript as if he would coax a child. "You'd have ended up burning it, you know. Like all your notes."

T.E. stood, rigid. "It's mine to burn."

"You left it at Reading Station in a Western Union bag! You were practically giving it away!"

T.E. remembered that one wild moment of relief—before the danger of the situation came crashing down.

"I thought at first," Ross continued, "that you were happier with it gone. The albatross cut from your neck. When you started torturing yourself to produce it again, I considered giving it back." His eyes gleamed as they did when he watched T.E. under the whip, a shine like the verge of tears. "But by then, I'd read more than the little excerpts you'd given me before, and I knew it couldn't be done. I decided to make some use of it instead. Don't you know how hard it is to get close to you? I've always cared for you, more than you could possibly know. Who else would do for you what I've done? So for a time I owned this piece of you. I knew just how much I had, by the way you thrashed to create it again. But you were still obsessed with Feisal, and he didn't even know what you are! When he came back to England after you ran away to the service, I seized my chance. I wanted him to hate you!"

"He should have hated me in any case, for the part I played," T.E. said bitterly. "Liars don't deserve friends, but I thought I could escape with a shred of honor, if I fought hard enough afterwards—if I could stop Britain and France from carving up his land for oil." A wave of revulsion swept over him. He'd halted none of it. He hadn't been true to Feisal, or himself. After Feisal gained Iraq—poor, shredded remnant of all they'd fought for—T.E. had resigned from the Colonial Office and crawled off to nurse his shattered nerves in the R.A.F. Ross was right—he'd run. With the book gone, he'd been frantic to protect his secret, afraid he'd be exposed as less than a man. But Ross had known—Ross, who had witnessed his humiliation countless times. The eccentricities and self-hatred of a celibate, homosexual friend hadn't mattered, Ross said.

He'd known the weak spot, and T.E. had fallen as blindly as the fool the Old Man said he was.

"Get out," T.E. said with quiet fury.

Ross smiled, as if he wasn't sure he'd heard. "You can't mean it." As T.E. stared, the smile faltered and the words spilled faster. "I've been your friend for more than twenty years. You need me. What will the Old Man do to you if I'm not there to carry out his orders?"

T.E. felt himself give way in a roar of fire. Everything he'd thought he'd known towered in flame. And yet, within the core, he stood like a pillar, unconsumed: a strength he'd thought he'd lost.

T.E. said, "There is no Old Man."

Ross stepped closer. "I know that. Sometimes, I wasn't sure if you did. Come on, Ted. After all this time—"

He stood close enough now—too close. T.E. had never been much at physical combat; his skills were endurance and logistics, and a certain talent for firearms. And Ross's handsome face could still disarm him. But this time when Ross advanced, arms open, a fist met him like stone.

"After all this time," T.E. said icily, "you should know how much I hate to be touched."

Ross's face twisted, his hand pressed to his chest. "I could have sold it to Lowell Thomas. Do you know what a splash it would have made with your adoring public? I can still tell them everything I know. All the parts you left out."

T.E. could see it all now, the road unwinding as swiftly as it did before his motorbike. There was one group of people who would hate to see his secret revealed even more than he. For the first time, he appreciated what Thomas had done, in making his a household name.

Ross stared back from the cage in his eyes—a mute appeal in which he recognized himself. Despite it all, T.E. felt the brush of sympathy. But he had done being chained.

"They'll laugh at you," T.E. said mildly. He picked up the manuscript. "No one will believe it."

Ross shouted after him, "Who do you think told the papers about you being in the R.A.F.? Don't you dare cut me off, Ted!"

T.E. straddled his motorbike and sped off, his heart roaring like the Brough's engine.

The land rushed up to meet Boanerges's wheels. The road curved to the tilt of T.E.'s body, the smooth turn of the wheel. Trees and hills streamed by as he flew along with the throttle open, the world unfurling as fast as he could think it into life. Power, speed, control: the bike responded instantly to the slightest touch, obeying each command without any conflict between body and will.

Moving onto busier roads, T.E. gripped the handles firmly, his feet planted on the rests as he dodged cars. Even here, slowed by the morass of city streets, he loved the open air. He threaded the London maze—pedestrians, automobiles, omnibuses, trams. Society's grooves had already dug a trench straight to the heart of Arabian oil. Neither the toffs nor working men truly knew the price, the horrors lurking behind the placid surface of "civilized" life—the steaming body of half a Turkish officer thrown at his feet; the wreckage of a train where mangled survivors were shot as mercy; Beduin women and children raped and massacred; wounded friends killed to spare them torture at Turkish hands.

Behind him in the pannier-bags rode a burden that, in contrast, felt even more shameful, for being so small.

This time, there was no trouble getting in. Feisal met him at the door.

Tall, regal, thin even in his robes, Feisal stood with his hands clasped. Those dark eyes assessed him as they had at first, giving nothing away. Then the bearded lips flashed in a smile as Feisal strode forward and took his arm. The warmth leapt through T.E. like a lightning bolt, even before Feisal grabbed him in a fierce embrace, with the strength of a brother's arms.

Feisal pulled back a little, regarding him with compassion. "It is good to see you, my friend," he murmured in Arabic. "Such a long road between us."

There was too much to say. The years blocked his throat. He gripped Feisal tight.

Feisal guided him gently into the room. Gertrude looked up from her chair, her green eyes eloquent with the question: but he didn't know the answer yet.

T.E. dropped to the rug as easily as he had when he wore Feisal's robes. He'd dressed as an Arab throughout the peace conference; when it ended in defeat, he'd put them aside. He'd been as unworthy of that garb as every other honor.

Feisal glanced from him to Gertrude, then picked a spot on the rug beside him, his eyes twinkling. Carefully, T.E. unwrapped the bundle and set it on the floor between them.

"I thought the government had it. I was only wrong about which one."

Feisal laughed. His teeth flashed like a sword; but Feisal's wicked humor seldom cut his friend. When he spoke, the words were as gentle as the light touch on T.E.'s hand. "You were already deep in another story when I got this one. You threw yourself at it so passionately I feared it would drive you mad to have this back."

One thing Ross had been right about: the strength of his feeling for Feisal. But there was a difference between love and obsession; and T.E. had never expected anything but friendship in return. The spark had been there from the first; but there was Dahoum, then Dahoum's death, now Feisal's wife and children. "Do you know what's inside?" he said.

Feisal nodded. "I asked Gertrude. We have agreed the current one is better."

"Because of what it lacks?" T.E. burst out.

"No. Because of what it contains. Your heart is haunted, but more complete, I think. You don't dwell on the insurmountable. It doesn't rule you. You simply live beyond it, even when your torment is great enough to shine through your words." From the sadness in Feisal's eyes, T.E. knew he meant it all: not just the torment of his secret, but grief over friends, over all their losses and defeated hopes. He had not spared himself any of it. And yet, this time through, he'd striven to detach himself enough to write with the same feeling about their camaraderie, their triumphs, their defeats and sorrows, his successes and mistakes—everything the same.

"You ought to hate me," T.E. whispered.

"You take too much on yourself, Aurans. We fought our own battles. We would have been fools to trust the English any more than the Turks. Fortunately, we trusted you instead." He held up his hand. "And before you harangue me again about your guilt, let me say now that no man has done more for us than you. You could not hope to win, one man against nations, yet you never relinquished the justice of our cause. Where you see a failure, I see a loyal friend."

"But I knew—Feisal, before the end, I knew what Britain would do—"

"You acted with heroism, then. Who else would have believed we could take the Turks with so few? Before you came, we knew that Britain, France, and Russia were bickering over our land, dividing the Turkish Empire before the Turks were dead. You helped us gain the best chance we had—Damascus."

T.E. stayed silent. Feisal watched him with concern, waiting. Beyond his shoulder, Gertrude sat in the deepening shadows, ready as ever to lend what help she could. She had never let her sex stand in her way, nor bowed to what anyone might think; and Feisal trusted her advice without regard for gender. She gave T.E. a tired smile.

They both knew his secret. For three years, they had not said a word to anyone. Neither seemed to care, apart from the worry they had as friends. Instead, they had given the secret back into his hands.

He asked gingerly, "And—that other matter?"

Feisal said simply, "You are the man I've always known and loved. My brother, heart of my heart. Were we in battle, I would guard your life with my final breath, as I know that you would mine."

There it was: the open question. He was surprised to find it was not whether they accepted him, but whether he could live with himself. There had been one place where, for a time, he'd been free to be and love whom he pleased—a place where he'd lived to his full potential. Among the Beduin, men had expressed their love for one another as though nothing could be more natural, their passion as fierce and clean as the burning sand. In the desert, there had been no place to hide, and the only way to be alone—that English luxury—was to be oneself. The extreme privations and extravagant luxuries of desert life taught both conquest and celebration of the body. A life spent entirely at the poles of existence had balanced and satisfied in a way that an easier English life had not. The stark, simple days in the R.A.F. had come closest, but there was no freedom there, for love or genius.

As if echoing his thoughts, Feisal said, "My friend, won't you come home?"

He'd last heard those words in 1922. But he'd brushed them aside. He'd never thought to hear them again.

Maybe Gertrude was right. It was not too late to start over. All the privations of his life had been leading to this. Nothing had ever been as sharp as those days in the desert. For once, the fame he'd hated could serve something other than the glory of the British Empire. He'd come to despise the name of Lawrence, which the government used to lend an aura of heroism to their ugly deeds. But he could use his own legend just as ruthlessly—to gain the freedom of those who'd earned it with their blood and courage. Thanks to public sentiment, the very men he'd feared would hesitate before contributing to the downfall of one they'd proclaimed a hero.

Churchill was still seeking ways to cut corners without losing access to oil. It was time for new alliances, new arrangements—time for Arabs to control their future. With one economy, they would be self-sufficient: what one tribe lacked, another had. If they alone controlled the oil, they'd have funds to promote both social welfare and defense from further interference. Feisal had already been working toward independence for Iraq. With both T.E. and Gertrude to help, they might see Arabia united at last. Feisal had dreamed of a land joined not by religion, but by freedom, where all Semitic brethren might stand together, as individual and strong a force as the colorful band of Beduins had been.

He would accept Churchill's offer to work for the Middle East Department, but this time on his own terms. Churchill was too wise to let his value be wasted. And perhaps that familiar shadow of despair in Gertrude's eyes might be erased with a friend to share the burden.

Best of all, he could spend his life in the company of the friend he loved best. Whether or not there was ever more between them, their brotherhood would be warmth enough.

He bowed. "Thank you. I ask nothing finer of this life."

Beside the long, straight nose, lines spread from laughing eyes. Feisal said, "It will be good to have the Wolf among us again." He gestured toward the manuscript. "And what will you do with this?"

"What I do with all first drafts, once they're superceded. Burn it."

With Feisal by his side, the words that had circumscribed his life went up in flames.

Author's Note:

I first encountered Lawrence of Arabia in an episode of Voyagers! *in 1982, and I've been fascinated ever since. The more I learned, the more I sympathized with a man who was haunted by guilt to the point where he renounced his own fame; who struggled with issues of identity (T. E. Lawrence became John Hume Ross, then T. E. Shaw) and with the constant effort to subjugate his body; who found freedom and happiness ultimately only by losing himself—in the speed of a motorcycle, his mind submerged in the moment; or in the regulations of the ranks, his identity subsumed in uniform purpose.*

Some sources trace the rise of Saddam Hussein to the coups and chaos that followed the overthrow of King Feisal's grandson in 1958. Might this have been avoided had Lawrence not died in the motorcycle crash in 1935, but instead returned to Iraq to assist Feisal along with Gertrude Bell? Both Bell and Lawrence had been instrumental in establishing the government of the Hashemite dynasty and the modern state of Iraq; Lawrence's considerable fame might have helped secure alliances to stabilize and protect Iraq once Feisal gained independence from the British mandate in 1932, and Lawrence's advice might have aided Feisal's heirs. One might even hope that Gertrude Bell herself would have enjoyed a longer life, had another friend been present to share her burdens.

Spellings of proper names are those preferred most often by T.E. Lawrence in Seven Pillars of Wisdom.

THE AUTHORS

Steven Adamson is the pen name of a 31 year old author from Guyana, South America. The hardships endured by the coolies in "Final Voyage" are well documented in the historical records and led the Anti-slavery Society to call indentureship "a new form of slavery."

Sandra Barret grew up in New England, where she spent more years than she cares to mention as a software programmer. She lives on a small sheep farm with her partner, two children, and more pets than are probably legal to own. She's an avid reader of SF, fantasy, and lesbian romance. Her books include the science fiction novel, *Face of the Enemy*, the lesbian romance, *Lavender Secrets*, and a YA novel, *In Keisha's Shadow*. Her website is at sandrabarret.com.

Steve Berman loved history so much he went back to college for a second degree in the field. He has sold over 80 articles, essays, and short stories. His YA novel, *Vintage, A Ghost Story,* was a finalist for the Andre Norton Award. In what little spare time he has, he runs Lethe Press. Actually, his cat, Daulton runs the press. Daulton doesn't care for the taste of tamarind, by the way.

Dale Chase has been writing male erotica for a decade and plans to never stop. Over one hundred of her stories have been published in various magazines and anthologies, including translation into German and Italian. Her single literary effort was published in the *Harrington Gay Men's Fiction Quarterly*. A native Californian, Chase lives near San Francisco and is at work on a collection of ghostly male erotica as well as an erotic western novel.

M P Ericson's short stories have been published in numerous magazines, most recently *Hub* and *Flashing Swords*. She lives on the edge of a moor in Yorkshire, England, with an assortment of spiders and mice.

C. A. Gardner served as editor for The Mariners' Museum (1999-2001, books like *An America's Cup Treasury: The Lost Levick Photographs* and exhibits like *Waters of Despair, Waters of Hope: African-Americans and the Chesapeake Bay*) and the Virginia Library Association (2003-present, quarterly journal *Virginia Libraries*). Now catalog librarian for Hampton Public Library, Gardner has had 23 stories, over 120 poems, and numerous articles and artwork published by venues like *American Arts Quarterly, Best of the Rest 2, Challenging Destiny, The Doom of Camelot, Legends of the Pendragon, The Leading Edge, Strange Horizons*, and many others. Learn more at gardnercastle.com.

Barry Lowe is a vegetarian Taurus whose short stories have appeared in *Hard, Cargo, Mammoth Book of New Gay Erotica, Flesh and the Word, Best Date Ever, Boy Meets Boy, Out of the Gutter*, and others. He is also the author of *Atomic Blonde*, a biography of 1950s blonde bombshell Mamie Van Doren. He co-wrote the screenplay to *Violet's Visit*, and his produced plays include *Homme Fatale: The Joey Stefano Story, Dutch Courage, The Extraordinary Annual General Meeting of the Size-Queen Club, The Death of Peter Pan, Seeing Things*, and *Rehearsing the Shower Scene from "Psycho."* His website is barrylowe.net.

Catherine Lundoff's stories have appeared or are forthcoming in over 60 publications including *So Fey: Queer Faery Stories, Periphery: Erotic Lesbian Futures, Farrago's Wainscot, Khimairal Ink, Caught Looking, The Mammoth Book of Best New Erotica 6, Stirring Up a Storm, Garden of the Perverse, Sex and Candy, Amazons, Best Lesbian Erotica 2008*, and *Girl Crazy*. She is the author of two collections of lesbian erotica: *Crave: Tales of Lust, Love and Longing* and *Night's Kiss*, and editor of the fantasy and horror anthology *Haunted Hearths and Sapphic Shades: Lesbian Ghost Stories* (Lethe Press, 2008). Her website can be found at visi.com/~clundoff.

Erin MacKay was born in Mobile, Alabama and raised all over the Southeastern United States. As a child, Erin was a voracious reader of fantasy and science fiction, much to the detriment of her schoolwork and social life. She began writing her own stories at an early age, most of which have mercifully disappeared. Erin lives in North Carolina with her husband and two dogs. Her interests include history, travel, football and gourmet beer.

Rita Oakes writes horror, dark fantasy, and historical fiction. A graduate of Jeanne Cavelos' Odyssey Writing Workshop, she enjoys history, travel, and Belgian beer—sometimes at the same time. Her work has appeared in Paradox, Dogtown Review, The Many Faces of Van Helsing anthology, and Aeon Speculative Fiction. She currently lives in New Jersey. For more information, visit her website at ritaoakes.com.

Emily Salter lives in Manchester, UK, where she studies acting, works any temp job she can get to pay the bills and writes to keep herself sane. She attended the University of Manchester, where she studied creative writing, and graduated in 2006 with a BA in Film Studies, Literary Studies and Drama. She was one of the runners-up in SFX magazine's inaugural Pulp Idol competition in August 2006.

Lisabet Sarai has been writing fiction and poetry ever since she learned how to hold a pencil. She has published three erotic novels and two short story collections, as well as contributing stories to more than a dozen print anthologies. She has also edited two erotica anthologies, and has just begun to explore the e-publishing world, working with Total-E-Bound, Phaze, and Eternal Press. Lisabet also reviews erotic books and films for ERWA (erotica-readers.com) and Erotica Revealed (www.eroticarevealed.com). For more information on Lisabet and her writing visit Lisabet Sarai's Fantasy Factory (www.lisabetsarai.com) or Lisabet's MySpace page (myspace.com/lisabetsarai).

Simon Sheppard is the editor of the Lammy-nominated *Homosex: Sixty Years of Gay Erotica and Leathermen*, and the author of *In Deep: Erotic Stories*; *Kinkorama: Dispatches From the Front Lines of Perversion*; *Sex Parties 101*; and the award-winning *Hotter Than Hell and Other Stories*. His work also appears in well over 250 anthologies, including many editions of *Best American Erotica* and *Best Gay Erotica*. He writes the syndicated column "Sex Talk" and the online serial "The Dirty Boys Club," and hangs out at simonsheppard.com.

The Editor

Connie Wilkins always intended to write speculative fiction, and did place stories in such venues as *Marion Zimmer Bradley's Fantasy Magazine*, *Strange Horizons*, and several anthologies including two of Bruce Coville's books for children. Then somewhere along the way she got sidetracked by the erotic side of the force. Her alter ego Sacchi Green has published short fiction in dozens of erotica anthologies, including seven volumes of *Best Lesbian Erotica*. Many of these have had historical settings, and a few have included specfic elements, the true loves that she's been overjoyed to combine in *Time Well Bent*. She has also edited or co-edited five anthologies of lesbian erotica, *Rode Hard, Put Away Wet*; *Lipstick on Her Collar*; *Hard Road, Easy Riding*; and *Lesbian Cowboys* (all with Rakelle Valencia, the first two being finalists for the Lambda Award), as well as *Girl Crazy: Coming Out Erotica*.

Lightning Source UK Ltd.
Milton Keynes UK
23 December 2009

147857UK00002BA/71/P